PRAISE FOR *NINEVEH*

"*Nineveh* is an astonishing modern fable about memory, belonging, and the mysterious forces of nature."

—Paul M.M. Cooper, author of *River of Ink*

"With its crisp style, infused with caustic humor, *Nineveh* places Henrietta Rose-Innes without contest among the most important voices of the new South African literature."

—Catherine Simon, *Le Monde*

"Disconcerting to the point of atmospheric weirdness and as chilling as the best apocalyptic horror... a beautiful and disturbing mystery about what lies beneath."

—Jared Shurin, Tor.com

"*Nineveh* is a sly novel. Never losing the ironic edge, Rose-Innes deepens the story and deepens it again, brilliantly probing the big question that reverberates through the book: who belongs? Rose-Innes's writing is entertaining and subtle, a rare combination. *Nineveh* easily pulls you onward, until you suddenly find yourself in the tunnel under the housing estate, with bugs and questions squirming all around..."

—Steven Amsterdam, author of *What the Family Needed*

The Unnamed Press
P.O. Box 411272
Los Angeles, CA 90041

Published in North America by The Unnamed Press.

1 3 5 7 9 10 8 6 4 2

ISBN: 978-1-939419-97-2

Library of Congress Control Number: 2016954665

This book is distributed by Publishers Group West

Cover design & typesetting by Jaya Nicely

NINEVEH

HENRIETTA
ROSE-INNES

A NOVEL

The Unnamed Press
Los Angeles, CA

For my mother,
who introduced me to the Assyrian and the tsetse fly.

And flocks shall lie down in the midst of her, all the beasts of the nations: both the cormorant and the bittern shall lodge in the upper lintels of it; their voice shall sing in the windows; desolation shall be in the thresholds; for he shall uncover the cedar work.
This is the rejoicing city that dwelt carelessly, that said in her heart, I am, and there is none beside me: how is she become a desolation, a place for beasts to lie down in!

Zephaniah 2:14–15

My possessions, like a flock of rooks rising up, have risen in flight. He who came from the south has carried my possessions off to the south – I shall cry "O my possessions!" He who came from the highlands has carried my possessions off to the highlands – I shall cry "O my possessions!" The swamp has swallowed my treasures...Men ignorant of silver have filled their hands with my silver. Men ignorant of gems have fastened my gems around their necks. My small birds and fowl have flown away – I shall say "Alas, my city"...Woe is me, my city which no longer exists – I am not its queen. I am not its owner. I am the good woman whose house has been made into ruins, whose city has been destroyed, in place of whose city a strange city has been built.

Lament for Ur
(The goddess Ningal weeps for her city) c. 2000 BC

I feel like an old war-horse at the sound of the trumpet, when I read about the capturing of rare beetles.

Charles Darwin
1854

1
SWARM

Caterpillars? Easy, thinks Katya. Even these, thick-clustered, obscuring a tree from bole to crown and shivering their orange hairs. Caterpillars she can deal with.

Still, it's a strange sight, this writhing tree: a tree in mortification. Particularly here, where the perfect lawn slopes down to the grand white house below, between clipped flowerbeds flecked with pink and blue. Off to the side, just in the corner of her vision, a gardener is trimming the edge of the lawn, his eyes on Katya and the boy and not on his scissoring blades. Rising behind the scene is the Constantiaberg. It's an autumn day, cool but bright. The mountains look their age, wrinkled and worn and shouted down by the boisterous sky. It's a lovely afternoon for a garden party.

But at the center of this picture is an abomination. This single tree sleeved with a rind of invertebrate matter, with plump, spiked bodies the color of burnt sugar. It's possible to imagine that the whole tree has been eaten away, replaced by a crude facsimile made of caterpillar flesh.

"Toby. Gloves," Katya says, snapping her fingers and holding them out stiffly.

Her nephew rolls his eyes – particularly effective, with those large pale orbs, green with the whites visible clean around the irises – but leans down from his superior height to press a crumpled ball of latex into her palm.

The gloves are important. Katya is not at all squeamish about cold-blooded, squishy things, but some caterpillars have irritant spines. Thick gardening gloves are too unwieldy for this fine work, and Katya also prefers the feel of the latex: it deadens, but in tamping down the background stimuli, it also seems to isolate specific sensations. The gravelly landscape of bark, the warmth of skin without its friction. The gloves are part of the uniform, along with the steel-toed boots and lurid overalls. Her signature color: poison-toad green, boomslang green. While they are working, the uniform separates her and Toby from the pastel colors of lawn and flowers. They are all business.

Katya shakes out the gloves and works them onto her hands. "We need to get some talc. Didn't I ask you to get some talc?"

Eye-roll. "Ja ja," he says, fiddling with his silver-blond hair, which is scraped back into a scraggy bun with a rubber band. He's been growing it ever since he left school a few months ago. He's always ripping off the elastic, or jamming it closer to his scalp by yanking at the strands, a sight that makes Katya's own hair prickle at the roots. Aunt and nephew both have their bangs pulled away from their faces in a practical way – although if you look closer the impression is diluted: the hairclips are sparkly, meant for little girls. Toby has supplied them and Katya wonders about their source. They are the kind of thing a teenage girl might wear, to be cute. One of several recent signs that her nephew might be in intimate contact with young ladies. What is he now, seventeen? Half her own age – a calculation that dismays her. What has she gained, in that doubled time?

"Come, pull it together."

He smiles at her appeasingly. Toby's smile has a comic quality: his teeth are small and gappy, milk-toothy almost. Pink, clean gums like a puppy's. With his mouth open, he seems much younger than his years. Katya often wants to tell him to relax. In repose, when he thinks no one is looking, his face falls into lovely somber lines; like his mother, slight melancholy suits him.

The uniform fits Toby better than it does her. They don't make them in short, busty women's sizes. Katya's is rolled in the leg and tight in the chest. You can get Chinese ones, made for smaller people, although not for ones with bosoms. But Toby, slender and tall, fits his like a bricklayer, ditch-digger. Like someone who's meant to be wearing it.

Toby's job, largely, is to do the heavier lifting; there is surprising strength in those spidery limbs. Katya watches him as he positions the first plywood box and the tin chute, all made to her careful specifications. Once everything is in place, he steps back and holds one arm behind his back at the elbow as he stares up at the tree. The posture is hard to pull off with excess meat on your torso. Or breasts. It's a pose Katya's seen adopted by lean farm laborers out in the country. Like them, Toby knows how to conserve his energy.

It is, in fact, the same stance as the lanky gardener's, who stands downslope with his arms and his bent leg mirroring Toby's, his overalls faded blue to Toby's bright green, his skin dark to Toby's paleness. It's like they're waiting to perform some kind of symmetrical dance.

Time to move into action. First, Katya appraises the swarm, walking around the tree and glancing up and down, guessing at numbers. Then she leans in, nose inches from the thin dorsal hairs of the creatures on the bark. You have to find the chief caterpillar, the general. (A general and not a queen. To Katya, disregarding the facts of biology, all caterpillars are male: foot soldiers. Perhaps it is their small, helmeted heads.) With one hand Katya reaches in, breaches the flow and picks out a robust individual, one who looks fat and juicy and determined, and with a particularly fine ruff of orange fur.

It is best if the client is there to witness this ritual, to see the skill involved, but in this case the client is so repelled that she's observing from a distance of a hundred meters. Katya can see her down there in a blue dress, hands on broad hips, watching as waiters and servants scurry behind her. Music is striking up. A classy party: they have employed a string quartet. There is a line of white-sheeted trestle tables, caterers laying out plates and glasses. Soon the guests will be here.

Katya places her prize wriggler on the rim of the tin spout, head downwards, urging him on with little prods. Then the trick is to get the next one in line latched on; and then the next, following on the numerous soft heels of his brother. Once they are in the narrowing chute, it's hard for them to reverse direction, back into the stream. The system is designed that way. Once you get some movement going, it's easier: caterpillars, like migrating wildebeest – very slow, small ones – have a strong herding impulse. They sense a stirring, they start to push. Perhaps they feel some dim invertebrate anxiety: that the swarm has not yet been consummated, that this is not the right tree, that a better tree awaits, that they will be left behind. This is as far as her study of caterpillar psychology goes.

Soon, there is a modest caravan of furry beasts marching down the spout. A conga line. Once it's happening, it is beautiful, in a way: a river of caterpillar flesh flowing down the tree, peeling away, leaving the branches stripped and affronted. Once the leader drops off the end of the spout and into the box, there's no going back, no turning tail.

"Yeehaw," says Toby. He jiggles side to side, excited by the slow stampede of the worms.

Caterpillars are easy.

The swarm is quite extensive: only the one tree, but it's a thick and comprehensive infestation. It takes two boxes. They're custom carriers, holes punched in the wooden lids to let the catch breathe. Katya closes the boxes up and latches them tight, then stacks them one on top of the other. Surprisingly heavy, and shifting slightly. Katya puts her ear to the lid and can hear them moving: a damp sound, not the dry scuttle you get with your hard-shelled customers. They're strong, these small creatures, working together. Individually, easily crushed beneath the heel; but if they all pulled together...she pictures them carrying her off, and Toby too.

"Alright Tobes," Katya says. "Mission accomplished. Let's get these cuties out of here."

Toby loops his long arms around the boxes and lifts them from her. Then he balances them on top of his head, a hand on each side, and ambles down the lawn, singing happily to himself. It sounds like "I Shot the Sheriff".

It can't be helped: Toby's a sweet-natured kid. He has a radiance to him that communicates alertness, good spirits, a readiness to greet the world and give it the benefit. Katya is fleetingly ashamed of wishing him older, cooler; for imagining the years of his youth away.

The gardener, who's drifted closer, looks at her and she smiles. She's easier with this man than she would be if she were out of uniform.

"How will you kill them?" he asks.

"We don't."

"What do you do with them?"

"We release them into the wild," she says. "It's a strictly no-kill policy."

This is the point at which most people start to laugh, or wrinkle their faces in disgust. But the gardener just nods in a thoughtful way, snipping closed the jaws of his clippers.

As they near the house, Katya can see that guests have started to arrive. Middle-aged men in pastel shirts and slacks, women in summer dresses. She and Toby are not dressed to blend in here, with their bright green Painless Pest Relocations overalls and their palpitating capture boxes.

Now Katya sees again, down towards the swimming pool, the figure of their employer, Mrs. Brand, gesturing tightly up at them. Shakes of the head, shooing gestures. She's ashamed of her caterpillar problem. The creatures have swarmed overnight, disgusting her; she cannot allow them to perform their congregation in sight of her fastidious guests.

Well, Katya has no desire to mingle with the party-goers; but the woman's rudeness wakes inside her an inner voice. *Fuck you, lady,* it says. Katya smiles and keeps on walking.

Toby peers at her from around the boxes.

"Just keep going," Katya says.

They pick their way down to the front entrance. A few guests stand next to the organically curved pool, drinks in hand; as the PPR work party comes through, they scatter instinctively. Katya and Toby are like people in hazmat suits, their catch pulsing radioactive in their hands. If Katya could rattle like a snake, she would.

Their employer is a foursquare, handsome lady, with short frosted hair. Her dress – waist cinched between broad hips and bosom – matches eyes so blue they look almost blind. Those eyes are fixed on

Toby and Katya with open hostility, as if they really are going to rip open the boxes and strew worms around.

"You were supposed to be done by three," she hisses.

Katya matches her stare with a blank one of her own. "Sorry. Coming through."

This job. It brings it out in her.

Specifically, it's the uniform. When Katya puts on her greens, something changes in her. She becomes cockier, more aggressive, but in the passive way of a servant. Also more stylized in her movements and her words: acting out the role of a working man. It's heady. But peel off her boiler suit and she's soft again, a lamb, a girl.

The house has a large parking area, at the end of a shaded driveway, which has started to fill up with luxury cars. Katya opens the back of the minivan, her pride and joy. The van's not exactly new, but she likes the fact that it's knocked and dinged and gritty, carrying traces of its previous owner. You can tell it was ridden half to death by some mean old bugger with a bony ass – the driver's seat is so hollowed out, Katya needs two cushions to see over the steering wheel. She's fitted the vehicle with bars, turning the rear into a cage like a dog-catcher's, and given it a bright-green paint job. It now bears the legend *Painless Pest Relocations,* with neat line-drawings of her own design: rat, pigeon and spider.

While Toby loads the carry-cases into the back of the van, Katya takes a wooden cigar box from the glove compartment and transfers four or five caterpillars into it.

"What's that you've got there?"

She snaps the box shut and spins around. The voice comes from the flowerbed – no, it's a rock garden, with an ivy-covered alcove behind it on a small rise. Katya makes out a figure sitting in its shady depths. Drinking. He raises his glass in a cheery salute and beckons her closer.

"Just a sec," she says to Toby. A paved path winds up to the grotto.

Closer, Katya sees he's a large man, sitting on a throne-like wrought-iron bench with armrests in the shape of dragons' heads. His legs are thrust out in front of him and a tendril of ivy tickles his brow. Shirt loose at the collar, a whisky tumbler askew in his fist.

She stands in front of him, waiting. This is another thing this uniform achieves. As it had eased her interaction with the gardener, so too it helps her do business with what is, clearly, a boss. Usually, standing in front of someone like this – evidently a rich man, powerful, older – Katya would feel awkward. She'd wonder how to stand, what to do with her hands, what to say. But here, now, her posture and her role are clear. He can talk to her if he wants. Or she can walk away. All part of the job.

It's also his evident inebriation that puts her at her ease. He seems to be a benevolent drunk, squinting up at her from behind the ivy.

Katya doesn't find drunken people difficult. Unless they are threatening or loud, they can be quite soothing company. She feels less observed around them; and there is something touching in the way they allow themselves to be seen, in this foolish, almost infantile state. And although they are in one sense blurred by the liquor, there is also a film peeled back, an occlusion lifted.

Right now, she feels free to pass her eyes over this man's suit, his watch, his hair, his fittings and fixtures. He is solid, meaty. His mouth and nose are strong, large enough to balance the broad face, and finely cut. The face of a Roman emperor, past his prime and in his cups. When he smiles he shows one grayed-out canine, the same color as his hair. In his fifties, maybe.

"Let's have a look at the merchandise," he says.

Katya opens the lid of the box, tilting it to show him the brownish caterpillars.

Most people would recoil, exclaim at least. But in his face there is nothing: no revulsion, no interest either. He sips his drink, and then, with a casual flick of the wrist, dribbles a splash of the liquor into the box.

Katya snatches it away. "What's that for?"

He shrugs. "They can't feel much, surely? Stuff's nutritious."

She scowls and closes the lid carefully on the squirming creatures.

"So," he says. "Caterpillar wrangling. Nice job for a girl. What else can you do?" He has a pleasant voice, smoother and more musical than his bulk would suggest.

"Caterpillars, snakes, frogs, slugs, cockroaches, baboons, rats, mice, snails, pigeons, ticks, geckos, flies, fleas." Katya observes his face for reaction. Men are generally more squeamish about these things. "Bats. And spiders."

He laughs – a laugh like the bark of a sizeable dog – and swirls his drink, as if her recitation has made him happy, has confirmed something for him. "I see. The whole gang. The unlovely. The unloved!"

He's not as drunk as she'd thought. His layers are shifting: filming and folding. One has just pulled back to reveal something hard and clear. Whisky sloshing back in the glass to show the ice.

"Would you like a business card?" Katya asks.

He's hugely amused by her, slapping a splayed thigh. "Sure, why not? Cards are good. A card would be fantastic."

There's a gold signet ring on his right hand. He looks at her with his eyes half closed in the late afternoon sun, wells of gray liquid glinting between the lids. Behind her, Katya senses Toby fidgeting with the car keys. The shadows are lengthening.

"In my top pocket," Katya says, leaning forward to him. It's a move that would show cleavage, normally, but as she is all buttoned up in froggy green, it's more of an aggressive gesture. What it does is tip her breast pocket open, enough to show him a pack of business cards.

He does not hesitate. Smiling still in that slit-eyed way that reveals little, he reaches up and tweezes a single card from her pocket. His hands are thick, nails broad but manicured. He taps the card across the open mouth of his tumbler, examining it seriously.

She's proud of the card: *PPR: Painless Pest Relocations,* it says. Plain font. Nothing cute, just the facts. Rat, pigeon, spider. Simple, accurate line drawings. It bothers her slightly that they are not to scale, but there is only so much you can achieve on a business card. Underneath it, her name: *Katya Grubbs.*

"Grubbs," he says, and she waits for the laugh. Most people make a comment, something about the name fitting the work, etcetera. But he's looking at it with a frown, holding it too long. "This is not you."

"Yes it is."

He looks up at her, sharp now. "I thought I told my wife not to hire you lot."

"Sir?"

"Grubbs, I wouldn't forget the name. Last year. Nineveh."

Nineveh? Katya shakes her head, mystified.

"Grubbs, Grubbs ..." He clicks his fingers. "*Len* Grubbs."

Katya's back teeth click together. She was going to have to say it. "That would be my father."

"Same crew, though?"

"No, I'm different – different company, different approach."

"How?"

"I'm humane. Painless. Different."

He taps his knuckle with the edge of the card. "Huh. Well, you better be. Because your father ripped me off quite spectacularly, you know that? Len Grubbs. Took my money, fucked around, fucked off. You can tell him I said so."

Katya is standing oddly, stiff and tight. The magic of the uniform failing. She makes herself shrug, casual. "I have nothing to do with that. I haven't seen him for years."

He looks at her, nods and tucks her card into his top pocket. Crisp in the heat: fine cotton, no doubt. The man is sweating booze, but his clothes are holding up. And now here is the bluebell hostess at the corner of the house, gesticulating with her glass. Irritation registers in a momentary immobility of the man's face but he gets to his feet, still smiling pleasantly. His movements are sharper and more energetic than a drunk man's have any right to be. "Well, we'll give you a try, I suppose. I might have some more work coming up." Then he leans forward and slips his own card – appearing magically in his palm, a trick – into her pocket. Katya feels it through the material, sliding in. "I do think I prefer my caterpillar wranglers, ah ..." – and he looks her up and down, the ghost of a wink – "painless."

As the PPR van labors up the steep driveway, Toby is uncharacteristically still. A capture box is on his lap, his long fingers resting lightly on its lid, and every now and then he drums on the wood with his index and middle fingers: a private, soothing rhythm. Poor little creatures, torn away: their pilgrimage denied.

"What was that all about?" asks Toby, rather sternly. "That dude."

"Nothing. Just the boss." And she changes to first so that the sound of the engine stops further conversation. But around the curve of the driveway, she pulls over and takes out the cigar box, slides it open.

"And now?"

She cranks down the van window and tosses the caterpillars into the shrubbery. "A bit of insurance. Gives us something to come back for, next time."

"Aunt Katya!" Toby laughs. "Wicked! Where did you learn that one?"

She takes a second to answer. "My dad," she says. "My dad taught me that one."

2

RELEASE

It's strange, what disgusts people. Who would scorn the friendship of a gecko, for example: golden-eyed, translucent-skinned, toes splayed on a farmhouse wall? Who could resent a long-legged spider, knitting its silver in the corner of a room? But they do: people will pay to have them killed, poisoned, destroyed.

Katya does not destroy. This is her skill, her niche. So she will relocate a wasp nest, reroute a caterpillar invasion, clear a roof of nesting pigeons, wrangle housefuls of mangy cats. She does not turn up her nose at cockroach infestations, gatherings of mice, strange migrations of bees and porcupines. She's even faced down baboons, although that's unusually robust work. Generally, she prefers the smaller beasts. She encourages spiders and is friendly to pigeons, which others unkindly call rats of the air. Her philosophy is to respect any creature that gets by in the city, ducking and diving, snatching at morsels, day by day negotiating a new truce with the humans among whom they live. Survivors, squatters, and invaders. Tough buggers. They have their place.

Mostly, they do no real harm. They're objectionable only because they've wandered from their proper zones, or because they trigger human shudders. But Katya does not shudder. Not ever. Slinging a snake round her neck like a scarf, the dry scales smooth as water on her latexed palms – no problem.

This is the job: helping these small sojourners in a strange land. Putting the wild back in the wild, keeping the tame tame. Policing borders. Sometimes, part of her wants to reverse the flow, mix it up. Take this box of caterpillars, for example, and tip it out in that Constantia palace they just left, even if it means chaos, screams and ruined dresses, soft bodies crushed into the lawn.

But that's her dad's voice. His angry humor.

Len Grubbs: a lifelong vermin man. An exterminator. He never bothered too much with keeping things straight or putting them back in their rightful places. Traps and poison, that was what he knew. He was often bitten – once by a puff adder. Even in that agony, he'd taken care to beat the snake to death. It was hand-to-hand combat, the way Len Grubbs did the job.

Katya's work, by comparison, is a relatively gentle business, one concerned with rescue and cleansing; but it brings out this mischief in her, this hardness. Perhaps because of what she deals in, what her dad dealt in before her: the unloved. The unlovely.

In Newlands forest, they carry the boxes up through the pines and into a stretch of indigenous trees. Katya's glad to have Toby with her on this lonely path. It can be nerve-wracking, going into the forest alone, although she likes to think that a woman with a box of repulsive caterpillars pressed to her chest is safe enough against most assaults.

They are in a part of the forest she doesn't often visit, off the path. This is Toby's idea. He's spotted a tree here, apparently just the thing for caterpillars. She notes, with interest, something else about her nephew that she did not know before: this lurking about in forests.

He's taken his shoes off in the car and his big feet pad confidently ahead of hers on the pine-needle bed. Seeing him move against the branches, some glowing pale in the darkening air, she thinks again that he is like a young tree. Despite his narrow frame, his lank hair, his liquid eyes, Toby is not a limp person. Indeed, he has a kind of springy resilience, like green wood. And there is the vegetable greenness of the veins beneath his skin, his slightly sappy body scent. *I'm a vegan now,* he told her recently. Perhaps that's why he's growing so fast: photosynthesis.

Over the years, Katya has seen him transform from stocky white-blond child into elongated teen. Not pretty; his face is too broad in the forehead and sharp at the chin, the nose overlong. But he does have those luminous eyes set deep behind long lashes, and the thinness of his lips is offset by their charm – the way he presses them together between smiles, restraining soft thoughts. Girls would surely go for that? His height would be in his favor, too, once he filled it out. Broad shoulders. Longshanks. Long fingers, right for guitar-string picking round fires. Tall like his father, no doubt, Katya thinks. Not like us. Toby's hair is also evidence of his paternity: of the pale father Katya never met, but who seems to be revealing himself in stages through the body of his child, stretching Toby's teenage limbs, flexing Toby's long, unGrubbsish fingers.

The Grubbs look is small but well muscled, with short legs and disproportionately long arms. Monkey-folk. Snub, monkeyish faces, too. In her sister Alma it's cute, with her long pale hair. Katya's always worn her hair trimmed short, and it's darker, like her dad's. They carry themselves the same, straight-backed and quick. Katya's ears, mysteriously small, must be from the other side; so too, perhaps, her large breasts. But in all other ways, their mother Sylvie's influence, like her memory, is faint and fading. There are many more body parts in which Katya can discern, all too clearly, Len's vigorous strain.

She wonders how age has changed her father. Bald, maybe. Last time she saw him, his hair was thinning. His face seemed less balanced, the features fiercer and more pronounced; the eyes and nose had come to dominate his small, rounded head. Len's expression remained largely the same, however: imperturbable, scornfully amused. She sees that expression often, although she hasn't seen her father for years now. It's in her mirror, most mornings.

Toby comes to a halt in a small clearing under a twisted tree. Round the base of the trunk are some planks and smooth stones, arranged in a circle. Candle wax melted onto the stones.

"How did you find this place, anyway?"

Toby shrugs, an exaggerated movement with his newly broad shoulders. "I come here with friends sometimes," he says.

"Huh," she says. "Really."

It is, clearly, a place one would come to smoke pot; she was a teenager too, once. Something else she had not known about Toby.

Katya touches a hard, furred seedpod. It's a wild almond, the same species Jan van Riebeeck used for his famous hedge, meant to keep Khoisan cattle-raiders out of the old Dutch settlement. Could this even be one of the original trees?

Dad taught me all that, she thinks.

The branches creak and shudder. Toby's high above her head, his broad feet gripping the trunk.

"Oy, get down here. No time for messing around."

He drops to the ground next to her in a scatter of twigs.

Funny child. Cartoon boy. He's always had these sudden energies and exhaustions, frisking one minute and dropping off the next, falling into a snooze on the spot. He lopes or lounges or mooches; he bops, he buzzes, he bounds. Katya pictures him getting out of bed on a good morning, leaping two-legged into his jeans. When he rests he is inert; awake he is effortlessly alert, bright and clear-eyed. There is no transitional state: Katya has never seen grit or sleep in his eyes.

He crouches next to the collection boxes and looks up at her, waiting.

"You do it, Tobes. You know how."

She watches him unlatch the lid, lift out a caterpillar in his long fingers and place it on the bark of the tree. He's developed a confidence in his work: the way he bends to stroke or scoop up some little hapless wayfarer. Some mangy cat or cockroach down on its luck. The family touch.

"How cool is this?" he whispers as the creatures resume their march.

Kneeling side by side, Katya and Toby watch the sinuous threading of the caterpillars' bodies. The tree is well chosen; the beasts approve.

"All done," he says, his voice softened and deepened by the dusk.

A vision from memory fits itself imperfectly over the scene. Surely it was here, or near to here, years ago, and at dusk...She'd been walking...No. That's not right. She was a child, she was not by herself.

It was the two of them. Her and Dad. She could smell his roll-up tobacco. They'd come out onto a path in the near-darkness, with the trees closing a tunnel above them. They were working.

Look. Dad was down on his haunches, intent, his whole body aimed at a spot on the ground. She crouched down next to him, carefully soundless. Proud of her soft feet, her silent approaches.

A black shape, twitching on the sand. At first she thought it was an insect of some sort, a dull butterfly moving its wings. But, leaning in, she saw it was mammalian: a shrew, the size of the top joint of her thumb, engrossed in some fervid action. So absorbed that it paid them no mind, even when she put her face close. Its pelt was slightly darker than the leaf litter, its paws delicate and fierce. She understood for the first time why shrews were emblems of ferocity, for this tiny creature was engaged in an act of carnage: it was gripping an earthworm that was trying to escape into a hole. The shrew was hauling the slimy pink-gray body out of the ground, hand over hand like a seaman with a fat rope, and simultaneously stuffing it into its jaws, wide open to accommodate the writhing tube. It was ridiculous, obscene, impressive.

They sat there for a long time, watching this miniature savagery, until all the light was gone. Her dad rose to his feet without using his hands. She admired his wiry strength, his woods-sense. She mimicked the movement, swaying a little to keep her balance. Another time, he might have brought the scene to a close with a shout or, worse, a foot-stomp, but that evening he stood quietly. It was not often that her father went so still.

The silence of that long-ago evening, the tree-trunks black against a luminous evening sky...the scene has a religious feeling in her memory. Is it possible that Len took her hand to lead her down through the trees? Surely not.

"Hey," says Toby. "It's not working."

It's quite dim under the tree where he released the caterpillars. Some cling to the bark, some have fallen to the ground, some are wandering off into the undergrowth. The discipline of the corps has been shattered, the general has lost his command.

"They're not swarming like they were."

She shrugs. It's true. She's tired. "We tried, Tobes. We can't win 'em all." He looks so downcast, she doesn't add that most of the catch will be devoured by birds, otters, snakes. The mountain is full of such tiny battles. It's all contested territory, overlapping, three-dimensional, fiercely patrolled. Millions of miniature turfs, the size of her palm, of her footprint, her fingernail.

Katya stands and brushes the leaf mulch from her knees. "Get us out of here, Tobes. I'm hopelessly lost." Although it's not really possible to lose yourself here in the forest, with the mountain on one side and the city on the other.

Toby points and moves, stepping long-legged over logs and pushing through dry bracken; not the direction she would have chosen. Some small thing goes scuttling away from them, unseen at their feet in the undergrowth. There is a chatter, a rustle, a clap of wings. She imagines the caterpillars finding their spoor, inching slowly home behind them.

Coming out from under the trees, Toby and Katya stand for a moment entranced by broader views. The switchbacking path pauses here on a bare shoulder, allowing them views up to the exposed face of the mountain, and down, out to the sweep of the city below.

"Let's go home, Tobes. Before it gets dark."

Driving home after dropping Toby off at his mother's house in Claremont, she feels tired and virtuous. She's not always so energetic. On occasion, she's simply offloaded creatures at the side of the road, or decanted the cold-blooded types straight into the Liesbeeck Canal. She feels bad about that, though. Fish are tricky. When she was younger, she sometimes went swimming up on Tafelberg Road, where the mountain streams collect in deep concrete tanks before passing under the road. Someone once freed their goldfish into one of those pools, where they reproduced madly and filled the water with lurid flashes. The feral fish didn't last: probably they ate the available tadpoles and then starved to death. The next time she checked, the tank was devoid of any life, piscine or amphibious. A relocation experiment gone horribly wrong.

There used to be a play-park right opposite her house, a small one but quite lushly treed, where she'd release the beasts if she was feeling lazy. Over the six years since she started this business, the park absorbed an astounding number of creepy-crawlies and minor menaces without ill effect, soaking them up like a sponge. For a while it became an object of slightly queasy fascination: how much biomass could that small square hold? It was a magician's handkerchief, enfolding and disappearing a thousand rabbits. Were all the animals eating each other? No doubt there was some run-off, some trickle of mice and midges out into the surrounding streets and drains, but she can't say she ever noticed, and the park's human inhabitants – the five or six vagrants living behind the toilet block, Derek and his friends – never complained.

Now, the park is off-limits. In fact, it hardly exists: it's been bulldozed. The demolition finished a week ago, but she's still not used to the change. Even now, steering the PPR-mobile round the corner to her house, her heart gives a lurch to see the road so altered. It looks unbalanced, as if the whole street tilts away from her house and down towards the disturbing gap on the other side. There's more sky than there was before. She can even see a piece of the mountain over the far rooftops, deep slate blue today and wearing a cap of cloud.

Katya stops the car in the driveway and walks across the road to look at the excavation. The fence is as chill as it looks, pulling the heat out of her hand and into its metal grid. As she moves, her fingers bump-bump in and out of the gaps in the wire, catching and losing grip. The sections of fence make silky looping patterns against each other, shimmering and aligning.

Fat tire tracks curve out onto the road, under the padlocked gate and over the edge of the pavement. A trench has been dug; old foundations lie exposed, strata of concrete and twisted metal pipes. Cloudy water pools at the bottom of the excavation. The ditchwater smells like long-buried coins. Leaning on the wire, she stares down into the pewter water and sees the wavering outlines of buildings and streetlamps, a sunken city that might still be raised, intact. But the surface of the water is opaque. Herself a blurred reflection in dirty milk.

Of course the destroyed park is no surprise. She's watched the deterioration from her upstairs window, stage by stage. First the jungle gym, the slides and the roundabout, the swings and the seesaw: each one uprooted and tossed aside, jumbled like the toys of a big, bad baby. Now the climbing frame is upside-down in the corner of the lot, paint chipped, concrete club feet in the air. The demolition made a surprising amount of ruckus and dust, considering that there wasn't much to start with: some trees, a few park benches of mundane municipal design, a yellow-brick toilet block. *Brick shithouse*, she used to say to herself in the mornings when she glimpsed it through her upstairs window, liking the sound of the words in her mind. Now that little joke is gone. One tall blue gum, pale-skinned and statuesque, an old-fashioned leaning beauty in whose branches multitudes had sung and nested: now that's a loss. A squad of men with chainsaws took the tree apart, hauling the pieces away like joints of meat; and then they came for the park's human dwellers. Derek and his gang came out stumbling, blinking, old soldiers led at gunpoint from caves. Their shopping trolleys dumped on the pavement, their mattresses like misshapen fungi pulled from the soil. And then the digging machines moved in, chipping their muzzles into the earth. Each stage brought its own wails of suffering and indignation. Now the excavating beasts have clamped their jaws and rested their topsoil-bearded chins on the ground. Something new will be rising up here soon.

This is what happens when you don't pay attention, Katya thinks. Things change; the pieces move around. She doesn't like it. She's troubled by change. Toby's presence, for example. It's not like she could turn her own nephew down when he came asking for the job. No, she's glad to have him. But she's lived and worked alone for a long time now, and to have someone tagging along is distracting. It's his vigor that she finds troubling, the speed of his growth. He's a new plant butting up from the soil, pushing her aside: her own roots are so shallow.

She plucks herself with a twang from the wire, and turns back to her house. Behind her, the water sloshes in its hole, a mud tongue clicking in a cold mouth.

The five houses in the row are two-story Victorians, high but narrow, pretty but decrepit, with a low wall fronting what once must have been five small gardens, now cemented over. She doesn't really know her neighbors. There's an old couple on the corner, and a family with a teenage girl who recently moved in two doors down. The other two houses are used as student digs. Katya lives at the end of the row, her garage right next to the alleyway. She crosses over the road, fishing out her keys.

There are many things she loathes about the garage door: its peeling wood finish, the perverse ridge on its steel handle that bites into her fingerbones, its pig-like keening when it does agree to open. She always approaches it like a wrestler heading into a tough bout, cracking her knuckles.

Irritable, she tugs at the rusted handle. The wood has swollen and it's sticking even more than usual. With spite in her heart she leans in to give it another wrench, really putting her weight into it. This time, the metal pulls right out of the rotten wood and her knuckles scrape across the door. She staggers back, clutching the detached handle.

"Damn it!"

She stares at her hand, stained now with a shit-like smear of rotten wood and rust and, yes, blood: the skin has been broken. The wet splinters in her palm, the wrench in her shoulder, the messiness of it all...She hurls the handle over towards the black municipal wheelie bins that stand in a row in the mouth of the alleyway. It bounces dully off the nearest lid and skitters into the space behind.

"Hey!" cries a hoarse voice.

"Oh fuck, what now?" She peers round the corner into the dark of the alley. There are a couple of draped brownish figures down at the far end. She makes out a mattress, a tangle of gray blanket, a black plastic radio held together with duct tape. One of the figures raises a ragged hand, and she recognizes the trailing bandage.

"Jeez, sorry, Derek man! Sorry."

Derek, who swathes his head and limbs in patterned rags, who leaves intricate sculptures made from toothpicks and cigarette boxes outside Katya's front door. There's a grunt from the dimness. "Got any smokes?"

"Nothing today, sorry."

"Eina, you hurt yourself, girlie," says Derek.

There is blood dripping from the side of her hand. "Flesh wound. I'll live." She blots the blood on her overalls.

Derek and his crew are mostly hospital survivors: of the psychiatric clinic in one direction or Groote Schuur in the other. Dazed and abandoned, patients who never made it home. There's the tall blind man who is led through the streets at a rapid clip by his squat, hawk-eyed companion. The slim woman whose features were once delicate, and who's always dressed in good clothes, but whose bloodshot eyes and ravenous panhandling quickly disperse any air of gentility as soon as she gets up close. Flora and Johan and their disappearing / reappearing baby. Dreadlocked Mzi, the shouter. A gentle bunch: the only bother has been the odd late-night singing and quarreling sessions. When they occupied the park, their nest of mattresses and blankets and tarpaulins was always tucked away discreetly in the bushes. Sometimes there was a small fire going – an almost pastoral scene.

Nobody else used the park: it would have been strange to see any actual mothers bringing actual children to play there. Turnover was high. Residents came and went, moved on or passed away, to be replaced. All but Derek. Derek has outlived them all, his age indeterminate but immense, his face not so much wrinkled as armored in plates of weather-toughened skin.

She gives him a wounded wave. "Goodnight." To hell with the garage. If anyone wants the van tonight they're welcome to it.

Inside her house, she kicks off her shoes and goes through the small lounge into the open-plan kitchen area. It takes half a dozen steps, wall to wall. The house is small, containing only a few gulps of sticky air; the carpet feels gritty underfoot. Katya runs water over the graze on her hand. The grime of the excavated hole has mingled with the rust from the garage door to taint her blood. Tetanus, lockjaw. A bath, that's what she needs. She climbs the narrow stairs – so steep! Today, more than most days, she feels how they've been shoehorned into the space.

She rented this place furnished, and since moving in she's changed nothing, barely added or subtracted a single item. She hasn't even moved the furniture, although some of it drives her mad: there's an old filing cabinet blocking the space between the kitchen and the stairwell, for example. The double bed is far too large for the small bedroom, and surplus to her requirements. But she likes the fact that this furniture has a history – a name scratched on the underside of the table, a seventies rainbow decal stuck to the bedroom window. It makes her own tenancy seem more plausible: someone else has managed a life here, in this same space. And if she starts shifting bookcases and beds around, she has a feeling the whole place might go haywire or just cease to work, as if she were trying to reassemble a complex machine she'd rashly taken apart. She'd do it all wrong.

Preparing the bath is a minor ritual. Katya likes it very hot, and always uses a great deal of bubble bath or cloudy bath-oil – the better not to see her own skin through the water's lens. Only the pale curves of her breasts break the surface. Sinking into the perfumed foam, she closes her eyes and goes through her day, emptying out her mental pockets, sorting the change into piles. But she can hear indistinct noises coming through the pipes, booming and sonorous, and the sunken pit of the building site keeps intruding into her thoughts. Its slick sides, its watery base. The mud like sweating flesh. The roots of the city, after all, do not run deep. A few meters down, and there you have it: raw earth, elemental.

She turns face-down and floats like that, eyes and mouth submerged. An unnatural posture, a sensation of slight risk; a person can drown in two inches of water. She summons again that sense of *downness* – of space under the surface – that the filthy hole across the road has opened up inside her. Depth, which the city conceals with its surface bustle. You forget what's underneath. A sudden vision of the deeps beneath the city, alive with a million worms, with buried things.

She surfaces with a splash of water over the edge of the bath. Rattled, that's how she feels. Headachey and wired and slightly nauseous, out of synch, not winding down apace with the day. Is it the stinking hole in the ground outside, the sense of things rearranging around her? Or is it the mention of her father – the old man popping up without warning after all this time? Seven years without a sniff of Len, and now here he is again, pissing on her territory.

Maybe it's just that damn garage door that's getting to her. All the wear and tear, the rot and disintegration, the distressing entropy of built things.

"What I wouldn't give," she says out loud. "What I wouldn't give."

For what? For a little bit of – not luxury, exactly, but ease. To be moved effortlessly from one action to the next, as she imagines some people are moved: the ground flowing like a conveyor belt beneath them, the world smoothing their passage.

That man she met today – he lives in such a world. Trimmed lawns rolling under his expensive shoes. She recalls his whisky scent. His mass. His handshake. She is something of a connoisseur of male handshakes, and that was a good one: dry, not a bone crusher or a loose parcel of phalanges either. She does not like being touched, mostly, but when she is it should be firmly. His hands made her think of the hands in the old Rothman's cigarette ads in magazines from her childhood – belonging to airline pilots, admirals. Solid and squarely reassuring. Those faceted wrists extending from naval cuffs, with clipped nails and a light dusting of hairs, holding out a pack of smokes.

She reaches a dripping arm over the edge of the bath and takes his card from the top pocket of her overalls. Quality card, textured, cream. Turns it over. *Martin Brand, Brand Properties* it says, under a blocky logo. On the phone, Mrs. Brand had pronounced the surname the English way, but Katya prefers the Afrikaans meaning. She likes the way the blunt sound of the word holds a secret conflagration. She touches the edge of the card to her lips.

On the bathroom ceiling, she spots a jagged new crack across the plaster. It's an accusatory shape: of smiting, of lightning bolts. The kind of thing sent from above, in punishment for some clear crime. The kind of thing one calls down upon oneself.

3

CRACKS

The call comes a few mornings later, as she's rubbing her hair dry after another bath and observing Derek through the upstairs window. He's on the opposite pavement, his back to her, weaving something – a piece of tape or ribbon – through the holes in the fence. It's absorbing, and the phone startles her.

The voice on the line is lush; she can almost smell the musk on the woman's breath, hear the smack of her lipstick. Sales call, Katya thinks, or someone following up on an unpaid bill.

"Miss Grubbs?"

"Who is this?"

"Painless Pest Relocations?"

Katya adjusts her tone. "That's us – how can we help?"

"Hold the line for Mr. Brand, please."

Silence, filled with furtive clicking. Derek's still busy down there. He must have been cold last night, she thinks. She could've gathered blankets, made food, offered coffee...but she's never done that, in all her years here. Never taken anything to Derek and his friends, never given them more than an empty Coke bottle to return for deposit.

"Grubbs!"

She remembers his voice, although now it's clear of the burr of drink. She looks down at herself – she's in a towel – and takes a moment to mentally slip into her overalls and button them up.

"That's what they call me."

"Then that is what I shall call you too. I believe we met at our garden party – perhaps you recall? You were wearing a rather fetching green." His voice is like marble, heavy but polished, evoking those giant stone spheres you see rotating in streams of water outside corporate headquarters. It would be reassuring, if not for its slightly mocking tone.

"White shirt," she says. "Too much to drink."

"And more before the day was out, I'm very much afraid."

Derek has moved on. The ribbon he's left behind makes a zigzag pattern in the wire, like those webs made by spiders on acid.

"So now," Mr. Brand's voice continues. "I have a problem, a persistent problem, and I would like to engage your services. If you're available."

"Depends," she says. "What sort of job are we talking?"

"What sort of job? Caterpillar wrangling, of course – what else?"

After the call, she sits quietly for a few minutes, considering. Down below, a schoolgirl – white shirt, gray trousers, Mary Janes– strolls past Derek's handiwork without a glance. She might be from the family that moved in recently down the road. Passing by, the girl casually pinches the end of the ribbon between her fingers, and as she walks on the zigzag unravels, lashing up and down through the wire, until the fence is empty again and the ribbon trails behind her like a tail.

A feather drops onto Katya's shoulder as wings clap across the space above her, and she looks up to see duct pipes, a blackened walkway. She takes it as a good omen: the beasts are here. City pigeons, in their proper place.

She's always liked parking garages, their in-between feel. No matter how glossy the shopping precincts that lie above or below, the parking garage is always a brute dungeon of raw concrete. Not a wild space, but not civilized, either. The dark corners and crevices make her urban-pest sensors prick up. Here you get your rats, sometimes your pigeons. Not a terribly varied fauna, but a resilient one, dark-adapted.

This parking garage is nothing special, the usual stained concrete and unfinished pillars. The old PPR-mobile looks dusty and out of place between the Beemers and Mercs. She lets her fingertips glide over the sleek flanks of the cars – metallic shells so like the carapaces of giant beetles – as she moves between them to the stairwell.

A short flight of stairs, and then a swing door and an abrupt change of atmosphere. There's a well-lit, carpeted lobby and a lobby-man in a cinnamon uniform; he takes her name and her picture with a webcam like a tiny Death Star. Then she has to press her thumb to a glass screen that glows with a bluish light. They say not a word to each other. He points silently to a space behind her right shoulder, in a banishing-from-Eden gesture, and she turns to see a large notice board of names and floor numbers.

Brand Properties, it says on the board: fifteenth floor.

"Thank you," she murmurs.

On floor two she's joined in the lift by a good-looking young man with satiny skin and a sharp black suit; on floor four, a bony woman carrying a tray of samosas. Nobody speaks, and none of them meet each other's eyes, although she attempts a brief flirtational skirmish in the polished metal of the lift wall with the young man. She tries to snag his eyes, but he's too good: she can't get an angle on him. He's staring off into a corner, not looking at anyone – not even himself. It seems unnatural, but also a skill: who could look at nothing, surrounded by mirrors? He gets out on the eighth floor, samosa lady on the tenth. Katya ascends alone. She imagines herself a cosmonaut in her green flight suit, trapped in a space-capsule. If it goes any higher, it might hit zero gravity.

When the doors sigh open on floor fifteen, she steps out into another white corridor, teal carpet with a diamond pattern underfoot. Disk-shaped light fixtures of smoked glass like flying saucers are set into the ceiling. She pads down the corridor, the only sound the sub-audible buzz of some electrical system – air-con, lighting. There are no windows, and it's impossible to say how far she is from real air and sunlight. This honeycomb bears little relation to the monolithic office block she circled earlier, looking for the parking entrance.

She counts the numbers on the doors. There are offices to the left and right, but no apparent occupants. Some show signs of recent activity, and a rapid exodus. Through doors ajar, she glimpses humorous postcards stuck to corkboards, a toppling pile of printouts on the floor, a chipped cup dumped in a sink in a tiny kitchenette. It's like the *Marie Celeste*. Can business really be that bad?

At the end of the corridor, where it turns a corner, there is at last a window, looking down onto the roofs of other city buildings. The foreshore: land stolen from the sea. The rooftops have been put to various uses. She sees gardens and stacked plastic chairs and heaps of scrap metal and even, on one, a gazebo and what seems to be a water feature. She can make out the fat torpedoes of koi fish circulating down there, the size of grains of rice but the shape unmistakeable. She has no idea all this had been going on above her commuter-level head. Most of the rooftops are grimy, though, not meant to be seen – like the top of the fridge in a short woman's house.

Down the other end of the corridor, just before it takes another corner, a cleaning lady leans on her silent hoover and stares down through a similar window. Katya wonders how the city's streets are marked for this woman, with what humiliations, curiosities and pleasures. The two of them, sole survivors of whatever mysterious plague has wiped out everyone else on the fifteenth floor, gaze down upon the grubby topside of the town.

The woman gives her a quick, flat glance and looks away, gunning the vacuum cleaner. It's a reminder. She is not floating here; she is working. Katya is working too. She passes the woman in the corridor without troubling her with another glance.

As she comes round the next corner, she sights life: not Mr. Brand, but another solidly potent figure, dark against the brightness of the corridor. It comes towards her with hand outstretched and a gleaming smile.

The woman is glossy and round and fragrant as a sugar plum, with toffee-apple lipstick, a deep but elevated cleavage and apparently knee-less legs that taper smoothly from nyloned thigh to stilettoed heel. Her globular haircut shines like black silk and is, Katya assumes, a quality weave.

She has no trouble recognizing the woman immediately: this is the owner of the satiny telephone voice. Seldom does a voice and its physical person correspond so closely. She has extravagantly bow-shaped lips, perfectly filled in, that part to reveal moist white teeth. There is nothing dry or cold or rough about this lady. She is all arcs and curves, sketched with a calligraphy pen and filled in with rich color. She proffers a hand and Katya feels the tips of enamelled nails touch her palm.

"Miss Grubbs? I'm Zintle."

Katya is at once a kid with skinned knees and frogs in her pockets. Puppy-dog tails. She shouldn't have worn the uniform; its powers are limited, in certain settings and with certain people. Zintle is tall, too. Being close to the ground has its advantages in Katya's line of work (nippiness, ability to creep into small spaces), but now she feels cowed before this substantial woman. She misses Toby's presence, pliant and wispy though it may be, by her side.

"Miss Grubbs," Zintle says, finding resonant depths in the name that Katya had not known existed. "We're so glad you came. Mr. Brand has been *so* enthusiastic about your work."

Her eyes, in finely wrought settings of copper eye shadow, dart around Katya's face, seeking data. She clasps Katya's upper arm and walks her towards an office door, a gentle but insistent escort.

"I understand that you've worked for Mr. Brand before?"

"Yes." She wants to say more – make something up, even. The woman seems so attentive.

But Zintle hustles them on briskly. "Lovely," she says, swiveling on one heel, batting open the door and easing them through. It's choreography.

Inside, it's all light and sky. The far wall is glass. Beyond, Katya can see the steep side of Signal Hill, the mosques and the forehead of the mountain. The sky is flawless, but tinted that sad, gunmetal gray of double-glazing.

"Have a seat," says Zintle, deftly installing Katya at one end of a leather couch. She sits too, flinging one silky leg over the other. "Well then, you know the outline of the project?"

"Well, no, actually. I don't know much, is Mr. Brand not—"

"He's in Singapore. Apparently." Zintle leans back and rakes a hand through her hair, which rebounds perfectly into shape.

The leather of the couch is taut and slippery, and Katya feels her overalled buttocks sliding off the edge. Crossing one's legs at the knee, she discovers, is not only ladylike but helps to lock one in position.

"You do...*do* extermination, right?" Zintle narrows her eyes and gives a teasing smile.

Katya appreciates this lady's style. She has a skittish, theatrical way of speaking, as if they're performing a slightly suggestive play. Katya is fluffing her lines, but that seems to be part of the fun. Zintle hasn't winked at her yet but there's a bit of a flick of butterfly eyelid in every syllable.

Still, Katya's responses remain clipped. How else do you converse with such a person, but play stone to their paper, rock to their silver scissor-blades?

"Right," she says. "Well, relocation, really."

"Precisely. So." Zintle leans forward confidentially. "We have a residential project which has been experiencing some problems."

"What kind of problems?"

"Various. Not very nice ones, to be honest."

"Cockroaches, rats, mites?"

"Well...let's just say it's a *comprehensive* pest situation." She's up on her feet again – when she moves she's fast – and holding out a hand. "Here we are."

There's something laid out along one wall on a table, under spot lighting. It's an architect's model, showing several buildings and their surroundings. Everything is white, the only markings the patterns of edge and shadow.

The scale is hard to make out at first. Katya sees a complex of four or five flat-topped, tiered buildings – ziggurat-like – arranged at angles around a central plaza. Elaborate walkways and arches and courtyards connect them, and tangles of what she supposes are ornamental plants drape over the edges of the stepped roofs. They look like tufts of white hair pulled off a hairbrush. A fountain, ringed by tiny benches, marks the center point of the plaza. A long driveway, decorated with a double row of miniature palm trees, strikes off to the edge of the model, and the whole is contained by walls.

"This is *Nineveh*." Zintle's dark fingers with their scarlet tips are vivid against the cardboard. A gorgeous giantess, reaching down from the clouds.

"Nineveh?"

Zintle shrugs. "It's just a name," she says. "Sort of a theme. One of the early investors was from the Middle East, I think."

Katya allows herself a moment to enjoy the calm of the miniature scene. There are model people down there, also colorless, frozen in attitudes of purposeful enjoyment: striding along a boardwalk, sitting at an outdoor table. A couple lean on a balcony railing. What they're staring at, though, has not been included in the model. The ground breaks off just beyond the boundary wall, as if some other-dimensional cataclysm has swallowed up a chunk of reality. The architect's manikins stare into the void – through the actual window, onto the vista of the real city beyond: full-color, blurred, gigantic. They look on the abyss with no discernible expression.

"It looks big," says Katya. She's never worked an entire estate before.

Zintle taps a nail on the roof of one unit. A smaller building on the border of the model, right up against the wall. "You'd have access to these, uh, servants' quarters. Or shall we say, the caretaker's lodge. It's two units, for the maintenance staff. The other buildings are shut up."

"Never used?"

"Not yet." Zintle clicks her tongue, suddenly exasperated. "Such a shame. Beautiful accessories, all furnished and ready to go. Show flats! It was built over a year ago, you know? Was supposed to be filled with residents by now. Top residents. But there was a string of disasters. All the copper wire was stolen, for one. Half the reclaimed area collapsed into the bloody swamp. Excuse my language. This disaster, that disaster. The landscape gardening didn't work out, everything got eaten by goggas. Had to redo all the interiors. It was a plague! We thought they were gone, the previous guy assured us... well." She splays her palms in a let's-not-go-there gesture. "Now the security staff tell us that they're back. We can't move anyone in until it's sorted. Losing pots of money. You understand?"

"Goggas?"

"They bite. Like I say, we got a guy in to sort them out, but between you and me, he was useless. Made things worse, actually. Creepy old guy." She crinkles her nose in remembered disgust, as if at a bad smell. "We had to get rid of him."

"Yes, well. Some of these older companies, they're very outdated. I have a different approach."

"I would hope so."

"You can't be more specific about these...goggas? You've seen them?"

She holds her palm towards Katya and wiggles her fingernails, evoking scurrying legs. "Yugh."

"Centipedes?"

"No, no. Here, sort of ..." Zintle grabs a pen and pad from the desk and scrawls a few assured lines. A cartoon bug. A button body with spindly legs sticking out in all directions – three on one side and four on the other, Katya notes – and a bundle of antennae like cat's whiskers. She's surprised Zintle hasn't included a pair of googly eyes.

"A beetle? Does it fly? Does it swarm?"

"Swarms. Eats the curtains, poos on the rugs. Nightmare."

"I see."

Zintle is suddenly brisk. "Well. Time runs short. I should just give you this dossier ..." She hands over a glossy cardboard file. "Perhaps you'd like to peruse that, and get back to us with a quote? It's a fairly urgent situation."

"Right then. I'll have to go out there of course, check it out."

Zintle is standing now, smoothing her suit down, shaping her hair back into its slick curve with a palm of a hand, taking Katya's arm and ushering her out. She's good at this maneuver, very professional. Before she knows it, Katya's back in the lift, doors closing behind her, on her way down to earth again.

Toby is waiting opposite her house, nose poked through the fence, the diamond wire pressing into his cheeks. He's staring at the demolition site. It's the first time he's been here since the bulldozers came through.

"Fucking hell," he says tightly. "How could they do that?" This place means something to him, too, Katya sees. She briefly feels their lives, hers and Toby's, overlap, anchored to the same plot of land.

"Here today, gone tomorrow," she says. "Nothing lasts forever, kiddo. What are you doing here?"

"Mom said. Your gutters."

"Gutters? Oh, okay, I suppose."

Alma is always doing this: worrying about Katya's living arrangements. It was Alma who'd explained to her sister about vacuuming, for example, and about painting walls. Who persuaded her to put a damn door on the garage in the first place. When Toby was only ten or eleven, she started dropping him off at Katya's place to sort out all the odd jobs that Katya had no idea needed doing. Now Toby comes alone, usually by minibus taxi along Main Road, with a screwdriver in his pocket and a dopey smile, eager to fiddle with a squeaky floorboard or mold on the bathroom ceiling. Katya suspects he's not very good at this kind of DIY, or any more interested in it that she is herself; but he's always willing to give it a shot.

It's Len's fault, that Katya doesn't know about houses. After the loss of their mother, when the sisters were little, they never really had a house, or not for long. Len kept them moving, job to job and place to place. They'd pass through with a nomad's contempt for the townsfolk. A dozen different schools. Many nights next to the spare tire in the back of the old bakkie, the pickup always stank of bird shit and pesticide and sometimes blood. They never did stand steady on the ground beneath their feet. But Katya always imagined that once you got to settle down, once you had that stack of bricks and mortar, it was solid. She hadn't realized how restless bricks and mortar are: how much effort it takes to keep them from falling down, from wandering off or spilling out in the wrong direction. It's disheartening to see that respectful inattention is not enough. That to keep things exactly as they are requires arduous maintenance, like a lawn needs cutting or a body needs feeding. Such ceaseless labor to shore up the world.

A rocking motion catches her eye. A girl has come to lie along the top of the neighbor's garden wall, on her back with hands folded on her stomach. She's wearing gray school trousers, one knee up and tossing to and fro. Eyes closed and dreaming, ears laced with the thin white cords of an iPod. Wire-fed, recharging. Fifteen, sixteen? So young, so weary. What could make such a new creature so tired?

She feels Toby's stare as a physical pressure, leaning on her right shoulder.

The girl sits up abruptly from a deep sleep of music. She pulls out the earplugs and regards them down her nose, head lolled back on her shoulders. Then she swings to the pavement and stretches her arms behind her back, pushing out her chest like a dove sunning its wings. Pretty. Katya recognizes her now: it's the girl from down the road, the one who unpicked Derek's spider web.

She's compact, with elastic-looking legs and calves: a body made for backflips and handstands. Coppery skin, short hair slicked back behind her ears, snub features and strong, clean cheekbones. Diamond nose-stud, to the left. Small mole on cheek, to the right. Dark eyes, more watchful than unfriendly. Maybe shy rather than sly; it's hard to tell.

"Howzit," says the girl. Not shy, then.

"Hi." Katya turns her attention to the garage door. Let the young deal with the young.

"See what they've done over the road?" says the schoolgirl.

"Uh, yes. Kind of hard to miss." Toby laughs and gives her his sweetest gape. Hopeless!

But the girl's observing him in a not unfriendly way. "So, have you guys got cracks?"

"Crack?" says Toby.

"Cracks, cracks in your walls. From the vibrations. From the machines."

Toby looks at her, worried. The girl quirks a shapely eyebrow. "Look." She points at the wall she's just been sitting on. Sure enough, there's a diagonal crack down to the tar. Has it always been there?

"And look, look there, it goes all across the road. I'm telling you." Now the girl is skipping out into the road – really skipping, like a small child – and pointing at the tar, which does indeed look ominously split open between her feet. She points out the length of the crack with a toe, hands in the air to balance. Her gray trousers ride up to show her ankles, thin relative to taut parabolic calves, in short white socks.

Is she younger than Katya had thought? Older? She has one of those strong faces where the bones set early and stay good for decades.

"You living around here?" asks Toby.

The girl ducks her head in a sideways nod. "Around. You?"

Oh, please.

Katya fiddles with the garage door a little longer before giving it up. It's now genuinely impossible to open without the handle. The girl is watching with arms folded across her chest. Toby has turned to stand by her side, similarly cross-armed. Copycatting.

"Toby, do you need a ladder, or what?"

"No, it's cool, I can get up by the garage roof. It's easy."

She notices the girl is spreading her legs wider across the crack in the tar, showing further, unanticipated lengths of calf. Toby's smile is stretched to breaking across his face.

"Now?" she says, snappier than she intends.

"Just now."

"You be careful."

Inside, Katya tracks onto the carpet some kind of khaki sludge from the road. She fetches the broom and pan from the kitchen corner – where a new black crack snakes up the wall.

The old house is built on sandy foundations that have been subsiding for decades, and she's used to the odd warp and split, the plaster running like a laddered stocking. Like the lines on her own face, she can't quite remember when each crack in the house appeared or lengthened; but she knows their shapes, their long italic slants, their seismograms. This one, though, she's never read before. Inky, sharp-edged, viciously jinking. It seems mischievous. Her first irrational thought is that the girl is somehow behind it, playing a joke.

Can it really have jagged all the way through the earth from the demolition site across the road? How deep does it go? Does it run through the whole house, bottom to top? She imagines it slicing through her walls, her foundations, through the earth deep beneath the road, straight and thin as a laser beam, cross-sectioning the cakey layers of earth, gravel, sand, tar. She shoves the broom back in the corner, although it can't conceal the flaw.

When the phone rings, it's so loud it seems it might split the cracks open wider still. She snatches it up before it can do more damage. "PPR."

The pause on the other end is ironic. "It's only me, Kat."

She makes her hand relax, lowers her voice. "Sorry. Hi. Your son's on my roof, if you're looking for him." This is usually the reason for Alma's calls.

Katya associates her sister strongly with telephones. Certainly, these days, phone calls – or more usually, text messages – are their main mode of communication. But it goes back further.

When Alma was thirteen and Katya ten, Alma started to run away. Sometimes she was gone for days, sometimes weeks. And then forever: at seventeen, Alma left and didn't come back. But Katya continued to hear from her. Alma would phone at odd hours, from call boxes, from unknown destinations, across immense distances. Sometimes there would be long gaps in their communication. This was before cellphones, and with Dad on the move, it wasn't always easy for Alma and Katya to find each other. But they made a plan with Aunt Laura, a distant cousin of Len's, who resided immovably in Pinelands. Every time she had a valid phone number, Katya would inform Laura, and receive Alma's current number in exchange – all while resisting being pumped by her aunt for further tragic family gossip.

One way or another, every few months Katya would hear her sister's dry whisper on the other end of a phone line, or sometimes a few moments of the kind of silence that was unmistakeably Alma's: a silver crackling static. Katya started to lose the memory of what her sister looked like. She saw only a delicate figure, floating in a cloud, somewhere very high and very cold. An ice princess, barely real, weightlessly revolving around the still point of the phone receiver which connected them. *Where are you,* Katya would ask, *where have you gone?*

Oh Kat, Alma would sigh, her breath filtering though the rosette of holes in the receiver, ice crystals forming in her little sister's ear. Each time Alma hung up, Katya was sure she had vanished entirely, like frost in the morning.

The next time she saw Alma, it was three years later and Toby had just arrived, a pale infant of mysterious provenance. By this stage,

Alma had started to peroxide her hair. Was it to match her child's? With her pale skin, it was indeed as if all that time Alma had indeed been out in some blanchingly cold world.

"Hey Al, it's so strange," Katya now finds herself saying. "I'm crossing Dad's path. He's working again."

"How do you know?"

"Somebody's hired me for a job. Apparently they used Dad before and thought I was the same company. He was there last year some time."

"God. So the old boy's still alive. When did you last see him?"

"Seven years ago. How about you?"

"Less than that. Three, maybe. I went to see him in that group home – you know that awful place he was in for a while, with the drunks? He borrowed some money."

"Really?"

"You sound surprised. I've done my bit for him over the years, you know."

"Oh, I know."

"More than my bit." Alma's voice is starting to rise.

Alma's everyday voice is distant, always threatening to flicker out and disappear from tiredness or lack of interest. An unimpressed voice. She's sounded that way since she was little. When she gets worked up, though, her voice slides up the register and she sounds like a child about to burst into tears: indignant, amazed to feel so much. Katya has never seen her sister weep – has only once seen her close to crying out from pain – and can't bear to imagine it.

"Anyway, it's creepy," Katya says. "Being in his footsteps, as it were."

"Huh. Serves you right, working in the same filthy business."

"It's not the same business."

"Ja, ja, relocation not extermination, I heard about it. Just do me a favor, okay? Think about what happened to Mom. What this business did to her."

Katya is silent. She cannot bring herself to ask the crude question: What *did* happen to Mom? Sylvie's vanishing has always been too grotesque, too central to discuss as if it were just another episode in their lives. One day, when Katya was three, Sylvie went to the hospital and never came back. Katya knows this means she died, although that has never been spoken. It must have been an accident: something so maiming, so traumatizing, that their mother was plucked instantly from the presence of her children and could never be returned. There is no shortage of possibilities. Any given day with Len, especially a younger Len at the height of his chaotic powers, could have brought a hideous demise.

But it was impossible to ask her father about Sylvie, and some kind of pride prevents her from asking Alma now. Anyway, she's always understood that Sylvie's loss belongs primarily to Alma. When it comes to their mother, Katya has no authority. Alma has three years on her, three years more of Mom; always has had and always will. Katya possesses only shadows: memories of a figure moving through a kitchen, in yellowing light; a taste in the mouth. These spectres are not proof of anything, nor are they weapons to be used in argument.

And so Katya simply says, "I'll tell Tobes to call."

Alma clicks her tongue and puts the phone down. Katya is not sure what that means: if Alma has cut her short, or if it's the other way around.

Above her, the tin squeals as Toby stomps across the roof, and she feels the noise in her teeth. She bites down on the scar tissue on her thumb, the place where she keeps slicing it open on the garage door. This is why she and Alma don't talk much. Their conversations tend to twist back on themselves and bite, like snakes.

Her messed-up hands. Len's. When they used to eat together in the old days, Katya would stare at his short fingers, attached to square, functional palms. When she looked down at the table, there they were again: those same hands, if smaller, less shop-worn versions, clenched around her own knife and fork. She was always scared of developing Len's bulbous knuckles, which he'd crack in their ears of his children to wake them in the mornings. Alma had the same hands – although Alma ate neatly, manipulating cutlery with neurotic precision. The tips of her index fingers pressed white against the steel as she dissected the food into smaller and smaller morsels. Katya ate loudly in response, chewing with her mouth open like her dad, showing Alma her teeth and her scorn.

In front of her on the kitchen table is Zintle's "dossier". She pulls it towards her, opens up the cardboard envelope. Inside is a sheaf of stapled paper – a brochure, phone numbers, maps, directions. Also a photocopy of a newspaper clipping. Katya spreads the papers out on the kitchen table. The newspaper article, dated June last year, is about a freak swarm of insects making their way through the southern peninsula. There's not much information in the piece: some people's gardens suffered, and a couple of motorists were disgusted by having to crunch their way through a tide of the things crossing a road. A small child suffered a bite on the cheek. A zoologist from UCT was interviewed, and he stressed that this was a natural occurrence, no cause for alarm: this particular beetle, "a species of metallic longhorn," swarms every few years, at unpredictable intervals – in recent times perhaps more flagrantly than before. There was no danger, but laypersons should not attempt to collect the creatures, "although they are attractive specimens".

A murky black-and-white photo shows a single nondescript beetle in the bottom of a laboratory beaker.

The brochure is much more appealing. The cover is an artist's depiction of a gleaming ivory building, tiered, lapped at its base by an impressionistic greensward. The sky in the picture is rapturous blue, the clouds artistic dabs. *Nineveh welcomes you,* it says in embellished cursive. The address is not one she recognizes, a suburb name she doesn't know. She'll have to look it up.

She props the picture up against the kettle: a fragment of color in the corner of her stuffy kitchen. It breathes of some foreign place, not quite of the here or the now. She wants to shrink herself down to that size, lodge on one of those miniature balconies, bask in the beams of that small but potent sun; or, better still, duck down into one of those tiny, immaculate rooms and close the door behind her.

Time for a new notebook. She selects a fresh one from the pile in the bottom drawer of the filing cabinet. It's a fine, old-school piece of stationery, A5, hard black covers with a red fabric spine. The top and middle drawers of the cabinet are where she keeps the old ones, filled with her working notes. They get used up surprisingly quickly: she starts a new one every three or four months. She's not really sure what she's keeping them for. Perhaps one day she'll write her memoirs: *Life Among the Vermin*.

Len never made a note in his life; his stories were all in his head. But Katya likes to do it. Making records is one way to keep things squared away.

She slides out the small pencil she uses for such things – so much more practical than pens for working in the field – and makes a neat heading:

NINEVEH

Katya negotiates a fee with Zintle for a reconnaissance trip to Nineveh. Mr. Brand, it seems, expects her to stay on the property in the "caretaker's lodge." Normally she wouldn't agree to this, but given the scale of the project – and the generous fee promised – she decides to make an exception. A few days should be enough to assess what needs to be done.

The day before she's due to go, she packs her bags. She has to stand on a chair to pull the suitcase off the top of the bedroom cupboard – it's been ages since she's gone anywhere, and the bulky old thing is buried under a mound of spare blankets and the pieces of a broken chair. The suitcase is one of the few things Len ever gave her – or rather, that he left behind.

Katya was twenty then. She'd been helping him out with the work full-time for three or four years, after she quit school. They were staying in a truly appalling hotel in Durban (cracked and leaking toilet bowl, dried matter – perhaps blood – on the walls). One morning he was gone, leaving her with the bill and a curious sense of gratitude: she would not have escaped in any other way. Later, their current employer came knocking, and she understood why he'd needed to disappear. Some expensive power tools had gone missing. Len had a habit – or perhaps a principle – of walking away from a job with more than he brought in.

But perhaps he'd just decided it was time to go. Katya suspected that Len was getting bored with her, now that she was grown. She was no longer so eager to please, but she didn't make much effort to quarrel with him, either. She was starting to apprehend her own boredom, too, and to sense the fatigue of the years ahead, grinding along with Len in the driver's seat. Len ever more whisky-soaked, their travels more haphazard and accident-plagued. At some point she'd started to be repelled by the stink of killing that clung to them both. She wanted to be clean. And she wanted to be still: to have one place that she belonged to, that belonged to her.

Along with the suitcase, Katya inherited a couple of nets and traps and the like, which she kept. And two pairs of Len's underpants, which she did not. She wrinkles her nose at the pungent memory.

Zintle had made the same face when recalling Len Grubbs, the exterminator, and Katya sympathises. It is the family smell, Eau de Grubbs. It comes from living on the road, from working with animals and chemicals. Not a bad smell, necessarily. Does Katya smell the same? (And could Zintle sniff her out?) Probably. Although, of course, this is famously the thing that one cannot tell about oneself.

Alma has it too, despite her potpourri, her talcs and creams. On Alma the scent seems to translate into a kind of sexual signal. As soon as she hit puberty, boys took one sniff and started to follow her around. While never once losing her composure, Alma used this power to pull herself away from her family and out into the world. Hand over hand. Grasping at the bodies of boys and men, hanging on like a drowning girl, desperate to be dragged clear of the swamp. And it worked. Whoever the faceless boy was who fathered Toby, he made Alma's return impossible. After that, she lost her enthusiasm for sleeping around: there was no need. And now that she's married to solid Kevin, Alma can devote herself full-time to eradicating the troubling odors of her former life.

It's something too intimate and shameful for them to talk about, but Katya knows her sister is still terribly self-conscious about the smell. As a child, Alma would scrub and scrub, any time they got close to a bathroom. These days, Alma has three bathrooms in the neat home where she lives with her husband, their young children – twins, a boy and a girl – and Toby. It's a place where every object has been carefully chosen and positioned. In the bathrooms and the main bedroom are dozens of bottles of expensive scent, body spray, deodorant. But they say the body has a signature, molecular; that it doesn't change. Under her perfume, Alma still has the family aroma.

Sylvie's smell was different. It is one of the few definite pieces of information Katya has about her mother: her musky, talcy smell has persisted more strongly than any visual memory. Going through her father's abandoned things that day when she was twenty, Katya found a loose photograph of an impossibly young, grinning Len with shoulder-length hair, arm slung around a voluptuous brunette. She recognized nothing about the woman – except a version of her own full bust, and something of Alma's distance in the eyes – but she accepted on the evidence that this was Sylvie, her mother, fresh out from England and newly married. Immediately, Katya felt the need to turn the picture upside down and not look at it again.

During her twenties, Katya held on to very little. Her possessions were so few that they fitted inside Len's: his suitcase and one of his old box traps – despringed, defanged – which she'd stuff with clothes and haul from house to house. Each time she moved, she threw out more of the heavy past. But the photo she has kept, all these years. Now it's hidden right at the back of the filing cabinet. Every couple of years she fortifies herself with a whisky and sneaks another peek. Over time, the woman's face speaks to her less and less. Young Len, on the other hand, seems to grow more vital with every year spent in the cabinet dark. She's never shown Alma the picture. It is her own guilty piece of Sylvie, kept for herself alone.

The suitcase tumbles down from the top of the cupboard onto her head, bringing with it a chair leg, the body of a fish moth and the smell of her father's things. He's here now, coming towards her out of the dust; his body is darkness crawling with the floaters of her sun-dazzled eyes. He smells strongly of campfires, of mothballs, of bleach and tobacco. He catches something from behind her ear, holds it tight in his hand: a conjurer's trick. He smiles and holds out his palm, and she sees it is crossed with gold, with something rich and glinting and alive: a dragonfly.

"Aitsa," he'd exclaim: "Surprise!"

The trick was meant to make her and Alma laugh, or flinch. She never knew which. Sometimes he let the little creature go, and sometimes not. And sometimes there was nothing in his fist at all. Sometimes it was just a fist.

4

AT THE GATES

Nineveh is so very new that it doesn't yet exist – not in the Cape Town street directory, and not on the maps in Katya's head. She stares at Zintle's map, but it's like a jigsaw piece for a picture she's never seen. She can't work out how these loops and forks correspond to any place real. When she tries to follow the route in her mind, she drifts into limbo: somewhere out past Noordhoek, between the new houses and the beach. Wetlands. Or so she thought.

She hasn't got used to Toby at the wheel, and has to stop herself from clutching at the handbrake. But he drives prudently, she'll give him that. Very upright in the seat, with his long legs cramped under the dash and his head poked forward off his shoulders, scowling into the headlights. Some young men gain grace with proximity to machines. Toby, clearly, is not one of these.

"Christ, relax," she says. "Take your nose off the windscreen."

She lets him do the navigating. This place obviously exists in a parallel universe, where nothing is quite what it seems. Some slightly future Cape Town, perhaps, one that Toby, being young, instinctively inhabits. Because he hasn't been alive long enough to have the roadmap stamped into his brain, he drives without directional prejudice, following Zintle's instructions to the letter, with no second-guessing. Thus they end up in the right place – which feels, to Katya, profoundly wrong.

On a dark stretch of road, Toby lurches the car off into a narrow avenue lined with palms. High white walls on either side, topped with electrified wire and set with evenly placed floodlights, turn the road into a corridor of light and dark. The palm fronds glow emerald, backlit, and they drive for ages through criss-crossing shadows. The avenue seems implausibly long.

How could she have missed this place? Katya thought she knew this city – she's fished creatures out of its cracks and crevices for years – and yet right now she can scarcely tell which way she's facing. Strange scenery has been cranked into place. The mountain is still there behind them, and somewhere up ahead is the ocean, where it should be; but everything else is turned around. This is somewhere else now. This is new.

Eventually they crunch to a halt in front of a set of tall iron gates where the avenue terminates. It's dark. Two giant lanterns are supported on bulky gateposts, but their light does not extend far into the gloom. Beyond the gate, the walls and the road and the trail of lights disappear. It's impossible to tell what lies on the other side.

Toby switches off the engine. Katya gets out and stands in the sudden country dark, and listens. The road is freshly tarred all the way up to the gate, but the ground beyond is raw, still to be landscaped. She draws her eyes away from the blackness between the bars and examines the gateposts. She sees now that they are ornate, elaborately shaped and tiled. A grinning lion paces either side, done in hard-wearing ceramic. Some kind of Babylonian fantasy, it seems.

Although the lions are hokum, the padlock on this gate is real enough: bright bronze and as big as a pack of cigarettes. There is no obvious keypad. No buzzer or handle. She has no phone number to try, and anyway, there's no cellphone reception.

Toby has popped his head out of the car. "Let's go," he moans. "It's dark, there's no one here."

Perhaps he's right. Perhaps this is all a huge practical joke, a trick. Peering through the bars, she has a powerful sense that there really is nothing there, that the street-map did not lie when it showed a blank. That they've reached the edge of the map and are about to drop off.

It's odd, and touching, too, to see Toby so discomfited. Katya herself feels eager to push open the gate, dip her toe in the blackness.

She's just about to turn away and get back into the car when a silvery sound tickles the air: an irregular *ting ting*. A small light wavers towards them out of the dark on the other side of the gate. It casts a modest halo on the ground as it approaches, slows and stops. Of course: a bicycle bell. She sees the glinting frame of the bike before she sees the uniformed rider. He straddles the bike, looking at them through the bars and breathing hard.

"You're the lady?" he asks. "The worm lady?"

"That's me," she says, and suddenly she's on familiar ground. He gets off the bike and fumbles with the big padlock.

"Step back, please," he says, and when she does the gates come creaking open after her.

"No car, please," he says. "It's still very muddy in here. You can get stuck."

Toby passes her bags out of the car. She doesn't have much with her: a small rucksack, the old suitcase. "Okay," she says to him. "This is it, compadre."

He's watching her with anxious bushbaby eyes. "Are you sure? Is this the place?"

"Seems to be. Go on, Toby, it's fine. This guy's expecting me."

She's taking a bit of a risk, leaving him the van. But they have several small jobs scheduled over the next few days, easy money that she doesn't want to give up. Some humane mousetraps to lay. Some mongooses that need transporting from the SPCA. Toby can handle it, she reckons, while she's living the life of luxury in Nineveh. She's made sure the first-aid kit is filled and ready to go, that he has enough gloves, enough of everything. He'll be sleeping in her house, keeping an eye on things.

"You'll be okay," she says.

"Two days?"

"Three maybe. I'll call you."

He nods in the dark. "No problemo," he says.

She should bend and kiss his cheek. The young are easy with their hugs, their kisses. But she doesn't feel that young. Awkwardly, she grips his cold hand with her free one. "Don't crash the van. That's all I ask."

She watches him crank the car through a five-point turn and rumble off down the corridor of palms and lights. The red taillights blink out at the end of the avenue.

The bicycle guard trundles the tall gates closed behind her. He does not offer to take either of her bags.

"Follow me," he says, and wheels his bike around. His taillight is a small echo of the van's, a strawberry firefly pulling away. She picks up her suitcase and follows.

The sky is overcast, with no moon or stars, and no blue ghost of moonlight on the sea which she knows must be ahead. Instead of waves, she hears a hidden chorus, multitudinous, massed in the night: the creaks and sighs and belling of the creatures out there in the vlei. The frogs and toads, the worms and the night birds. The ones she's come to parley with.

Ahead is a confused collage of shade, with black, vaguely geometric shapes rising out of the general dark. The ziggurats must be arrayed around her, but it's too dark to make anything out. Close by is a much smaller building with a lit window. The guard has leaned his bike against the wall; now he comes towards her with an oversized torch. He hands her a clipboard, a black ballpoint attached with a piece of grubby string. The beam of the flashlight lances off at an unhelpful angle – she wonders if he's any better at aiming that gun on his belt – and she has to shield her eyes to fill in what seems a tedious number of questions. Name, address, three phone numbers, fax number, email, place of work, age, occupation.

"Age? Why do you need that?"

He shrugs. *Reuben*, says his name tag. He has a delicate face: full lips and long eyelashes. His neck is wrapped in a gray woollen scarf, although it's a warm night. He barely looks at her answers as he takes back the clipboard.

"So ja," he says, "they've put you in Unit Two." He writes the number large next to her name.

"Two? Is that good?

He pauses. "It's okay," he says. And with that he's on his bike again, heading off towards the looming buildings, taking the flashlight. She can hear his tinny bell growing faint. Once more, she's following through the dark.

Beneath her feet, the path is hard and slightly unstable: wooden planks. The bicycle man pauses for her, turning to shine his flashlight onto a place where the planking is laid over a dark trench. She can hear the sound of running water.

They come up against a two-story building. The guard brushes a doorway with his flashlight, finding *ONE* in silver letters. "Unit One," he says.

"Where's the lights?" she asks.

"They'll be on tomorrow. For now, it's just emergency power. We go up."

There's an outside staircase leading up to the next floor. Katya ascends carefully: the banister is disconcertingly low. At the top, she has the sensation of stepping out into nothingness. They're on a stone terrace, white in the flashlight but smeared with arabesques of mud: whorls and streaks left by muddy boots, as if an army of mud crawlers had emerged from the vlei and done a dance outside Unit Two.

Reuben steps forward and his flashlight finds a doorway. Black matte surface. A silver *TWO*. He hovers his thumb – nicely manicured, she notes – over a small black square next to the door handle.

"You do it," he says. "I'm not authorized. You press it like this."

She puts her thumb to the pad. The door lock makes a soft cluck. "Wow."

"You see, you're in the system."

This gives her a funny feeling. Like she was already built into the fabric of the building, long before she got here. Like her whorls and loops were there on the blueprints, inked in, microscopic. She remembers now the guy in the lobby of the Brand office block, scanning her thumbprint. She flexes her fingers uncomfortably.

"Go in," he says.

Inside, it's utterly dark, but she can feel the hollow darkness of the night pushing at the small of her back. She steps in, and then steps back out again immediately.

"I can't see a thing."

Reuben shrugs. "No lights tonight."

"Well, can I have a flashlight?"

He looks down at his own big light with a frown. "Let me just show you quickly rather."

He goes ahead of her. In the flashlight beam, small details spring into life and are immediately doused: a picture frame, a door handle, the legs of a table.

"Ah," he says. "Bedroom. You'll be okay here."

"Okay, no, wait ..." She feels her way forward, touches the edge of a bed. It feels inviting: cool, crisply made up. "Is this where he stayed? The other guy who was here. The exterminator."

She can't make out his face behind the bright disk of the light. "No," he says at length. "He was Unit One. Underneath." The light dips briefly to the floor and back up. A sniff in the dark. "Okay, I say goodnight now. Electricity's on again tomorrow."

And then he turns and herds his light back out of the door. She sees the illumination bounce once or twice off mirrors and pictures, and then the front door clicks shut again.

She's sunk in absolute darkness. She drops her bags at her feet and waits, feeling the disturbed space settle around her. Her knees are pressed against the bed. The best she can do is to stay very still, and not make any unnecessary motions. Carefully, she turns and sits. She works her cellphone out of her pocket. The small blue screen winks on reassuringly, but there's no reception.

She kicks off her shoes and fumbles her way between tight sheets. Small movements. The sheets smell clean. She coughs in the dark, just to hear the acoustics of the place, but there are none: sound sinks into the air like a footfall on thick carpet. Wrapped in her black sheets in a lightless world, there's nothing for Katya to do but vanish into sleep until the morning comes to show this place to her.

5
BULLY BEEF

In the blurred night that follows, Katya wakes frequently, rising with difficulty out of patches of dense, dreamless sleep. She can hear her own heartbeat in her ear against the pillow, a scraping sound, too loud. Each time she wakes there is the same disorientation: she can't tell which way round the bed stands, in what room, in what house, what city. In the dark, she has no sense of the size of her body, or of the space in which she lies. There might be a high cathedral vault above her – or her nose might be two centimeters away from the roof of a cave.

Morning comes with a tearing sound, like a knife through foil. She's lifted out of the deepest trough of sleep, bobbing to the surface, head clearing the waves.

She doesn't drink now, not much, but there have been times in her life when she did. The worst part was always the waking, the panic of erasure. The laborious pulling-together of time, of the body. She has the same sense now, lying here in this strange bed, of having to reconstruct everything from nothing. How her limbs lie; whether she's face-up or face-down. But unlike the drinker's morning-after dread, she feels a dreamy, unfettered kind of elation.

For a good few minutes, she lies there in the limbo of the dawn dark – mysteriously different in quality from evening dark, or midnight dark, or small-hours dark: with a luminous lining, the promise of something on the other side. Like pale blue silk showing through black lace, or sand through shallow water as your night-boat comes to shore.

Inevitably, her body settles into itself. Gravity seeps into the room along with a seam of light near her face, as if light creates mass. As her body returns to her, she finds that it's a childlike pose she has adopted: hand shoved against her mouth and drool on her knuckle. She watches, a little fearfully, as the blue line of radiance gains intensity, and then becomes decipherable as the bottom edge of a curtain. Below her, a bed. These arms, these legs, this heavy head: all the same as they were before.

It's an old sensation, this: opening her eyes on an unfamiliar ceiling. When they were kids, in the old days with her dad, they moved around so much, flat to shabby flat. They slept in spare rooms, on floors belonging to Len's dodgy acquaintances. For a while in a caravan. A couple of weeks here and there with distant cousins or long-lost aunties. Dumped with Laura on and off. Once they stayed in a converted garage, with a rolling door that opened their entire life for inspection every morning, like the lid of a sardine can. Once, a few nights in a small concrete room in the back of a mechanic buddy's workshop, among the carcasses of engines and the smell of rancid motor oil.

As an adult, though, she's found a home and tried her best to stick in it. She doesn't like to spend nights away. As far as lovers' beds go...she doesn't stay for breakfast. Katya is one of those creeping girls, who pick their shoes from the floor and vanish at midnight. She prefers to deposit the scents of the night back in the fug of her own bed.

In the night, Nineveh's sheets have lost their cool neutrality and taken on her own smell, but they are still tight and smooth around her, as if she's been held in a motionless swoon all night. She wonders how long this bed has been waiting for an occupant. Is she the first?

The night before comes back to her in pieces, like stepping stones through the gloomy swamp. The firefly light of the bicycle. The damp air and the darkness. The Halloween face of the security guard above his torch. The dense conversations of the frogs and insects all around.

The morning is casting a grain of texture onto the curtain next to her head. Her arm dangles towards the light and touches fabric. These drapes are not cheap, thin things like she has at home, but heavy stuff that resists the light. She lets them slip back between her fingers. While the curtains are still closed, there might be anything out there. Any landscape at all, any place in the world.

A bicycle bell rings somewhere. That silver sound fills her with a flood of nostalgic delight: it is the sound of childhood, or clear days, of cycling with no hands down hills...where does it come from, this memory? Did she have such a childhood? Did anyone?

Another sound: the ripping again. She pushes the curtain aside. And lies there, propped on an elbow, staring out at the dreamy scene that fills the large window. The light is quenching in its early-dawn blueness. There is a vlei, very still, with a complex, broken frame of tufts and fronds. She can make out the heads of bulrushes, etched against the milky water. She sees now what made the tearing noise that woke her: an Egyptian goose, raking its wingtips on the water, then climbing away with a clap. It leaves behind a serrated wake.

It is not a completely lonely scene. There's some kind of construction site on the far side of the vlei. Another housing estate going up. Stationary bulldozers and tractors, dim in the early dawn, a tiny tin-drum brazier burning like a thimble of heat. A nightwatchman, still on duty.

She sees the building from that lonely watchman's perspective: hers must be the only window showing any movement, the only one in which the curtain has been pulled aside. She closes it and in the dimness pats her hands along the wall, looking for a light switch. Her fingers find a square of smooth plastic, which doesn't even require a click: her touch alone triggers it, and the lights fade in, dim and yellow. The electricity is back.

She gets out of bed, assuming once more her body's weight. She's still in jeans and T-shirt from the night before.

The light switches are in obscure places, not easy to find. A girl in a maze, Katya makes her way out of the bedroom and into a dark passageway by trailing a hand on the wall and not losing contact. In this way, she was once told, any maze is solvable. It's one of those pieces of information she's stored up, in case of need. She has many imaginary stratagems of this kind; plans for escape.

By means of this cunning technique, she locates a small kitchen. The fridge buzzes to itself, cycling; she opens it, letting a rectangle of white light into the dark. The shelves are empty. Something she hasn't given much thought to: how she will sustain herself while she is here.

Opposite the kitchen, a door opens onto an empty living room. She wades through white linen curtains and finds the handle of a patio door. It slides back smoothly on its runners, letting her out onto the terrace and into morning light. She surveys the field of operations.

For a moment, she feels a vertigo of scale. She is inside the architect's model that she saw in Mr. Brand's office. As advertised, a high wall rings the property, topped by the parallel lines of electric fencing. She can make out the main entrance, with the lions on the gateposts looking small as cats, and the corridor of palms beyond. Just inside the gates is a small wooden hut: the guardhouse. It seems much closer than it did last night on her torchlit march. Her own block, the modest "caretaker's lodge", is built into a corner. The guardhouse and the lodge both face an arc of larger, grander buildings, all pale plaster and stone and designed in a vaguely Babylonian style: stepped terraces, ziggurats, archways.

A central plaza separates the staff quarters from the residential buildings. But this is not the landscaped garden that's meant to be there: it's a raw field of mud, criss-crossed by temporary plank paths and tracked by bicycle tires. A small stream bisects the area.

Close to the base of her building, down to her right, a couple of milkwood trees grow up against the perimeter wall, their trunks bending low to the ground, their leaves dark and glossy – the only sign of organic life within the walls. White garden furniture is arranged in their shade.

There is no other greenery: no trace of the hanging gardens suggested by the brochure. The built-in planters on the terrace are filled with nothing but flakes of gray stone. Clearly, the planned vegetation was never planted, or has been devoured by the mysterious goggas. Also, there are no small human figures, save herself.

Zintle mentioned that the land was reclaimed. Katya wonders how much of the wetlands they had to drain, how many thousands of vertebrate and invertebrate souls were displaced or destroyed to make this place. In her experience, a poorly drained property is a magnet for all kinds of damp-loving pests: water-snakes, slugs and especially mosquitoes. The rising water and its travellers always find a way back in.

Indeed, beyond Nineveh's perimeter, everything is insistently alive and pushing to enter. Heaped against the outside of the wall is a mass of green and silver: low bushes and stretches of pale grass, threaded and patched with water. It is a beautiful scene, the colors pure Cape fynbos. She can smell the sweet pungency from here. Beyond the green, further gradated bands of color – a line of white beach and then the sea, an opaque blue today like a turquoise inlay. And above all that, a chalky morning sky, the subtlest blue of the spectrum. The sudden rush of light and sea air is the visual equivalent of that shining bicycle-bell sound – all sparkle and fizz.

Katya is a princess in a white tower...another childhood fantasy, but not a childhood she recognizes as her own. Some other little girl, one she never was. Where do they come from, these confusing visions? But never mind – she claims them. She stretches her arms out into the sunlight, and she is small again, a child cradled in a big, bright world, alight with possibility. She hasn't felt this particular pleasure, this animal wellbeing, for a long time.

The unfinished feel of the estate does not depress her. She can see the potential here: this is a place still forming. Unlike Katya's usual environs, Nineveh is a brand-new world, made from scratch. She'd been uncertain about this job, but now she's eager to get on with it: to open negotiations with her fellow residents, small or large. She sees the days set out before her – three? Perhaps she could stretch it to more? – as empty and capacious as these pristine quarters, this golden prospect. She sends a message, an invitation, to every crawling scuttling creature out there: come in, come in, infest, invade, give me reason to stay!

Some movement down there. A man has appeared, is sitting at one of the tables smoking a cigarette. She's disconcerted to have company in her new world, but then she sees the dark-blue uniform. He's a security guard. At once she feels glad: they both belong here, they're part of the crew. He sees her and gives her a languid salute, leaving his hand raised for a couple of seconds. It is from the expansive panache of his greeting, more than anything else at this distance, that she deduces it is not the small, slightly morose Reuben who guided her last night.

She sends a regal wave back in his direction, and retreats through the white curtain layers, a royal bride in seclusion.

The bathroom walls are plain, tiled in frostbitten white, with a border of stylized blue flowers. Her every touch leaves a fingerprint, matte against the gloss. If this place was immaculate to start with, it won't be for long. Briefly, a vision of her father intrudes. Pissing in the basin, stubbing his foul cigarettes out on the windowsills. She runs water loudly. Mind on the job, she tells herself.

She showers in the brand-new bathroom – the taps snapping briskly on and off, the water gushing hard and hot from a sunflower-size shower head. Quality plumbing, this. She takes pleasure in buffing herself with brand-new soap, a brand-new towel. From habit, she avoids looking at herself in the long bathroom mirror. She combs her hair back from her forehead and behind her ears, the way that feels clean and sharp, the way she likes it.

First things first: the uniform. She has brought three sets of greens with her, each crisply pressed by the lady at the laundromat down the road from her house, a luxury Katya allows herself. She puts one on, straight over her underwear.

Now: the notebook. She opens it to where she's put the heading: *NINEVEH*. She underlines *NINEVEH*, then writes underneath it in a confident hand:

Day One: Thurs 11 May

Underneath that: *"A species of metallic longhorn"* ?

That's all she can think of for now. Time to make a thorough survey of the interior conditions. Although already her sense of these things – her spidey sense – tells her that the walls and floors are as sterile as a swabbed-out surgery. But she sets about performing the necessary routines. She opens the windows and pulls back the curtains until the place is aflame with sunlight. Takes in its dimensions and geography.

At first it seems as if the place is quite plain. But soon she realizes that everything in this "servants' quarters" is of the most luxurious quality, if minimal. The rooms are simple cubes, but there are alcoves and cupboards cunningly inset, shelves that whisper out from recesses at a touch. She investigates each one with professional eyes and fingers. Diligent as a secret policeman, she kneels, running her hands along the seams of skirting boards, opening cupboards, checking in every dim corner for lurking spiders or geckos. She strips down her bed and shakes out the bedding. Turns the mattress over – quite a task as it is a heavy, high-quality one – and examines the seams.

All the time, she is loving the slate floors, the carpets in silvery shades, the subtle not-quite-white walls. Here it is: cleanness, simple lines, plush finishes. This is the comfort and ease that she was thirsting for, back in her crumbling, cracking old house. It's as if she has imagined Nineveh, dreamed up out of her own cluttered mind these volumes of coolly defined space. All the place is missing for real luxury are the electronic items – TV, wi-fi – but she doesn't even want to play music here; it would complicate the upholstered silence. She examines a beautifully constructed built-in cupboard – stands running her hands along the bevelled edge of the door – and then folds and stacks her clothes on its shelves. She never does that at home; she is an inveterate jeans-shedder, bra-scatterer. But here, for a few days at least, it seems possible to imagine that she might really be the inhabitant of these immaculate chambers. It occurs to her that if her own house, her home, were to evaporate, conflagrate, sink into a sudden marsh or sinkhole right now, she would feel only the smallest quiver of loss.

In short, Katya has never seen a less parasite-infested place in her life. If there are any creepy-crawlies here, she's brought them with her. There's something odd about the sterility of the place. She looks out of the window again, and the frank morning sun makes it clear that there's not so much as a field mouse, a cabbage butterfly, stirring on the property. It's strange. After all, there is a big sticky swamp out there – hard to prevent contamination. Such an unworkable combination of elements: mud and cream carpets, goose shit and pale stone. If Toby were here with her, she'd say something, make a joke of it. A smart remark remains unspoken on her tongue. She swallows it.

But wait. She's not completely alone: there is some human presence, as clear as a word spoken in the silence, although it takes her a second to locate it. There, on the kitchen counter, which is a lovely gray marble, delicately streaked with white veins like stratus clouds, is a single piece of thick, cream letter-paper, on which is written, in a looping, over-large hand: *Welcome!* She does not need to wonder whose it is. Those lush, rounded vowels, the curlicued W, the oversized exclamation mark: it can only be Zintle.

As she picks it up, a musical note rings out. It is so exactly synchronized that it takes her a moment to disentwine the sensations, to realize that the paper itself is not chiming a melodious welcome. By the time she works out that it's the doorbell, a knuckle is rapping on the door – a harsh jiglike rhythm that makes her heart jump and the paper slip from her fingers.

Through the peephole, she makes out a stooped blue back.

"Hello?"

The figure turns and presents two large eyes, mantis-like in the peephole's distorting lens.

"It's me. Reuben."

"Oh, right."

She locates a recessed intercom in the hallway and presses its unmarked buttons at random. The door unclenches its lock. Standing there is a small man with receding black hair. Reuben seems reduced in the daylight: his features still delicate and pleasing, but now showing the cast of his true age, which is closer to forty than twenty. He has hollow cheeks and pale-brown skin, and large, anxious eyes in an unusual shade: warm hazel, what one might even in certain lights call orange eyes. She see this all particularly clearly because he stands in a shaft of light like some harassed administrative angel. He has two large shopping bags from a budget supermarket weighing him down on either side.

"Reuben, good morning!" she says, perhaps too cheerily; he looks startled. But she is, in truth, delighted to see him.

"Electricity back on, everything okay?"

"Everything's great, thank you, I slept really well."

Too chatty, she thinks: he looks at her oddly. "Yes. So." He gestures with his wrists – the bags' weight is cutting into his hands, preventing a more expansive gesture.

"Oh! Oh, sorry, can I take those?"

He rubs his feet on the mat at the door and shuffles inside. His shopping bags seem exceedingly heavy. She tries to take them from him, he looks so frail under his burden, but he flashes her a look from under his well-shaped eyebrows and struggles on towards the kitchen.

"Is this all for me?"

In answer, he starts to unpack the bags, laying out their contents in neat rows, sorted by category of food. He unpacks: two cans of corned beef; a loaf of white bread, sliced; a tube of polony; a block of processed cheese; three bottles of bright red Sparletta; a tin of pilchards in peri-peri tomato sauce; a tin of condensed milk; a can of instant coffee; two rolls of toilet paper; a sack of sugar. She's amused but not disturbed by the proletarian cast of the food before her. It's clear that Reuben has taken it on himself to buy the food for her – she cannot imagine the glamorous Zintle stocking up on bully beef. Perhaps this is what is considered suitable fuel for a pest-relocation expert, a Worm Lady. Looking at the glutinous polony, she wonders whether two rolls of toilet paper will be sufficient for the days ahead.

Although the bags had seemed stuffed and heavy, now that the food is laid out it seems rather meagre. He looks at it sadly and shrugs. "Okay?" he asks.

"It looks great," she says. "Fabulous. Thank you so much for doing all this. What do I owe you... ?"

He waves both hands before him. "No, it's fine, paid for. So ja, if there's anything else, just let me know. Any," – he casts around, looking at the ceiling and then at the floor – "... problems."

"Sure, thanks, I'm good though."

But it seems as if he is not quite ready to let the matter lie. He's still looking fixedly at the floor. "Or any...you know. If anything troubles you. We're down there, by the guardhouse, all the time. Me and Pascal?"

"Yes, of course."

"Panic button." He points at a small red knob next to the door. She's seen them; they're all over the place, in every room, insistent dabs of red in the otherwise colorless decor.

"It goes through to the security node—"

"Node?"

"The guardhouse, you know. Press it, we'll be up here like that." He snaps his fingers. "And if we're not there at that time, the signal gets routed to Central Control. Someone will come. Okay?"

"Sure thing," she says. "Oh, hey, Reuben? These insects...you've seen them?"

He nods.

"What do they look like? Do they really bite?"

He pushes up the sleeve in answer. Under the uniform he has attractive skin, a smoothly muscled, youthful arm. An oddly intimate view.

"See?" he says. "There. And there. Bites – this is from last week still. You see?"

Could be. Tiny red pinpoints. But maybe not. Anyway, she nods. "I haven't seen any insects at all."

"You will," he says. "They come out after the rains. They bother the dog."

Dog? There's a dog? Katya's left buttock tenses in painful memory.

Her expression must be plain, because Reuben's looking at her thoughtfully. "The other man, who was here before about the goggas? He didn't like the dog either."

6
SWAMP

She slings her rucksack over her shoulder. It's an old khaki thing, something left over from her dad – it looks like a piece of military kit. She supposes Len would have been in the SADF in his unimaginable youth, although it's difficult to picture him marching on command. He never mentioned it. She never asked.

Inside the bag: notebook, camera, binoculars, pencils, tape measure, water bottle, extra gloves, dark glasses. She has contemplated getting a more professional-looking bag; perhaps a hard case with proper clasps, like something to transport pieces of electronic equipment or refrigerated body parts. It would make a good impression on clients, give her an air of forensic expertise. With the money from this job, she might be able to afford some new gear.

Stepping out of her front door onto the terrace, she looks down and sees that the traces of the mud ballet she noticed last night have been mysteriously mopped away: the tiles beneath her feet are spotless. Did Reuben clean up? She checks her cellphone again: no reception, even up here on the terrace. Who would she phone, anyway? Toby. Hassle him about work.

She takes the stairs down to Unit One. This is part of her assignment too, surely? She presses her thumb to the sensor next to the door. Nothing. It seems there is a hierarchy of access here, and she has not been cleared for certain levels.

No matter. She puts on her sunglasses and ventures out across the mud to explore the main apartment blocks. The buildings at first look bland and repetitive. But the compound is bigger than it appears and soon becomes confusing, with culs-de-sac and blind corridors and connecting walkways, all done in the same silver-flecked white stone. The place seems in perfect repair, but nonetheless it feels disappointingly...frayed. Worn, but not by use; more like a brand-new item that has sat on a shelf too long, losing its crispness. It corresponds exactly to the neat architect's model that she was shown in the office, but somehow, in its sudden expansion to full scale, the place's edges have been blunted. Nothing that couldn't be fixed, though. She can see how the place would revive, if properly lived in.

The concrete culverts that let the stream in and out of the property are deep, steep-sided, and fitted with fine grilles to sift the water. Nothing much bigger than an undernourished tadpole's going to come in or out that way. Where the water enters, the grille is choked with grass and plastic bags denied entry: no wonder the stream's reduced to a grudging trickle.

She presses her finger to the doors of one or two ground-floor flats, and these all open for her readily enough. Inside, everything is on a much grander scale than in Unit Two. Here is the visual language of the brochure: the huge high rooms, the lush finishes, all gleaming in expectation of first use. The layout of each is identical. The decor is luxurious but oddly erratic: she notices doorknobs and sections of carpet missing, as if the rooms are awaiting finishing touches. Certain things one might expect in a furnished flat – chairs, appliances, cupboard doors – are absent, while other details are in place.

In several of the flats there is framed art on the walls: reproductions of old engravings of ancient monuments and ruins. She examines these with interest. Stepped towers, pyramids, statues. She recognizes the lions from the gateposts as well as the daisy-like flower motif from the bathroom tiles.

Alma would like it here, she thinks, and briefly imagines a life complete: Alma and her family in one of these apartments, Toby perhaps with a studio flat of his own, herself – well, she can only imagine herself in that caretaker's flatlet, really: it's just her size. She could wave to them all from her terrace, not too close and not too far away.

Really she should search each block scrupulously, top to bottom, but she's soon bored by their sameness. After looking through four identical ground-floor flats, a disconcerting series of rewinds and repeats, she decides to move on.

Making her way between the buildings, she gets turned around and comes out, unexpectedly, near the guardhouse. She heads back towards Units One and Two, completing the circuit. The guard she noticed earlier under the milkwoods is still there, lounging with his jaw on his hand, a thin stream of smoke escaping from a cupped cigarette. He inclines his head slightly and she understands that she's being beckoned. The man has powerful body language. She walks over, ducking under the low branches of the milkwood into the shade. He's long-legged, dark-skinned and wearing sunglasses.

"Hi," she says.

"Good morning. I am Pascal," he says, brushing a fingertip across his nametag. Did you have a restful night?" His voice is French-accented and precise, the words carefully chosen.

"Very. I'm Katya, by the way."

Another incline of the head. "Yes. I understand you are here to deliver us."

She smiles. "That's the plan. Tell me, though – I thought this place was supposed to be infested? It seems so clean. Is there really a problem here?"

He nods. Drags on his cigarette.

"You've seen them? The goggas?"

"Yes. I have seen them. Last year, many, many, everywhere. Now this year. They have started to come again: one, two, six. There will be more."

"But what are they? What do they look like?"

Pascal plugs the cigarette into his mouth and for a moment she doesn't think he's going to answer, but then he brings his hands up before his face and links the thumbs and wiggles his long fingers at her. It says: *creepy crawly*. Something with many legs. "You will see them," he says, "after it rains." He claps his palms together. Then he pushes up his dark glasses and lets her see his close-set eyes. "You have been paid?"

"I'm just here for recon. I get paid when it's done. Why?"

"No, nothing. I am just wondering."

There's a pause; she hesitates. "Can I ask, where are you from? Originally?"

"DRC."

He offers nothing further, and she doesn't press. Refugee stories always make her feel a little shy, awed even. She imagines in Pascal a rootlessness far more wrenching than her own, and also a sense of determined purpose that puts her to shame.

"Are you going somewhere now?" he asks, rescuing her from her clumsy silence.

"Maybe. How far are the shops?"

"Reuben will go in," he says. "Maybe today, later, maybe tomorrow only. You could ask him to fetch you something."

Behind him, set into the white perimeter wall, is a pedestrian gate. She starts towards it, then freezes when she notices the giant dog lying spread-eagled on its back before it. A mastiff cross, or a Rottweiler, one of those meaty dogs with huge jaws. Maybe a boerboel. It's black and tan, close-haired, solid as a young bullock, with a thick member and scrotum lolling between legs splayed to receive the sun. The animal raises its heavy muzzle to look at her, having no doubt picked up the molecules of anxious adrenaline she's wafting into the air.

"Is that thing friendly?"

Pascal whistles a note through his teeth and the dog heaves to its feet and lumbers over, pressing its black flews against his hand. Pascal grips the dog's collar. "His name is Soldier."

Give me baboons any day, thinks Katya.

She edges past them to the gate. It's made of wood reinforced with steel, narrow but high. Another thumb-pad next to it: it seems that whoever designed the system was just as worried about people getting out as getting in.

"What's through here? Can you get down to the beach?"

"You can walk. It's dirty though. Full of mud, full of these things, these little things ..."

"Snakes? Goggas?"

"No, no, different ..." he pinches the skin of his neck, makes a sucking sound through his teeth.

"Oh...mosquitoes? Ticks?"

"Maybe ticks."

"Oh, okay. I'll give it a try anyway. Thanks." She presses her thumb to the pad and hears the click as the gate releases itself. Pascal drops his shades over his eyes and dismisses her with a nod.

As she passes through the gate, there's a physical change in the atmosphere, as if she's stepped into richer air. The spring-loaded door swings shut behind her, and she finds herself on a boardwalk. The walkway is L-shaped: it runs parallel to the wall, and then opposite the caretaker's block it turns at right angles and strikes out into the wetlands – towards the beach, she assumes. The peeled pine is smooth and bright yellow; it dips and flows like a ribbon. Her feet curl inside her steel-capped boots: it would be nice to go barefoot, feel that texture with her soles. Another few months, she imagines, and the planks will have darkened with damp, rotting away into the vlei.

She hesitates, trying to read the landscape. The beach is a public place, relatively safe, as is the walled compound behind her, but she's not sure about the stretch of ground that lies in between. Instinctively she scans for dodgy signals: no litter or other signs of human habitation, no stands of alien wattle. This place seems pristine. Surely she is alone? And anyway, how long would it take to traverse this uncertain zone – fifteen minutes? She'll be at the sea in no time. It's a perfect day. And a boardwalk, especially a new, fragrant one such as this, is a lovely thing to travel along; the spring in your step is involuntary. A black bird darts past, almost touching her face with a wingtip: a benediction. Katya zips her uniform collar all the way up and steps out, with the authority of Nineveh at her back. She's on a job here, after all.

Ahead, the vegetation masses: stiff ruffs of dakriet higher than her head, grass and a profusion of small flowers, orange and pink. The yellow road of the boardwalk turns sinuously to enter a maze of reed – and stops abruptly; they've built thus far and no further. The ground is about a meter down, but seems solid enough, and she jumps for it – calf-deep into brown mud.

It makes her laugh, until she realizes that she's stuck. She can't even reach the boardwalk – she's leapt too far. For a second, she considers the extreme humiliation of dying this way. She can feel hands of clay around her ankles, pulling her down. With some rude sucking noises, she manages to work one foot to the surface; and then in a burst of panic lunges full-length, casting herself skydiver-style onto the raft of the surrounding reeds, nearly wrenching her boot right off. She claws herself onto dryer ground, gasping then laughing again.

She is lying in a field of flowers. She turns her head and her gaze alights on a beetle nuzzling its way into the heart of a yellow daisy. It's a wacky-looking creature: jointed feelers and legs sticking up at acute angles, a narrow, armored head equipped with pincers, and a pair of long, precisely tooled wing-sheaths – all coated in the most fantastic blue-green iridescence from feeler-tip to the ends of each of its legs. Sipping peaceably at his satiny bloom.

"You're pretty funky, aren't you?"

She picks herself up and knocks the worst of the mud off her boots.

The wetlands are extravagantly beautiful and full of life, brimming with pools of amber water that flash where the sun hits them. In some places the water runs clear, elsewhere it stands still over a precipitate of slime. Spider webs gleam with dew in the shadows. Wafts of meady scent alternate with the sulphur of vegetable decay. At times Katya finds herself fording a shoulder-high field of flexible, pinkish swords, or wading through waterlogged grass. She can see that the place has suffered a fire not too long before: the alien vegetation has been burned down to the sod, making way for new growth. The gaps between the stumps are lush with banks of tiny flowers in lavender and pink and white, the stubby raised fingers of succulents, daisies with yolky centers and bees in their mouths.

And the beasts! They are everywhere, scuttling in the grass. Here and there are patches of pale gray sand, tracked with the symmetrical indentations of tiny paws and tails. Every now and then a hidden bird will give an outraged but pure cry as she passes. There are bees and muggies, and a fat jointed centipede struggling to get away from her curious fingers, and two small geometric tortoises clambering over the sand. One tree holds a mud sculpture in its boughs; it proves to be filled with scurrying ants when she taps its sides. She wants to touch everything – the knobs on the tortoise's back, the soft explosion of the fat bulrushes. Katya is not wearing gloves today.

As she walks, she feels her heart lifting. This is a child's landscape of mud and splashing pools, nothing big or tall, no dramatic cliffs or giant trees. The beauty is in modest treasures. A watery patchwork place, shifting and uncertain. There are no markers here, no distinctive great trees or boulders – or any stones at all. She's lost sight of Nineveh now, but she can't yet hear the sea. Great bunches of dakriet stand up in her path, but each one looks the same from every angle; there are strands of water which lead in no clear direction, seeming to sneak left and right behind her back as she blunders on through thigh-high grass. Sun and shade dapple her eyes. At times she runs up against a larger patch of water that seems to be part of the vlei she saw from the bedroom, but its outline is amorphous, cluttered by reeds and green-scummed, only revealing itself when she's already one bog-soaked ankle deep in what had been solid land the moment before.

At length she gives up on finding a path to the beach. Some odd curvature of space occurs here, leading her in circles like Alice in the flower garden. She suspects it is not physically possible to wade straight through to the other side, to get back to the map.

A golf ball nests in the undergrowth like a rare egg to gather up. Once she's seen one, her eye picks out another and another: a dozen. An atavistic impulse compels her to gather them all and make a careful pile in the grass. It's odd, that pyramid of white spheres: the only human marker in this watery landscape.

Then she comes out of a stand of reeds onto an emerald plain, and stumbles into a strange midget village. Municipal workers, she presumes, have been cutting down alien vegetation and have left the dead branches in evenly spaced heaps that look like small collapsed huts. On the other side, the ground starts to hump itself into dunes, the dank succulence of the vegetation toughening into beach scrub. Low barricades of milkwood appear, although still the sea remains elusive.

She climbs in under the umbrella of one of the milkwoods. It must be close to midday now, and getting hot. She zips down her overalls. The air is a relief, and she succumbs and pulls her arms out of the sleeves and lets the top half hang around her waist. She's got only a bra on, and soon her torso starts to sting pleasurably where the sun dapples through the leaves.

This is the most peaceful she's felt in forever. She lies there in the sleepy warmth and feels that this might be where she really belongs. Tree roof, soil floor, and the beasties buzzing around: a sweet spell.

Through her eyelashes, she makes out an odd shape in the leaves. Directly above her, a rust-holed cooking pot has been hung on a branch. She sits up quickly and puts the top half of her overalls back on. A small chill has entered the air.

She stumbles out of the shade and up a slope of white sand. From the crest, she can at last see the breadth of the sea, and between her and it a tough pitching landscape of dunes. Small flies plague her. She slaps them away. Slaps her head also because sly music has entered her head, a thread of a tune. Whistling. Coming from where? Down there, on the beach.

There is a horse and rider cantering along the shore. In their path, an ambiguous shape stands or leans, dark against the beach. If she had Toby here with her, she could send him coursing down there to investigate. *Check it, out Tobes, double-quick.* The horse floats like a mirage, its hooves beating silently. As it approaches the still figure, the horse appears tinier and tinier, until she realizes that the tilted black shape is a piece of boat wreckage, much larger than a man.

The horse and rider move on out of the scene, but the whistling remains, displaced by distance, like the soundtrack of a film slightly out of sync with the image. It makes her shiver. She lowers herself, putting the body of the sand dune between herself and the distant wreck. The whistling ebbs.

A chilly breeze has sprung up. Time to go back. This time, the swamp relents and lets her find her way home. She doesn't see the pyramid of golf balls, though. It's as if they've sunk straight into the ground, which might actually be possible in this boggy earth.

Back at the gate, the fingerprint magic doesn't work. She realizes that she is too coated in mud, and even when she spits on her thumb and wipes it off on the clean underside of her collar, the door refuses to know her. At last she raises her fist to the gate: the thick wood gives a muffled thump. She tries harder, with knuckles. Before she knows it, she's doing *rats-in-a-rattrap, squashed-flat*. Everybody responds to that one. It works a charm: soon she can hear the spin of bicycle wheels on the other side, and the door clucks its acceptance. She pushes it open cautiously, but there is no meaty dog body pressed against the other side.

Reuben is there, straddling his bicycle. When he sees her, he laughs, rings his bell and pedals off again. Reuben and Pascal: she's pleased that these two will be her companions here, crossing paths with her at clockwork intervals. Pascal appears to be the dog man, Reuben the biker.

"Are you going into town?" she calls to his back.

"Tomorrow," he shouts, and spins between the buildings. She's got him to smile, at least.

Her knuckles sting as she heads across the mud. *Rats-in-a-rattrap!* Len coming home at odd hours, rapping that out on the roof of the bakkie or the side of the caravan. *Squashed-flat!* Alma and Katya would jump out of their skins, every time. Instantly awake, crouching to receive whatever their father might be bringing home. Sometimes it would be a treat, sweets or a comic book. Sometimes he'd be in a mean mood, and they'd have to duck. If he'd been fired again, or lost money, or had a fight, he might be on fire with indignation, waking them to tell them about this new injustice. Sometimes he'd be in a high good mood, whistling, rubbing his hands, ready to pack their bags. Or he'd bring home something for them to play with: a grass snake or a frog.

It's possible to get addicted to that kind of lottery. But Alma shrunk before it, grew silent and thin and secretly hard, laying her plans for escape. Katya tried to play the game. She slept with one eye open, ever alert to her father's moods, ready to engage.

Once, years ago, one of Katya's fleeting boyfriends used Len's knock on her door when he came to visit.

"You scared the shit out of me!" she shouted. "Why did you knock like that?"

"Doesn't everybody?" the poor boy said, bewildered.

And she couldn't explain.

How to explain her father? He was a frightening man, a physically dangerous man. It wasn't that he abused them or hated them. But he was rough company, always dropping hammers on their feet or keeping them out all night in the rain. He didn't lift a hand without bringing it down hard, didn't touch if he could shove. He never could respect the fragility of bodies. Len made his living from perilous things, from animals with teeth and stings and claws, and various poisons, and a range of implements fitted with blades and weights and protruding nails. All this compounded by his nature, so impatient, so given to rapid and unconsidered movements, to extravagant gestures of rage and enjoyment. Her father was proud: he would rather collide with the world than bend to it. And some of life's shrapnel inevitably ricocheted off him and struck his close relations.

As a family, they were remarkably accident-prone. Len broke Alma's collarbone when she was ten, swinging a gas tank off the back of the bakkie. It wasn't deliberate. Katya remembers feeling pleased that it wasn't her, and hoping her father had noticed the nimble way she jumped aside. And once he took Katya with him to clean birds' nests from a roof. She was eight. He didn't hold the wobbly ladder for her, and as she was coming down it twisted away from the roof on one leg and toppled, and she landed heavily on her arm with a rung across her neck. She was brave; she didn't cry and she carried the toolbox back to the bakkie with her left hand, and clutched her fork awkwardly that night at supper. Alma noticed, but Dad didn't. Katya refused to meet her sister's eye across the table. It was only the next day, when she couldn't dress herself with her strengthless and swelling right arm, that her father grudgingly took her to the public hospital. He paced up and down the waiting room while a trainee doctor pressed and manipulated her arm, trying to persuade her to confess to pain. She didn't, she wouldn't. At last the young medic, frustrated, gripped her upper arms and lifted her bodily into the air. She bit her lip. She didn't yelp.

Her father did magic tricks. He could make coins come out of their ears, he could hypnotize a frog. He could do accents and jokes and funny songs. He could make Katya weep with laughter, the only kind of crying allowed. He called her "Katyapillar". Sometimes he slapped his daughters in annoyance, and that stung but it wasn't the worst of it. The frightening part was the sense that they, the Grubbs, lived in a merciless world, full of hostile objects that could at any time rear up and hurt them. And the best you could do was be prepared to hit right back.

These days, Katya often wakes with a jolt, ready for anything, her father's knock still echoing from the door of her dreams.

7

GOLF

Something's changed: there's a new sound in the air. Irregular, emphatic. *Thwuck,* it goes. And then after, a long pause: *Thwotch.* It seems to come from above. Katya walks quietly up the stairs to the terrace outside Unit Two.

At first, she fails to recognize the figure with the golf club. A man's body looks different in moments of muscular tension. There's a line of golf balls lined up on the edge of the low wall around the terrace, and Mr. Brand is perched up there too, screwing himself into a chunky pretzel to swing at them one by one. *Thwop.* It's an odd sight, the ball flying sweetly from such an earthbound figure as Mr. Brand, sweating in his shirtsleeves.

But when he turns she sees his face alight and boyish, and the exuberant flight of the ball makes sense. His joy changes to something else when he catches sight of her. He stares and then roars out a laugh, doubling over his club. The mud cracks on her forehead and cheeks, and she realizes how dirty she is. So that's what Reuben was grinning at. At least Mr. Brand won't see her blushing under the mud.

"Grubbs!" he yells. "You filthy child!"

He hops down – surprisingly lightly – from the wall and comes towards her, club in hand, the silver wand vibrating in amusement. Despite the sweat, he's as clean as ever. Cream suit trousers, white shirt; cream suede shoes, even. How on earth has he moonwalked, spotless, over the mud?

"I didn't realize we had a meeting," she says.

"Just popping in. I used to drop in on your father. Grubbs Senior. Check in on the old crook every now and then." He says this with relish, whisking circles in the air with the head of the club. "He and I, before things turned sour, we used to line up the balls, just so, and whip them out into the bushes. Good fun."

"You're kidding me. My father played golf?" It's not to be imagined.

"Not very well, no. Had to watch my head. A bit on the wild side." He acts out ducking under a low-flying ball. "You play?"

"Please. Can you picture it?"

He pauses and considers her. "Some other sport, perhaps. Mud-wrestling."

"I'm very dirty," she remembers.

"Grubby Grubbs," he says, rather childishly she feels. "Go on, get yourself cleaned up, and then let's have a drink and you can tell me what's been going on with this *gogga invasion*." He widens his eyes on the last words, teasing.

Katya lets herself into the flat. A drink – does he mean she should invite him in? It's too late now, he's turned back to his balls. She's not sure what she is here, exactly: employee? Hostess? In the spirit of compromise, she leaves the door unlocked, but only slightly ajar.

In the bathroom mirror, she sees she is coated, pretty much from toe to crown, with a silky dark mud, like the finest of spa treatments, drying now and starting to pull at her skin in a not unpleasant way. So much for the dignity of the professional pest-relocation expert. Her spattered trouser-legs are also speckled with small travellers: ticks, dozens of them. She sticks her foot up on the edge of the bath and tweezes them off, one by one. Other leg. It's hard to do, with her short fingernails. Into the toilet bowl, and flush – it's not exactly killing. She gives her trousers a last smack with her palms.

Now she'll have to check every fold of her skin for their nasty, flat bodies. She strips down warily, on the lookout. Her body looks freakishly pale, cuffed with deep brown ankles, hands, neck and face: an interesting effect. It all stinks worse indoors – as if the muck is starting to spoil. Mud tracked in onto the carpet, too, she sees with some dismay.

Perhaps this is why she so dislikes ticks, more than any other insect: searching for them is the one time she has to look at herself unflinchingly, examine every inch of skin, with mirrors too.

Alma and she are both cursed with skin that scars. It keeps the marks of her father's inattentions forever, like paper keeps ink. Her wounds are not as deep as some, she knows that; but fathers have different ways of marking their children. Katya's scars are evenly distributed across her body. Cuts and scrapes and badly set bones. And cigarette burns, lots of those. She treasured those scars when she was a child. They were the family brands, they showed they belonged to each other. And Katya had a child's contempt for Alma, who mourned the loss each time her skin was split.

The mildest of Katya's marks are a sprinkling of tiny flecks all over her body, which only she would notice. Her father used to hold a match-head to the skin to get a tick to pull out its mouthparts. The girls would be left with tiny blisters, which they'd scratch away after a day or two, leaving a freckle. There's a better way of doing it, of course, as Katya now knows: you dab a little Vaseline on the tick to smother it, and it backs out. Painless all round. But Len had no patience for such niceties.

The worst of her scars is from the dog-bite, humiliatingly on her buttock, received on a job with her dad when she was eleven. She still bears two narrow arcs of puncture wounds, now shiny and slightly indented. A small triangle on her foot is from when Len dropped a box of engine parts on her when they were setting rattraps in a warehouse. Many of her scars have interesting shapes, suggesting the imprints of man-made objects. If you transcribed them, copied them all down neatly on a page, they'd make an expressive alphabet.

It has been a problem, with lovers: lying alongside another naked body, is it not traditional to count off the other's scars, to touch them and hear their stories, to read the skin? Like being granted a peek into a diary. But so many entries! And it's embarrassing to confess how many were written by her father.

In the shower, she rinses her body, and under the mud her flesh is slick and thin, almost translucent – as if the troublesome outer layer has been burnt away, leaving infant skin beneath. Through the falling water, she can hear Mr. Brand moving around inside the flat. What's he up to? Of course he has a right to enter his own building. It was probably rude of her not to invite him in. But still, it feels odd, showering with a strange, fully-clothed man only inches away through the thin wall. She turns the water off and listens. Footsteps, chinks and rustles: objects picked up and set down? Drawers opening?

She towels herself dry, and the scars show up again, white against rosy skin. She has only one not-quite-large-enough towel, which she cinches firmly across her bosom before opening the bathroom door. Mr. Brand's nowhere to be seen, but the front door's open. She scuttles for the bedroom. What things has he touched? She looks for displaced objects, but nothing is obvious.

Clean clothes – and not the uniform, this time. There isn't a lot to choose from, but it takes her longer than it should to consider the permutations of two pairs of jeans, three shirts. In the end she goes for a dark ensemble: black jeans, navy long-sleeved shirt. She leaves her shoes off; they just make her legs look shorter. She brushes her hair back behind her ears in the usual way. In the mirror, she looks like a teenage boy on a date, a fifties boy, Brylcreemed and eager and angular. She should have a cigarette behind her ear. She bends savagely at the waist, throwing her head between her legs and shaking out the hair. It makes her dizzy, crazed-looking, like one of Derek's more agitated colleagues from the park. She runs her fingers one more time through the wet hair and leaves the room to avoid changing her outfit all over again like an anxious fifteen-year-old.

In the kitchen, she casts an eye over her stash of unappealing eats and drinks. She's starving, but that will have to wait. Eating in front of a stranger can feel undignified, especially if one is hungry: Katya tends to wolf her food. After the "grubby Grubbs" remark, she won't give him another opportunity to scoff. She rather wishes Reuben had thought to include some wine in his purchases. Vodka, even. She fetches two glasses and carries them outside, along with the bottle of water from the fridge. Impeccably sober drinks.

Mr. Brand's sitting on the edge of the terrace, one leg folded across the other. It's hard to laugh at cold water, but he finds a way: "My, how Spartan," he says. "That's no good, no good at all. Look in my jacket, won't you? Inside pocket, on the right."

The jacket, cream fabric, is draped over the terrace wall. She picks it up, feeling the warmth of the fading day in its cloth. The lining is even warmer: body heat. He must have put it on and taken it off again while she was in the shower. She's not the only one fussing over her outfit. She fleetingly wants to wrap the coat around her shoulders and push her arms into the too-big sleeves, they are so silky and warm.

Thinking of Alma, who never wears a piece of clothing without pockets to hide her hands, Katya runs her fingers over the lining. There are numerous slits and pockets of different sizes. Some of them contain objects: business cards...handkerchief...pen...she must guess what he wants her to find. But then her fingers touch a cool weight and she knows what it is before she pulls it out. A stainless-steel hip flask. Nice thing, heavy, elegant lines. She weighs it in her hand. Half full, she would say. She tosses it across the space to him.

"Careful with that," he says, catching it easily. "Antique. Or so I'm told."

Already Mr. Brand is screwing off the cap and putting the bottle to his lips. A greedy action. He watches her with slitted eyes over the silver flank of the bottle, like a jealous baby suckling. She's pleased when he pulls it away and his bullfrog throat relaxes, showing off his strong jaw to better effect. He's a handsome man, when the angles are right.

"Your father liked a drop," he says.

"Hm." What, were they drinking buddies, too?

"Not good with the booze, was he, your dad?"

She doesn't want to talk about her father. She shrugs.

"Go on," he says, "have a hit." He holds the flask out to her.

But this is too much. She is not ready to apply her lips to the spout he's just sucked on. She pours a measure into one of the tumblers. She makes sure it's a good tot, though, two fingers – his not hers. Whisky. She lifts it to her nose and drinks in the scent. She's no expert in these things, but this smells awfully expensive. If that gold signet ring he wears on his finger could be turned into vapor and sniffed, then this is what it would smell like.

"You know, it will be magnificent," he says. "This place."

"Yes, it's beautiful," she says lightly, looking out at the perfect sea, the green profusion of the vlei.

But his attention is focused in the other direction, down onto the muddy grounds of Nineveh. She goes towards him and he stands at the same time, so they almost collide, but he doesn't seem to notice.

He points. "You don't see the full effect, obviously. The greenery will be established, it'll be lush. Magnificent in the summer. And the guardhouse will be replaced by something more permanent. All of this area, here: parking." He shifts his hand a little, tweaking and molding space. As he talks, gesturing with his right hand, his left reaches out and pats her gently on the shoulder for emphasis. "Do you see?"

She's not really listening. She's watching Mr. Brand sidelong. He is a physically easy man. In his body. Towards her body. He touches her without thinking, persuading her into his vision with taps and nudges. Shoulder, knee, and once – it burns – her cheek. She does not withdraw from it. He has the unthinking generosity of touch of someone who lives in the body, and who likes to be touched in turn. It's hard not to feel warmed – physically warmed, as if each time his big hands touch her skin or her clothes it passes on some of his heat, until the whole side of her body facing him is glowing, ear to ankle. Now he's leaning out to show her something on the far border of the property, gripping her shoulder for balance.

She tries to take in what he's saying. He's using more extravagant language now. He says he wants to expand. There are plots across the road that belong to him, too, that will become more luxury estates, perhaps a shopping center. There will be nature trails through the wetlands, beach access. And not forgetting the poor: he talks of the people in the informal settlements, how they can be put to work, and how in turn they can be provided with better homes, roads, electricity. He speaks without enormous animation, but rather in a tone of calm surety. She'd like him to carry on talking for a long time, as she replenishes herself on his frequent touches, the scent of warm gold coming through the fabric of his shirt. It is all she can do not to lean in and press her cheek to his solid breadth. He is so confident: his gestures have the power to raise palaces, cities. Beneath his hand, the model town comes to life. She wants to be touched the way his hands touch the landscape: tenderly, boldly, burnishing her into something better than she actually is.

She realizes that he's stopped talking, is looking at her for a response. It takes her a moment to pull back from the bright vistas.

"You see what I mean," he says. "You see how big this is, how big it could be."

There is a chill patch on her shoulder where his hand had weighed. She swigs her whisky, he takes another shot from the hip flask. If he asked her, *What do you think about all this, really?* she would have to answer in her father's voice. She would have to say: *Bullshit, Mister.*

But her father is not here. And she remembers the architect's model in the office, perfect under its yellow light. If there is such a golden city being built, she wants to be one of the calm little figures on the battlements, looking out – not out in the big, cold world, staring in.

She shivers. Mr. Brand is reaching for his coat. The far reaches of Nineveh have turned chilly and blue. Down there, Soldier and Pascal pace the perimeter. Man and dog look slow, damp and shuffling, profoundly unsatisfied. Pascal guards this place but does not inhabit it; and neither does she.

He claps his hands. "So. What's your verdict?"

"Sorry?"

"How long is this all going to take? When can you wrap it up? It's been a year...we need to move you out and the tenants in, pronto."

She swallows down the last of her drink. She was just starting to like the place. "Well. Just as soon as we sort this gogga problem out."

"When? How many days? How bad is it? Are they going to swarm again? I can't say I see any of these famous bugs ..."

"You'll get my report," she says. "Shortly."

"Give me a clue."

Thinking hard, she pours herself some more whisky. "You'll see all the details in my report."

He's staring at her, drumming his thick fingers on the balcony rail. Then he barks like a dog: his laugh, she has to remind herself. "Grubbs!" He chortles to himself, suddenly decisive. "Fine. Come by...let's say Sunday? You can tell me what it'll take to get us a clean bill of health, a no-bug certificate or whatever, and then we can get on with things around here."

She puts her glass down and wipes her palm in readiness for a businesslike handshake. Instead he grips her arms above the elbows and swivels her body slightly, to the left, to the right, like she's a loose bolt that needs adjusting. "Sort it out, would you? Would you do that for me? Not like your dad, eh?" Then he runs the flat of his hand over the top of her head.

She watches him as he makes his way down the steps, across the open ground and to the gate. He confers briefly with Pascal at the guardhouse. He's patting Soldier on the head, with the same hand that just touched her hair. The dog genuflects, bowing down on his forepaws. The gates open. There's some big, pale, luxury car out there. It slides away, almost silent in the fading light. Pascal pulls the gates closed, giving her the briefest glance over his shoulder.

Why did he come, Mr. Brand? It couldn't have been just to check up on her. Maybe he's a lonely man. Maybe his wife is tired of listening to his grand plans. Or he just wanted to knock a few golf balls into the gloom. The club he's left behind is a rusty old thing. She picks it up and strokes an imaginary ball out towards the horizon. Hole in one.

It is a perfect evening, no wind, the sand on the beach clean and trackless as if pressed by giant hotel staff. The sun is sinking, quite lovely as it glances metallic off the vlei and starts to polish the sea.

She can hear, rising now on the cool evening air, the sounds of people. The noises are faint but distinct, and although she cannot see from her vantage point where they are coming from, she can tell from the quality of the sounds that it is a township or an informal settlement. A radio, a crying child, companionable shouting – not a mix you'd find in the suburbs. She's surprised; she hadn't noticed anything like that close by. This place is not so exclusive, then. You can shut out a lot, but not the floating sounds of human life. When she goes to the edge of the terrace, she can see it clearly: a group of maybe thirty shacks standing close together in the bush, balanced precariously between the vlei and the road. Are these the people that Mr. Brand plans to set to work on his grand new projects?

She closes her eyes and listens. A densely patterned chorus of frog-song is building beneath the human sounds. The waves are a distant bassline. Two dogs start barking at each other, one near and one far. The near one has a gruff dark-chocolate sound to it; she thinks it might be Soldier. The other sounds like a young dog, filled with the happy excitement of puppyhood, and they seem to be tossing the sound back and forth not in hostility but in playful communication. Then the guard's bicycle wheels sizzle past, the familiar *ting ting* bell...and there it is: a fragile symphony.

When she opens her eyes, the daylight is gone. The lamps on their ornate poles have turned on automatically, and cast soft handfuls of light here and there on the muddy grounds of Nineveh. You'd have to wade right out into the vlei to get the country effect of purple sky and bright stars. Out beyond the wall, the bush is dark, and beyond that the beach glimmers ghostly, completely empty now.

She can feel the building growing cool towards her, becoming a stranger again. It doesn't belong to her. No more than Mr. Brand's hand on her arm meant any kind of belonging. She will see him again on Sunday, she will give him her empty report and he will take back the keys of the city. She had hoped for more time.

Get it together, kiddo. Scowling, she stomps back inside, briefly startled by a motion-activated light switching on over the front door. She leafs fretfully through her notebook, but there's nothing more to say. Her usual note-making procedure is to state the problem and propose a strategy: plan of action, schedule, goals. Then make out a list of tools and equipment. Conclude with outcomes and resolution. There's a discrete and obvious mission: borer beetles to be persuaded to change their ways, snakes to divert from their crimes, kittens to talk down, spiders to cajole. Even if the situation is overwhelming – a plague of locusts – at least it's clear what's wrong. But here, the pest is elusive, its goals obscure. She can't even give it a precise name. "A species of metallic longhorn" indeed. That's about as helpful as "gogga."

In the kitchen, she fills the place with her own noise, shoving chairs aside, grabbing at forks and knives: things to hold on to, tools to use. Food! That was something of Mr. Brand's she could incorporate, that could not be taken away.

The bully beef sits on the shelf in its round-edged, perfectly designed cans, which haven't changed since, oh, at least Len's boyhood. The contents, according to the label, are largely filler and very little meat. This stuff might not even offend Toby's vegetarian sensibilities, despite the tubby, oddly pink bull in the picture. As she would remark to irritate him if he were here.

It all comes back to her in a wave: the way the loose paper label comes off the shiny, scored tin; the flat key that you have to insert just so – the first time she fumbles it, sticking it in the wrong way round – and its satisfying winding action. The tin hinges back to show a plug of white fat. She takes a teaspoon from the drawer and spoons off the tallow to expose the pink flesh beneath. It gives off a rich, slightly metallic odor. The processed meat looks toxic, fluorescent almost, but she can't resist. She spoons out a chunk and puts it in her mouth. Salty, fatty, pungent ...

A dim afternoon. A kitchen table, dirty yellow light coming through the window, and the feel of a tacky plastic tablecloth under her arms. The hard edges of a spoon in her mouth. Fingers, smelling of soap, wiping the grease off her lips. She remembers: their mother would spit on a tissue and clean the girls' faces with it, like an animal grooming her young. For a while, Katya and Alma must have shared that smell: the musk of her mother's mouth, underlying the waxy sweetness of lipstick.

Katya swallows quickly and pushes the sprung-open can away from her. Pain strokes her fingertip. She remembers now, the peril of those cans. The sharp edges surrounding the meat.

"God knows what they put in this shit," she says into the silence. Then she pulls some paper from the toilet roll and presses it to the finger. Red blossoms through the tissue. She squeezes, focusing on the pain.

"That stuff will kill you," she says again, addressing her imaginary Toby, who is, for once, listening attentively to her advice. "Close your mouth," she says to him.

She puts the rest of the food away in the fridge and in the cupboard, one of those numerous cupboards that are so cunningly concealed, with doors that snick closed so trimly that she's not sure she'll ever find them again. She sips the red, fizzy drink. It's warm and excruciatingly sweet, like drinking flavored lip-gloss. She tips the bottle immediately down the sink, the stuff hissing and frothing and giving off a pungent raspberry whiff, wondering, as she does, if this is the first organic substance to foul up these drains. If it is even organic. As she runs the taps to clear the sink, she imagines the course the water is taking, down the pipes laced into the walls of the flat, down two storys and into the sewers; flowing ultimately, perhaps, into the depths of the swamp itself.

8
SCRITCH, SCRATCH

Every hour through the night, it seems, Reuben does his circuit. She can trace his movement by the squeaky bicycle wheel, and she pictures the wavering lamp seesawing around the perimeter, then across the middle, and across it again. There's something ritualistic, pentacle-like, about the motion. The sound makes her feel more alone than before. It's as if the guard is inscribing a juju shape into the ground, a spell to keep her out.

The truth is, she doesn't want to go home. She wants more of that grand entitled feeling she had up on the terrace, with Mr. Brand's one arm around her shoulders and the other raised in invitation, urging her on through some portal into the glorious prospect. She wants to go there, she wants to buy that ticket. But her only currency is the usual: bugs and beetles. And she can't seem to lay her hands on enough of those in Nineveh.

Perhaps the force of her desire pricks something into life. She becomes aware that the bicycle has been joined in counterpoint by another sound, closer. A tapping. Then a scraping. She sits up and listens; she switches on the bedside light. The sound is faint, and moving. She walks from room to room, cocking her head. Human hearing – tragic. She feels like a pigeon, trying to use its own weakest sense, turning its head this way and that to pursue an elusive fragment of sight. Is it in the floor? The walls? *Scritch, scratch.* She runs through her mental archive of pestilential noises. Something with claws? With a rapping beak? It sounds larger than an insect, certainly, but noises can be misleading. Now another element: a repetitive clucking. A bird's cry, a creaking in the masonry? But it seems too rhythmic, too clear, too regular: it's electronic almost, not an organic sound. Not unlike the ticking of a large, resonant clock – except there isn't one. She turns in a slow circle, echolocating. The more she hears it, the more unnatural and ominous it seems: the countdown to a movie bomb-blast. And then it stops. It has gone silent, tjoepstil, and although she stands for a good ten minutes, utterly still except for her eyes searching the room, the sound does not return.

She scrabbles in the innumerable drawers and finds a stash of glassware. Wine glass or tumbler – what's best for eavesdropping? She chooses a juice glass and presses the base to her ear, the mouth to the wall. Louder, certainly.

No wall is ever silent; always there is a subdued orchestra of knocks and sighs and oceanic rushing. The hum of pipes, the creaks of bricks and mortar settling. Or unsettling: such sounds are the minute harbingers of future destruction, the first tiny tremors of a very, very slow collapse that will end, decades or centuries from now, in a pile of rubble.

She can't tell if the clicking noise is loudest in the walls, the floor, or higher up. After some experimentation with combinations of furniture, she takes a high-back chair from the kitchen and puts it on the bed, and then climbs up and stands wobbling with one palm pressed against the ceiling, the glass in the other hand and her ear to the glass, wedging herself thus in a teetering tower between floor and mattress. What she hears is the sea.

The chair starts to tip and she jumps clear just in time, hooking her foot in a corner of the white duvet and declining in a slow-motion pratfall to the mattress and then the floor. She giggles at herself for a while; there's no one else here to do it.

There's a clear black handprint on the plaster of the ceiling. Hers? But she's clean. She lies there for a long time, looking up at it.

When at last she turns off the bedside lamp, the handprint vanishes, as does she, into the general dark of Nineveh.

In the morning there is still no sign of the elusive infestation, although she has a crawling sensation, as though tiny mouthparts have been probing her. No marks on her skin, though. No new ones, at any rate.

She rises from her bed with new determination, and hungry again. From the unlikely ingredients in her pantry, she manages to construct a processed-cheese sandwich, but when she bites down she finds it has somehow attracted sand grains: it grits startlingly between her teeth. She throws the cheese away, leaving the fridge empty except for the Sparletta bottles, one now holding chilled tap-water.

Decent groceries: it must be possible to obtain them. She is not a particularly discerning eater, but there are a few things she craves: tea with milk; wholegrain bread, proper cheese, tomatoes and avocado. To say nothing of a bottle of wine or two. She remembers, now, passing some shops with Toby on the way in: a cluster of a mall and petrol station and McDonalds. A pleasant stroll. Only about a kay or so, surely?

It's a perfect pale-blue morning. As she heads off down the driveway, a breeze rustles the fronds of the palms on either side, making white fire flicker in the green. But the day turns warm fast, and, in another clear manifestation of spatial distortion, the avenue grows longer and longer the further she goes. There's sweat coming down her temples and dripping through her eyebrows by the time she gets to the end, where she pauses in the square shadow of the billboard advertising Nineveh's charms. *Welcome!*

The main road is bleaker and longer than she remembers: dunes and bush, and every now and then a stretch of blank concrete wall topped with razor wire. More of Mr. Brand's developments? Whipping past in a car, one gets the impression that the road is inhabited, busy even, with a press of traffic, people selling firewood at the side of the tar or walking along it. But time and space are different when you're on foot. The spaces between the human events open up and elongate and the individual becomes smaller. The pavement appears and disappears. For stretches, there's only a foot-worn track. Here and there she can see inlets and ochre paths that head into the bush. The cars are infrequent; it's still quite early. She's left all alone on the side of the road for long minutes between the vivid flashes of passing vehicles. When they come, they come fast. There's no reason to stop here.

A few faces turn to watch her from behind filmed windscreens. She doesn't fit in here: a white woman, not even jogging. Does she need petrol? Has she burst a tire? She gives a random guy in a van a reassuring thumbs-up. The uniform, that complicating factor, does give her a certain confidence that she wouldn't normally have. Someone in overalls always has a job to do, a reason to be there. Again she mulls over the necessity of getting a more workmanlike bag. A toolbox: even if all she carries in it are cheese sandwiches and slug bait.

She glances back over her shoulder in the direction of Nineveh. She's come surprisingly far. The long wall is now visible only as an intermittent stitch of white through the bush, with the tips of palm trees poking up at regular intervals from its battlements. Seeing it from this angle, in daylight, the palms look completely artificial.

She passes one, two, several people selling stacks of firewood. Wicker chairs and small herds of wire animals are also on display. They're the same designs that you see everywhere, and not for the first time she wonders about the clandestine workshops where these styles are hatched and then released into the networks of roadside wire-benders.

Now signs of life peek through the dusty greenery: corrugated iron, smoke, voices. Funny that she never noticed this settlement before, on the way in. People look up and nod to her cautiously as she passes. Shackland. She doesn't often find herself so close to this world, on foot, but she feels safe. The passing cars are just in touching distance, and up ahead, about two hundred meters away, she sees the familiar yellow and red of the McDonalds. What could go wrong?

She almost stumbles across the things laid out for sale in the next dusty lay-by. The usual trinkets and piles of rooikrans firewood, and something else: ice-white tiles laid out on a piece of plastic sheeting. Each has a figure at its center. They look small and orphaned, lying there in rows.

"Where did you get these?" she asks the young girl selling.

The girl shrugs, laughs. She has a pleasant, square face, with a plump chin and small smiling eyes. Perhaps she's just squinting into the sun.

Katya goes down on her haunches for a closer look. Her overalls pull snug over her thighs, making her wonder if she's put on weight in Nineveh. In two days? On bully beef and Sparletta? Quite possible.

The bathroom tiles have been carefully removed: no broken corners, scuffs or smears. Tile adhesive carefully chipped off the back. Little blue flowers in their centers.

"These are from Nineveh, right? Over there?"

Shrug. "Do you like them?"

"I like them very much. How much?"

"Two rand a tile."

"That's not bad." She doesn't bother to haggle. "I'll take all of them – how many is that? Six, seven – nine."

The girl seems pleased. She stacks the tiles up and wraps them in a Shoprite bag, and Katya takes them carefully. She gives the girl a twenty-rand note and tells her to keep the change. The tiles are heavy, and all stacked together they make a pleasing brick, almost a cube, which only just fits into her bag.

"Do you have anything else like this?"

Again, that squinting-into-the-sun look, although this time the girl seems less amused and more assessing. She bites her lower lip with slightly skew incisors.

"I could ask for you," she says at length, carefully. "We have many things for sale." The girl turns and meets the eyes of a man who's been watching. When he comes over, Katya sees he has the same face as hers, but fleshier, with a strong, arrow-shaped nose.

"John," he introduces himself.

"Hi," Katya says, and puts out her hand. His grip is dry, silky and limp, as if he is unaccustomed to the form of shaking hands. It's an uncertain moment; if handshakes are meant to be a show of trust, this one has failed.

"You are interested in these tiles? I can get you more, many more. How many do you want?"

He's polite but pushy, and it adds to her wariness. She's not sure why she started this.

"If you want these things, you need to talk to me," he presses. "Anything, anything – bathroom fittings, electrical – I can get it for you. But you must talk to me."

She nods and smiles, backing away. She understands.

Her bag is considerably heavier now. Quality tiles weigh a ton.

The mall is a small, new, rather homely one, with a temporary feel. It looks like it's been made from a kit, slapped together rapidly out of plywood. It wouldn't take much more than a good push to knock the stores over like a row of dominoes.

She watches with professional interest as a rat scuttles out from behind a skip. Katya has a sentimental fondness for rats: they were her first humane conquest. For most of her twenties, she led her own solo version of Len's nomadic life, living in rented rooms and working in bars. It was a rat infestation in one of these establishments that got her started. The manager let her have a crack at the problem before he laid down poison. After much painful and unsanitary experimentation, she managed to trap every last rat, letting them loose one by one on Rondebosch Common in the dead of night to avoid suspicious passers-by. That was the beginning of her vocation, and it led in time to PPR, the van, the uniform and at last, with great trepidation, to the house: a permanent base of operations. To everything.

The rat dashes past a figure standing, hands on hips, in the corner of the parking lot. Katya does a double take, but it's just some poor guy trying to cadge a few coins. The real car guard, in his fluorescent bib, moves him along. It's become a bit of a habit, to watch out for her father's figure among the homeless and abandoned. She ducks her head and hurries on.

Inside, the boxy space contains the usual array of clothes and electronics stores and fast-food joints; they all seem very exciting to her, as if she's been away for months instead of days. The clothes so bright and clean, the tilted trays of perfect vegetables, the books and CDs with their covers shiny as varnish. She picks up her basic groceries and gets some cash from the machine, then browses for a while in a bargain bookshop. It's one of those odd places stocked with a random selection of publishers' remainders, books rescued from being pulped.

There's a reference section, and she finds the *Complete Guide to Southern African Insects*. She rifles through it and glances at the pictures, the maps, the Latin names for grasshoppers and dragonflies. Len, otherwise unschooled, had all that knowledge at his fingertips. For any given indigenous bug, he could tell you names in half a dozen languages. Somehow, Katya never got it together to learn those things. Laziness, she supposes. For all her business cards and logos, this knowledge haunts her: Len was the true craftsman. She pushes the field guide back onto its shelf.

Next, she finds one of those old photographic books where vintage black-and-white photos of Cape Town are compared with the same views taken in modern times. Long Street, Camps Bay, now and then. District Six, alive and then in ruins. The antique harbor with its elegant pier, and the bleakly triumphal foreshore that was built on top of it – pushing back the sea by force of will, shadowless in the sixties glare. What is striking is how everything is different – the point of the book – but also how neither the old nor the new seems obviously preferable. The monochrome pictures of Victorian Cape Town seem dreary, stricken with a kind of lassitude, the streets strangely empty. The fifties snaps are stultifying in their own way: those over-bright Kodachrome skies, the street scenes populated entirely by white people – except for the picturesque flower-sellers, of course. In none of the pictures does the city seem to be sitting easy with itself. Only the mountain and sea are serene, altering at a far more dignified pace. A disorienting experience, looking at this book. Each person snapping the shutter had been trying to fix the city as it was, but there is no fixing such a shifting, restless thing as a discontented city. If you strung these pictures together in a giant flip-book, or put them together to make a jerky film reel, year on year, the city would be hopping and jiggling, twitching and convulsing in a frenzy of urban ants-in-the-pants. Colonial cities are itchier than most, no doubt, fidgeting in the sub-Saharan light; harsh, even in a sepia world.

So little of the original Cape Town remains. Just the heavy star of the Castle pinning down its surroundings like a brooch – or a five-pointed policeman's badge. How silly to imagine that anything built now will stand for years to come. She shelves the book again, butting it carefully against the flimsy partition of the shop wall. This place, certainly, will not last long enough to feature in photos of the future.

She leaves the mall through the automatic doors and stands at the edge of the parking lot to make some calls. First, Mr. Brand's office.

Today, Zintle disappoints. Her voice is as mellifluous as ever, but lacks its previous rise and fall. She seems subdued, as if she has a slight cold or a case of the sulks or even a slight hangover. "Oh, Miss Grubbs," she says absently.

Katya misses the sense of being playfully manipulated – does Zintle no longer care? "Just checking in, reporting in, you know," she says. "To my employer."

"Uh huh."

Zintle has no faith in her after all, no faith whatsoever.

"I have an appointment with Mr. Brand on Sunday. I thought I should just confirm the time and so on."

"Sunday?" She sniffs. "I don't know anything about that. I don't work Sundays."

"Well what should –"

"Try him at his home. He'll be there. Maybe."

"Oh, okay. Also, I need some money for expenses?"

That gets a laugh out of Zintle, at least. "You're not the only one, my dear," she says. "Good luck." And puts the phone down.

After that, Katya feels shy to ring the Brands' house. Instead she tries her own. On the other end of the line, she imagines the old house ringing like a bell, cracks widening with every vibration. Pick up, Toby, before it all comes tumbling down. She gives up after ten rings and phones him on his cell.

He answers at once. "Yo PPR, what can we do you for?"

"God, that's terrible. Why are you answering the phone like that? This could be a work call. Shit, this *is* a work call!"

"Jeez, sorry. Howzit, Katya."

She's immediately penitent. She didn't mean to be sharp. His voice seems wispy and insubstantial on the end of the line. She has a moment of vertigo, of panic: where is he? How would she ever find him again, or he find her, if one of them hung up now?

"Where are you, Toby?"

She knows it's an irritating habit, to ask a young person on a cellphone this question: the reflex of an older generation. And she accepts the rebuke: "I'm just...out."

So wavering, so faint. A boy in a bubble in the sky. It's his mother's voice: a million years ago, Alma's whisper reaching her from another world, unmoored, drifting, ever more distant.

Suddenly there's a yell on the other end, and the line goes dead.

She rings again. "What's going on?"

"I'm busy," he says ungraciously. Judging from the agonized howls, Toby is now contending with a pack of wolves.

"Toby, what the hell? Are you okay?"

He grunts. "Yes yes – it's just...Can't talk now!"

"Wait wait wait! I need you to come and get me. Tomorrow."

A tense and panting silence on the other end.

"Tobes? Tomorrow?"

"No! You fucker!"

An unearthly yowling in the background. And he's hung up. She tries again: no answer.

She thinks, and then dials her sister. "Is Toby okay? I just had a weird phone call with him."

"Well, he's on a job. For you. Mongeese, I think he said to me."

"Mongooses?"

"Whatever. Why? What's wrong?"

"No, nothing, never mind." Alma freaks out enough as it is. "Just tell him...tell him two o'clock, tomorrow. I need to get back for a meeting on Sunday."

Katya hangs up, wondering whether she's got her lift or if her driver has been ripped limb from limb by raging mongeese. The flimsy partitions of the mall building seem to clatter and shake behind her. Across the parking lot, the wind is smacking at the rather sad banners on poles, rolling an unattended centipede of trolleys across the tar and – bang! – into the side of someone's car.

Everything is in motion, distressed by the wind; steel and concrete shivering like the waters of a lake. She hovers at the edge of the lot, weighed down by her grocery bags, unwilling to start the long trudge home.

Something strikes her like a bird from the sky, gripping the back of her neck with fleshy claws. She yelps and ducks and twists around, dropping her parcels to beat away the attack.

The figure behind her jumps back and yells too, and for a moment they're like cats in a fight, all arched backs and snarling. Then she sees who it is and she stops cold. Her hand goes to her neck.

He's got his fists on his hips, grinning, pleased with himself. "Katyapillar! Fancy meeting you here!"

She digs in her fingers until she can feel the nails.

The first thing she does is buy them both a drink, and a stiff one too. She's not sure she can do this sober. Remembering Mr. Brand, she chooses whisky. They sit in the dim rear section of a franchised steakhouse, one that has a bar with polished wood and fake brass and very few customers.

"What are you doing here, Dad?"

He smirks. "Heard you were about."

"Heard from who?"

"Heard you got my job."

"My job, Dad," she says. "Mine."

He laughs and cracks his knuckles, making her flinch at the sound. He's got a distinctive way of doing it: pushing his palms together prayerfully, forcing the wrists back at ninety degrees until they click, then deliberately moving the pressure onto the fingers to get at the knuckles, producing a riff of meaty pops. Katya clenches her teeth to stop the sound getting into her head.

She can see them both in the mirror: up on bar stools with their ankles hooked around the legs, identical poses, each swiveled a half-turn away from the other. It could be late at night in this boozy amber light, the two of them strangers drowning their sorrows, and in fact she can feel that late-night drowsiness coming over her, a kind of inertia. When he turns his face to the side she catches the gleam of an eye, the angle of the brow. Each glimpse delivers a soft blow of recognition. Dad.

She's not sure if he looks bad or good. Older, certainly. He looks like someone who's spent seven years in a forest, chopping wood and eating squirrels: lean, battered, dirty, but tough and full of wily energy. He's wearing cheap jeans and an old yellow T-shirt that says *Tropicana* and shows his arms, still knotty with muscle. Looks like he's lost a front tooth. His skin is lightly wrinkled, like paper that's been dropped in the bath and left to dry, and he's darkly tanned and sun-spotted, except for the right forearm. That one is flayed. It's the snakebite, the old healed one. Puff adders have an evil bite: the venom necrotizing the flesh. She vividly recalls the shape of the scar, which used to remind her of the smooth skin of a gum tree where the bark's stripped off. He used to flinch away from a touch to that arm. Now the discoloration is worse: the damaged skin is red and looks even thinner than before. On the backs of his hands and around the edges of his brow the skin is freckled with age, which, along with the missing tooth, gives a paradoxical impression of boyish mischief. Even the wisp of tarnished hair that remains at the back of his head, floating above his balding scalp, has a youthful exuberance. The only really dispirited thing about him is his footwear: the running shoes are worn down almost to the uppers, with holes at their seams through which she glimpses horny nails. Shoes: always the biggest giveaway of hard living.

He leans forward, smelling of sweat and tobacco and...what? Mold? He tweaks the corner of her collar. "Snazzy."

She can't help it: she pulls away. Len pauses, hand in mid-air, to note her reflex; then deliberately continues, taking a big handful of collar. She stays completely still. She allows it. His thumbnail scrapes at the logo sewn onto the cloth. "PPR. Stands for what?"

"Painless Pest Relocations."

"Relocations? Very fancy." He lets go of her collar at last. "And what's this about Painless?"

"I remove animals, I don't destroy them. It's humane."

He whoops in amusement. He rocks on the bar stool, so that the front legs rear back from the floor and slam down with a mirthful explosion.

"Humane!" he snorts. "Fucking painless!"

She straightens her collar and buttons it all the way up. "Dad, enough of the bullshit. Where have you been? All this time? Do you live around here?"

He points his weather-beaten finger at the ceiling and traces a circle, points at the ground and does the same. "In and out, around and about. Lying low." He winks, reminding her queasily of Mr. Brand. "So, you having any trouble with that job, then? Hit any snags? Need your old dad's help?"

"You've got to be kidding. No."

He snaps his fingers for another round. The bartender is a young girl and seems suitably cautious of them, staying over on the far side of the bar.

"So you know what to do with those bugs, do you? When they start to swarm?"

"Which bugs?" she says without thinking.

"Which bugs, she says! Which bugs!" The bartender smiles politely, and he jerks his chin at her. "Packet of chips, darling? Salt and vinegar."

Katya perches on her bar stool and watches him. She can smell him, see the mash of potato chips revolving behind his snaggle teeth. The more he eats, the more animated he becomes, shifting his bony rear on the slippery bar stool, raising his eyebrows at her comically.

"Go on, get some of these down your neck," he says, pushing the greasy foil packet towards her.

She shakes her head.

"What's the matter? Pressure at work?"

She rolls her eyes. But she is, in fact, thinking of the blank pages of her notebook. About Mr. Brand, and the meeting she's supposed to have with him, and the invisible goggas that she is unable to see. Beside her sits a man who knows more about vermin than anyone alive. She clamps her arms across her chest and grinds her molars together.

"Dad. These goggas. You know what I mean."

"Pretty things, eh?" He lifts his eyebrows, waiting.

"I haven't seen them. Nothing, no infestation. If there ever was one, it's gone now."

He chuckles into his glass.

"What? What's so funny?"

He leans forward and tells her in a vinegar blast: "They're there. They come and they go. Sometimes you see 'em, if you've got the eyes, sometimes you don't. One day there'll be one or two, and then the next day..." He widens his eyes, takes a sip.

"Well, maybe you got rid of them all last time. Maybe they're not going to swarm this year."

"Oh no. Oh no no, they're coming alright. Soon, too." He gives it a beat, but then can't restrain himself: "Go on, ask me how I know. Ask me."

She thinks about it. "Oh."

"Oh, she says! Oh!"

"Insurance."

He snaps his finger at her: got it in one!

"Dad. What have you done?"

He waves her question away modestly. "Oh, not much, not much. Originally it was nothing, a pisswilly job."

"The goggas?"

"*Promeces palustris*. Best to catch them when they're still in larval form, of course, if you know where to look. Get in there with the poison. But a few of them had popped up and were doing their thing – eating the carpets, biting babies and so on. So they called your old dad in to get rid of them."

"But you didn't get rid of them. They swarmed – they destroyed the place."

"Think you could have done better? Sure, it was a bit late in the day by then, already July, but I did what I could. Plus there were other problems – cockroaches, guinea-fowl shitting on the roof, that type of thing. I was there two months, and it would've been a lot worse without Len Grubbs, let me tell you." He sniffs. "Not that you could tell that cunt Brand anything. He was quibbling about payment from the get-go. Stiffed me in the end. So I thought, fuck him. When the job ended I made sure I left a calling card or two.

Took certain precautions. Made sure there was always something going on, you know? Greenfly. Wood-borers. Our furry friend the rat." He wheezes a laugh, showing his missing tooth. "Plus a little general chaos. It was beautiful."

"What about the other stuff? The missing copper wire, all of that – was that you?"

He shrugs, modest. "Maybe, maybe not."

Despite herself, Katya is impressed at the scale of the operation. He'd single-handedly made Nineveh unlivable. "And you've been hanging around here all this time?"

"I've been in the vicinity, you could say."

"But why? What's in it for you now?"

"See, I was waiting for beetle season to roll around again. I made sure enough of those buggers survived last time to lay eggs, and I've been keeping a paternal eye on the kids, as it were, as they go through their growing pains."

Metamorphosis. Katya wonders whether her father has not, finally, gone completely insane. "Come on, Dad, you expect me to believe that? You've been, what, herding larvae?"

"I know the places where they lay their eggs, the hidey-holes. I've made sure they're protected. It's a good crop. A bumper crop. The swarm's gonna be a knockout. My plan was, I'd let them hatch, and then Brand would come knocking on my door in desperation. Easy money. I'd make him kneel down in the mud and beg for help. But instead, what happens?" He leans towards her, poking her shoulder with his forefinger. Katya leans away.

"*You* pitch up, just as the beasties are starting to pop up again. You get the benefit of it. Hardly fair, eh?" He pulls back and slugs his drink, then shows her his missing tooth again. "But never mind, we'll make a plan."

"What do you mean, *we*?" she asks. Oh no.

"You'll be needing some expert assistance, my girl. I know these creatures, I've dealt with them."

"Dad. I can do it. This is my job. They hired me."

He scoffs. "You think this is going to be easy? You think you can play *P. palustris* a little tune on your painless pipes" – spittle lands on her cheek – "and they'll follow you out the front door?"

"Yes," she says, stupidly, stubbornly, wiping her face with her sleeve.

"Ja. Maybe so. Maybe not so much." He shows her his teeth. "Here's an idea, though, listen to this. How about I'm your 'assistant'? You're going to need one. Can't rely on those morons, Pascal and whatsit. No, no, my darling, I think your old dad better come along. We'll get it done. It'll be just like the old days, eh?" He stretches, lacing his fingers together and turning them inside out and pushing them up above his head. His whole body pops and he grins in relish. "See, I'm in good shape, I'm ready to work."

"I don't do your kind of work. I don't use poison, I don't kill things. I told you."

"What do you do with the critters then? Put them up in a nice hotel?" He chuckles at his own joke, slaps a knee.

"Boxes. I use boxes."

"Oh, *boxes*. Oh well that's alright then. How many *boxes* have you got? You got twenty boxes? Fifty? Five hundred? You have *no idea*! These little guys will stick *you* in the boxes if you don't watch out! They're tough. You'll see. You try on your own, it'll be a fuck up. Then what will you tell your Mr. Brand, eh?"

She looks down into her glass, rotating the last mouthful of amber.

"Here, I'll drink that if you're not going to."

She lets him take it; he gulps it down in one.

"Tell you what," he gasps. "I'll tell you what you do. You go to your precious Mr. Brand and you say, here's how it is, you tightwad bastard, you've got a serious invasion on your property of noxious animals, noxious *endangered* animals, and it's going to cost you a pretty penny to keep them away, and it's going to take months to sort, and I'm going to need a special assistant. And then," – he's miming it now, flinging something down on the bar like a lightning bolt – "then you slap down a toxic frog, or a nice little scorpion, right there in the lap of his Italian fucking suit! That'll get him!"

He cackles, and Katya laughs too, a burst of tension. She quickly disowns the laughter with a frown. "Thanks, but I can handle it. On my own." She struggles off the bar stool – not made for shorties, these things – and gathers up her bags.

"Can I get a ride then?" he asks. "I believe I'm going your way."

"No car."

"Oh." At first she thinks he's going to offer to walk with her, but he seems to lose interest. "Oh well." His gaze drifts across the bottles lining the back of the bar.

"Dad," she says.

"Hm?"

The roll of money she withdrew is still in her pocket. She peels off a fifty-rand note and puts it on the bar. "If you need anything ..." She hesitates. "Call Alma, okay?"

"Likewise, sweetheart," he says as he pockets the cash. "Likewise."

9
UNDERWORLD

Afterwards, she goes back to the bookshop and buys, bloody-mindedly, the *Complete Guide to Southern African Insects* and – what the hell – a field guide to frogs and one for snakes and reptiles too. Fuck it, she can learn to throw Latin around too.

The books add considerably to the weight of her load. Struggling back along the road with her two bags of groceries and the tiles and the field guides, Katya is flushed with whisky and bile. How dare her father follow her here, with his dirty shoes and fingernails, making claims, making demands? Will she ever find a home, a life, that he can't worm his way into?

When she spots the tile-seller standing by the side of the road, sucking on an orange and standing on one foot, Katya feels a sudden flare of righteous anger at her, too. Another shyster!

The girl sees her coming from a distance and squints in her friendly way. Before she can say anything, Katya takes a fifty-rand note from her pocket and pushes it at her.

"I don't have any more tiles ..."

Katya takes out another pink note and thrusts that into the girl's palm too. She's never done this before, giving money away: it feels powerful. The girl looks at her, uncertain, fingers half-curling around the notes.

"I want to know where the tiles come from. Tell me." Katya takes out a blue hundred. Her food money for the week.

The girl rolls all three notes together into a thin tube, looks briefly over her shoulder, then nods. "Okay, let me show you." Another backwards glance. "Five minutes. I'll meet you down there." She gestures with her chin at a bus stop down the road.

Katya waits in the piss-smelling shelter with its broken bench, watching the intermittent traffic pass. Soon the girl joins her, taking her sleeve in her fingers and pulling her round the back of the shelter and down a narrow lane running along the edge of the shacks. Wood smoke and eucalyptus are strong in the heated air, as well as the faint sweetish stench of sewage coming from the bushes. People watch them curiously, and her guide nods and greets one or two. A small battered-looking dog follows them for a while, yipping suspiciously, but then they move beyond its turf and it leaves them alone.

The homes here are built of tin and wood and scavenged scrap. Some of it, Katya realizes now, quite possibly liberated from Nineveh. Resting the groceries briefly on the ground, she squeezes her wallet and feels for the cellphone in her pocket. And then sees how silly that is, considering that she's just given away all her money, and the fact that, no doubt, most of the people living here have better phones than her beaten-up old clunker. Phones are important here, she imagines: if home is flimsy or uncertain, a cellphone number can be a permanent address.

They're moving out of the shacks now, following a narrowing track into the bush. Around her, the swamp is still and hot. It's an unseasonable, humid heat – almost thunderstorm weather, strange for Cape Town. Another thing that's changing about this town: the weather patterns. Autumn used to be a slow cooling, a prelude to the gently persistent rains of winter. But this steamy pressure promises a deluge.

Katya's disoriented, but the girl walks confidently, striding more easily now that she's out of sight of the shacks. Katya wavers. This feels wrong, against her instincts. This is not pristine wetland, birdwatchers' paradise. This is the urban bush: utilized, compromised. There are paths here, but they were not made for people like Katya to use. She has the overpowering feeling of walking into a complex trap.

But the girl turns and smiles at her. "It's okay," she says, and her pretty grin is reassuring. Katya wonders how old she is. Fifteen, maybe. A little younger than Toby. Increasingly, Katya seems to be shown a path through the world by children.

"There," the girl says, pointing.

Katya blinks in the sunlight and sees that they have come quite far – far enough, in fact, to see the boardwalk extended into the swamp. Behind it, Nineveh looms like an ice fortress. Approach is everything, she thinks: how different this landscape seems if you come to it from the outside, through a village of shacks. How things change, according to the routes one takes to them. She can hardly believe she belongs behind those battlements.

"Okay," she says. The girl has come to a halt. "You get all this stuff here? From who, from the guards? The builders?"

The girl's shaking her head emphatically. It's clear she plans to go not a step closer.

"Who?" Katya's question is too loud, bullying.

The girl's finger is not pointing at the back gate. It's pointing to Katya's feet – between her legs. Into the shadows under the boardwalk, where the ground dips down.

Katya peers into the dim and clammy space. There's nothing down there. And yet: that is where the imperious finger of youth is directing her. Katya steps forward onto the mud. She's learning how to walk on this slipping, uncertain foundation. It takes a light touch, a hesitant tread, nothing too demanding or insistent. The walkway is chest-high here. Katya puts her bags to one side and ducks under the edge. When she looks back, the girl has gone.

The darkness continues in. Some sort of tunnel seems to go right under the perimeter wall, under the caretaker's building. The foundations, she sees now, are supported on cement uprights, creating a long, low cavern floored in mud.

The girl had pointed: insistent, jabbing.

Katya shuffles forward, head bent. Soon it's easier to crawl. This is, so often in her line of work, the proper approach: to get down on all fours, to emulate the beasts. Pest's eye view. The air is dense with moisture and the dank perfume of the under layers of the earth. There is mud under her hands and knees – a surprisingly pleasant sensation. It takes a moment of suction to pull the heel of her hand out of the muck. Daylight has narrowed to a long, low slit behind her back. The cool encloses her.

Worms and crawling things. Snakes. She puts on her small headlamp, the elastic band tight around the back of her skull. The beam flares and points. She switches it off again. She turns her back to the slit of light at the entrance and lets her eyes absorb the darkness. She waits.

There. Up ahead and above her in the dark, she sees a slim trapezium of light floating somehow against the ceiling. At first she thinks it's a reflection from water, thrown up against the concrete. But no: it is steady. She crawls towards it. The ground slopes gently upwards, the space becoming more cramped the further in she goes.

It is a kind of trapdoor above her. A plank half conceals the gap, but a crack of weak light shows through. She puts her hand up tentatively and pushes at the damp wood. And the weight of the building pushes back. She has the distinct feeling of being pressed back down into the mud, of the space squeezing smaller, the dark cave pinching shut ...

Panicked, she twists around in the dark on her belly and struggles back the way she came – crawling, slithering – until she's passed under the boardwalk and climbed out of the trench and there's sky above her again.

She rolls over and lies on her back. High, high up in the bluest of skies, a bird paddles past. Flying, it is bathed in sunlight under and over. No downside to that world.

Back in Unit Two, the floor seems less firm beneath her feet. Everything sways. She has seen the cavity beneath the structure, now. Nineveh contains another, lower story, an underneath that did not exist before. She feels the same disorientation she felt looking down into the hole of that demolition site back home.

She lays out the tiles on the floor of the living room, placing each like a piece in a game. The nine tiles seem an unimpressive haul, but she senses they are merely a sample, a calling card. They have travelled mysteriously to get here: passing through the walls of Nineveh and back again. This place is not as impermeable as she had thought. There are channels, trade routes out and in. And now she has made herself part, in a small way, of these illicit transactions. As if she's stolen these things herself.

Len would always take something away with him: motorbike parts or cigarettes or silverware or, on one occasion, the entire back seat of a car. Sometimes to sell, sometimes just to show that he could. It was a point of pride, not to come away with empty pockets. She feels his presence here now in Nineveh, as surely as if she's smuggled his smelly old bones home with her from that depressing bar. Staining the air with his tobacco breath, dulling the clean surfaces with his worn fingerprints.

Katya stacks the tiles away on a kitchen shelf. She strips off her dusty clothes and redresses herself in a new uniform, still stiff from the laundry. She paces the white hallway like a general, plotting to reclaim lost territory.

There's no help for it. She will have to employ extreme techniques to lure the critters out, wherever and whatever they are. It's entrapment, sure, but what can you do? She needs to know what she's dealing with before she talks to Mr. Brand again.

She's not going to eat any more bully beef, so she spoons half of it onto a plate, using heavy cutlery she finds in one of the whispering drawers. Chops it into chunks the size of sugar cubes with a ferociously sharp knife.

Then she moves around the house, looking again behind cupboards and under beds. Everything is so snug, so well butted together and carefully fitted, it is almost impossible to find a nook or crevice. Instead, she deposits the chunks of flesh straight onto the floor, in corners, into the backs of drawers. It's an old trick of the trade. Draw the vermin if they do not come to you. Call them out, if they are not being sufficiently pestilential.

Reuben has done well. The foods he selected are not ideal sustenance for a pest relocation expert, it is true, or at least not a high-class one such as herself; but they are absolutely ideal, in fact the preferred foodstuffs, for a wide range of pest and vermin. Bully beef! Chemically addictive, and it lasts forever.

If she has any small housemates, they will show themselves now, if only for the love of processed meat.

Dreamland turfs her out into the middle of impenetrable darkness. She lies on her back listening to the night silence, which now has an added intensity. A listening quality. The house, which seemed muffled and lifeless before, is now more like an ear: whorled, attentive, magnifying every faint sound – including her own small bodily noises.

There. A scritching, a scratching. Pause. And a *rattle-rattle*. Despite the thickness and quality of the walls, the sounds vibrate through them, through the headboard of the bed and into her skull. The hunted creature inside her wakes, sits up and cocks its ears. The tentative scratching seems extraordinarily loud, but she knows from experience that the smallest creatures make the biggest racket, particularly when you cannot see them. A mouse pawing a packet of Tennis biscuits in a tent can sound like a pack of wolves. A lone cricket suggests a maniac with an electric drill.

The bedside light does not respond. Electricity must be gone again. Katya's feeling for the headlamp she keeps on her bedside table, an old habit, when another noise makes her pause. Because this noise is completely unmistakable. Footsteps in the corridor: one two, one two. Human. Nothing else sounds like that.

The unseen feet proceed down the corridor. Now they are passing her door, but she sees nothing in the blackness. Dark though it is, the steps seem confident, as if their owner knows exactly where he or she is going. She knows they've reached the kitchen when she hears the fridge sigh open. A furtive pause. Feeding?

More footsteps, and a metallic gushing. Deciphered: it is the sound of pissing, of piddling, of urination. She believes it is a man, from the echoey, reverberating quality of the noise; this is someone standing up, boldly. As they do.

She could, conceivably, make a dash for the exit while the intruder is thus preoccupied. She could slither out from under the covers, crawl through rooms, feeling her way by touch across the variously slippery and padded, rough and smooth surfaces of the flat, navigate her way to the front door, scuttle downstairs to Reuben and Pascal. This thought traverses her analytical forebrain as she lies motionless in the dark. The deeper, more primitive regions revert to small-animal mode: lying very still in the dark is always the preferred course of action. She's certainly not going to leap naked from her bed to confront the bad man in the gloom. It is too tempting to squeeze her eyes shut – an extra layer of blackness in all the dark surrounding her – and hope for morning.

A final scuffling is followed by a mysterious silence. A length, she starts to wonder if she did in fact hear anything, whether it was some seepage from a dream. And anyway, it's not possible to keep rigidly still, primed, listening urgently into the silence, for very long; eventually the persuasion of the mattress and the swaddling sheets and the darkness will coax you to lower your guard. The body might clench in fright, but the mind, eventually, lets go.

She waits and waits, but she hears nothing more.

And so the tension leaks from her body like water, and she sleeps.

Fuck. The knowledge is in her the moment she wakes, as if it's been waiting by the side of the bed like a faithful hound. In the house. A *man*. Her heart wakes a second after her brain and gives a bound of alarm.

Is he still inside?

Nothing happens for many minutes. Her heartbeat slows and her mind calms. As she tries to pin down a precise memory of the nighttime sounds, they grow more indistinct, and the longer she lies there, the less and less likely it seems that anything really happened.

Nonetheless, she makes an effort to be swift and silent when she gets out of the bed. First, she dresses. Once more she slips on her defensive greens. Removed from the care of the laundry lady, these are becoming worryingly soft and creased. They are losing their effect. Still, she zips up briskly. The overalls are something, at least: some protection. Now if she needs to flee the house shrieking, she can do so without shame. She picks up her notebook. She will approach this in a professional manner. Anyway, she needs the toilet.

Cautiously she pokes her head out of the bedroom. All clear. No menacing thugs, no bodies. Once more she does a careful tour of the entire flat, peeking into every corner, heart in mouth. Nada. Nothing seems missing from the fridge, but she can't be sure. She checks the front door. No sign of a break-in, but something must have come in this way. Some*one*: there are very few creatures, barring the odd monkey or clever cat, who can open closed doors. And none that she knows of that can do so when the door is locked. With thumbprint recognition, no less. Surely one requirement would be to have a thumb?

The bathroom looks precisely the same as it did before. She scans the white surfaces. More than most places in the flat, the bathroom is of an immaculate blankness. It would take a criminal of vast confidence to transgress in a place of such lustrous surfaces, receptive to the lightest touch. An intruder would surely have left something of themselves: fingerprints, even DNA, displayed on the tile as on a microscope slide. But the porcelain is unsmeared. The taps are tightened.

To catch a beast, you need to be still, as still as she'd been in her bed last night; you need to let things come to you. She scans the bathroom quietly, moving only her eyes, focusing on each square inch in turn.

The toilet. Is that a foreign droplet on the rim? And in the bowl... she recalls no flushing sound from the night before. Is there a yellow tinge to the water? She goes down on her knees and inspects. Perhaps. The slightest tint. Is there a musky, sweet and salty tang in the air above the bowl? Has it been...polluted? She could put her head down there, take a sniff – but something fastidious rises up in her. Although she has done worse in her quest for fruit flies, mites and larvae, has rolled pigeon droppings in her palms to test consistency, has savored the rarest of animal exudates (snail urine and moth vomit, meerkat piss and gecko ejaculate), she will not do this. She flushes the toilet once, twice. Runs all the taps.

In its secret places, she notices, the bully-beef bait is untouched, the chunks of processed meat still crisp-edged, incorruptible.

10
VIP

From the outside, the security box is a child's drawing, a Monopoly house, with its four walls and neat pitched roof. There is a voice coming from inside: a sports announcer.

Peering in, Katya sees a man's face, unnervingly close. Reuben is tipped back in his seat, with his feet on a small table and his shoulders against the wall just below the window frame. There's a narrow sill there to support his head. He seems peaceful, despite the apparent discomfort of this position. She notices his hands folded on his belly, over the thick leather gun-belt. His one finger is tapping.

She knocks on the window right next to him and he jerks upright, kicking the table askew as he looks around wildly for the intruder. She smiles at him through the glass and gives a wave, but he stares at her with a kind of horror.

Jumpy, jumpy. His hand, she sees, has gone to his hip, although now it floats away. She notes again that it is a real, large gun. Perhaps she should be a bit more cautious around these guards, despite their smiles, their pixie bicycle bell.

"Hi," she says. "Let me in for a sec please, I just want to ask you something."

There's a surreptitious movement behind him in the gloom. She recognizes Pascal, concealed in the small but unaccountably dark, almost purple, confines of the Security Node.

Reluctantly, they let her in. She can smell hot electronics and dagga. Inside, the space is compact, containing the fundamentals of life. She notices with interest a gray telephone in the corner: an actual landline. There are other, more intimate artifacts. Stubs in a tin ashtray. An empty two-liter plastic Coke bottle by the door. A blanket folded away on a thin mattress in the corner. The sweet and sour smell of men living in an enclosed space, with a strong base-note of dog.

Although there is barely room for one person in here, they manage to shift around the puzzle pieces of furniture – table, two rickety chairs – to offer her a seat. She notices Reuben hastily stubbing out a joint and tossing it through the cracked-open window, while Pascal, presumably giving him cover, edges forward to shimmy the chair into place on her side of the table, extending an arm as he does so to mute the TV.

Finally, after all this furniture-moving has been concluded, they find themselves arranged as follows: the two guards standing stiffly together on one side of the small card table, Katya sitting on the other as if she's interviewing or firing them. It is not an arrangement that affords any of them much comfort. Reuben looks nervous, Pascal bored – his eyes keep sliding sideways to the screen, where an apparently enthralling soccer match is playing out.

It's very stuffy and crowded in here; they're all closer to each other than they would normally be, adding to the sense of crisis.

"Hi guys, sorry to bother you," she begins – and then pulls herself up short. She is an investigator, she thinks, and as such, it is no bad thing to develop a certain distance from her subjects. In this situation, her greens are not the ideal outfit. In authority, they rank somewhat below a security guard's uniform. Especially when they're not accessorized by socks or shoes – she dressed in a hurry.

"Pascal, Reuben." She pushes her feet firmly forward under the table, then recoils when her bare toes nudge something warm and solid, like a heated cowhide bolster. The bolster growls, and Pascal snaps a command and reaches down to grip something – Soldier's collar, she hopes.

"Sorry," she says, shifting back in her chair, her feet tucked in as far as they can go. "Okay, this is going to sound strange, but did either of you come into my apartment last night?"

Pascal controls his eyeballs' irresistible drift to the TV screen. Reuben sucks in his cheeks.

"Inside? Your place?" asks Pascal. "We couldn't do that even if we wanted."

"We're not entered into the system," says Reuben, lifting his thumb to illustrate, a faintly insulting gesture.

"Why?" asks Pascal, catching on a little faster. "Did you have problems?"

"I heard someone come in last night. Someone used the bathroom."

They look at each other. Silence. "This was on Two. Unit Two," says Reuben slowly.

"Two. My floor."

"It's not possible," says Pascal. "Are you sure you didn't dream?"

"Yes! God. You can come and see for yourselves, upstairs. Someone was there!"

They shoot their eyes at each other again. The soccer game is forgotten.

"Well. Why didn't you call us?" Reuben asks. "Next time, call us. You got our number? I'll write it down for you." He makes no move to do so, however.

"Or this." Pascal leans down and slaps a hand against the wall, startling her – and Soldier, too: she feels a displacement of warm air under the table as the dog jumps. They're used to slower movements from the tall guard. Next to his hand is a bright red button, like the ones in her apartment but bigger and closer to the floor.

"Right," she says, momentarily thrown. She'd totally forgotten about those buttons.

"Press it. It is battery-power, too."

"Right."

"So ja, we'll come and have a look, if you like," says Reuben. "But I really don't think anyone was there."

"Yes, we will deal with it," says Pascal. He touches the gun on his hip. "Don't worry about it."

And they wait for her to leave. As she walks away from the hut, she hears the soccer game cranked up to full volume again.

She sits at the kitchen counter and opens her notebook. It's still terribly empty. And dirty –dappled with blackish thumbprints. And Mr. Brand requires a report. She tries to concentrate.

Here's how it is, you tightwad bastard.

She bats Len's voice away. But what else is there to say? She's stumped. On the one hand, there is Nineveh's sterility. There's something odd about a place where there's no sign of life whatsoever: no fly bothering the windowpane, no tiny transparent spider abseiling on its filament from the edge of a doorframe. Nothing but curious sounds in the night.

And on the other hand, in extravagant contrast, there is this profuse and teeming wilderness that lies beyond the white retaining wall: a tangled knot of bog and root and stem, chattering and scuttling, through which she has waded, which has caked and splattered her blackish-green. The rich pungency of the mud alone is evidence of the life force out there. The wetlands must be the hangout of ten million species, jeweled, slimy, creeping, thrashing, slithering, biting. On one side of the wall, there is nothing that one might consider a troublesome pest; on the other, everything. Perhaps it is the swamp itself that is the problem, one gigantic pestilential creature. Nothing less than complete drainage would solve that one. But how to express this in a neat, professional note or diagram?

Because it is essential that she does. Because if there is no pest problem, then there's no humane solution and no reason for her to be there. And one thing she's realized is this: she is not ready to go home.

She must try to be methodical; stick with the program. She has a tried and trusted routine, a way of going about things. Observations, course of action, outcomes.

She underlines *NINEVEH* one more time. She writes: *Observations.* She underlines this too, and then goes back and puts a box around the main heading. Then she sits for a while, biting down on the butt of the pencil. She draws a rough map of Nineveh. She writes: *Prome-*

ces palustris. She draws a floor plan of her flat, a cross-section. She thinks for a while more. She draws an inchworm smoking a cigar.

Nothing.

Now it comes again: the noise, the measured tick-tock. It seems to be right next to her ear. This time, finally, she tracks the radio beacon down to the bathroom. It's coming, *Psycho*-style, from behind the shower curtain. She approaches. When she whips the curtain open, the sound stops abruptly. At first she sees nothing: white tiles, white grouting, silver taps and shower rose.

It's only when she looks down that she sees the source of the clicking. It is so much smaller than the sound it generates. She crouches down low and, although she's not wearing her gloves, she scoops it gently into her palm.

Her captive flickers in her cupped hand like a secret. She takes it through to the kitchen, where her notebook lies open.

She doesn't claim to speak the language of animals; often, they speak in imprecise tongues. But then again, sometimes a living creature is as clear and unambiguous a message as the world can give you.

She opens up her hand, and transfers the creature slowly onto the page, like a thought.

Aitsa.

At two o'clock, she waits for Toby, sitting on an ornamental bench at the main gates of Nineveh. A lavender pigeon perches on the wall behind her back. Staring.

"Sorry, china," she says to it. "Nothing for you here today."

The pigeon, sensing the obvious lie, cocks its head and directs a red-ringed stare at the bully-beef tin in her hands, holes punched in its sides.

"Oh no no no no, not for you, this is precious shit in here." she says, shielding the tin with her bag, giving it some shade. "This is VIP."

She can feel nothing coming from within the tin, no shifts or vibrations of life, and she fervently hopes that her little passenger is sitting tight. They're good at that, of course – squatting, saving up their strength for the right moment to make a leap. She opens the lid a crack and peeks at the subdued jewel gleam of the creature within, careful to keep a hand over the top of the tin in case of jumping incidents. She (or he) sits there quite still in the bully beef can, on a cushion of damp toilet paper, in the inscrutable manner of amphibians.

Frogs are ambiguous gifts. They are what naughty boys are supposed to give to girls they like, in order to disgust them. They are what Len gave Alma and Katya to play with when they were little.

These frogs were received by the sisters in very different ways. When Katya found her frog – on her pillow, or in the tin trunk where she kept her tangled clothes – she knew it was a gesture of secret recognition, and her delight only proved that she was more beast than beauty, just like Dad. There was unthinking cruelty in it, though, like there was in so much he did. Len never considered that she might want to keep her frog, after its dramatic appearance. That she might grow attached. She tried, of course, the first few times, with jam jars and pond water and captured flies, but she had no technique then and all her frogs died. So each gift of a damp, glossy-eyed creature was also the gift of its corpse. She sensed a lesson in this, although it's unlikely Len intended one.

What did these presents do for her sister? They gave Alma the opportunity to release the scream she held always in her chest. Her father would bloat his throat like a bullfrog and make belching croaks, and was not above chasing Alma around and slipping a frog down the front of her dress. She never got rid of the feel of the slime, Alma once told Katya. These days, Alma's children have no pets.

But that's Alma's issue, not hers. Katya and frogs, they've always got on well. And she knows quite a bit more about them now than she did, especially as she spent the previous night studying her new field guide. She checks again on her friend. No movement. "Come on," she tells it. She reaches in with a fingertip and taps its cool back. It flinches, flexing its toes. Alive, then.

At last, she sees a shape making its way up the long white corridor of palms, growing larger and assuming the unmistakable outline of the PPR-mobile. She clutches her tin can to her chest and waves. She's pretty pleased to see it, and Toby at the wheel.

Mongooses prove to be stimulating van-mates. Toby has done his best, trying to confine seven of them in two of the maximum-security, specially designed humane carrying boxes, but they're slippery customers, liquid and lithe and with a nasty bite too. As the van bumps out of the parking lot, already they are starting to slither out of the boxes, popping latches, squeezing through holes the size of keyholes.

"Oh shit," Toby mutters as one of them comes poking its head through the sliding window that separates the cab from the back of the van.

Katya beats it back with a light bop on the nose, and tries to wrestle the window closed again; it sticks halfway. There's a mutinous jostling going on in the dim rear.

"So this is the SPCA lot, then. What's the story?" she asks.

"Someone was trying to export them as exotic pets. Cashing in on the ferret trend, you know? Unbelievable."

"Huh."

She's not sure she likes the terse worldliness of his tone; this is her business, after all. Nor does she appreciate the casualness with which he is spinning the wheel of the PPR-mobile. But Toby is not half as cool as he'd like to make out. He's somewhat wild-eyed and white-faced after his three days at the helm of Painless Pest Relocations.

"Slow down. God. No wonder they're getting overexcited. So let me get this straight – they've been in the back of the van *all night*?"

"Well, shit, I didn't know what to do – getting them in there was hell, and then – well, they're crazy, Katya! I didn't know where to put them, or, or anything. I chucked in some water and some muesli, and – *yaouw*!" He jerks the wheel, skids and comes right.

Another jailbreaker has got through the barricade, shinned up the back of his headrest and dug its claws into the top of his cranium.

"Oh hell," she says, thrusting the tin at him. "Grab this for a sec."

He grabs it blindly and steers with one hand while she untangles the mongoose from his hair – ignoring a lance of pain in the ball of her thumb – and forces the animal into the rear. It's chaos back there: mad eyes and sinewy loops of fur. She jams the window as far closed as it will go and examines her thumb.

"Shit! The little fucker bit me!"

"I told you."

She presses the bleeding puncture to her thigh. Her poor bloody lacerated hands. She should get a rabies shot, but knows she won't get around to it. She's been gnawed on by all sorts, and has been lucky so far.

"Maybe I should drive, Tobes," she says, taking back her tin.

"I'm fine!" he snarls, weaving.

"Out of control, Tobes. I can't believe you left them in there all night."

She taps her fingertips lightly against the tin in what she hopes is a soothing rhythm: like raindrops on a tin roof, like rustling leaves, that's the effect she's going for.

"Did I mention that we don't kill animals, here at PPR?"

It's true: not even by accident. Some injuries, some nasty bites of her own, but thus far no casualties. Let's hope Toby himself won't be the first, she thinks. Alma would murder her.

In the end, they just drive on out to the sandy wastes of Baden Powell Drive, out to the Wolfgat Reserve, reverse the truck into the dunes, open up the back and let the outraged mongooses pour out of their busted cages. She counts them off, one to seven, as they slither into the bushes, and Toby mutters "Voetsek" after them with what seems to her to be unseemly, and not very PPR-ish, venom.

On the other side of the road, in a dip in the low dunes, Khayelitsha begins: a dusty ocean of tin roofs and walls, wind-battered, the color of sand and smoke, stretching to the horizon. Table Mountain a pale rumor, far on the other side. The place is bigger every time she drives this way. The road is barely holding, lapped by drifts of sand. The wind relentless. The dunes walk halfway across the tar and the cars have to swerve around them. From the other direction, the shacks are being forced towards the sea by the pressure of the makeshift metropolis behind them. She thinks about the cluster of wood and tin homes near Nineveh. That's growing too, creeping outwards through the marshland. Reaching out to the next informal settlement and the next, linking up, sewn together by taxi routes and shortcuts through the bush. Perhaps this is the real city, and the patches of brick and plaster are the oddities, the stubborn holdouts, too rigid to move or grow.

They pull away, sand crunching under their tires. Katya can see that Toby, like her, is tired. Adult responsibilities, even three days' worth of them, seem to have worn his natural good cheer a little thin. Try another twenty years, kid.

But there's something new about his manner: a tension that she senses has nothing to do with the trials of the job. He's chewing his lip and, she notes, every now and then ducking to observe himself in the rear-view mirror. He rearranges his fringe to no effect.

"How do I look?" he says. "Do I look tired? I think I look tired. Check these rings under my eyes."

She lets the comment hang in the air a beat or two. "You're gorgeous."

He shoots her a glance. She's waiting for his gappy smile – she's missed it.

"So what's the can all about?" he asks.

"Bully beef."

Toby wrinkles his nose as if he's never heard anything so gross in all his life.

"But look. Inside. Observe." She hinges open the top. "Pretty, huh?"

"Oh!" His eyes widen in appreciation. "She's lovely." For Toby, the beastie world is female. He beams down at the VIP in the manner of a doting father peeping into a bassinet. "Can I?" He picks up the can and upends it on his hand; the captive slides out and squats on his palm.

"Careful. It's a jumper."

But Toby has the hands; the creature sits there quietly, untroubled. It's no bigger than the top joint of his thumb, a beautiful dappled gray-brown with a pale golden line running down its spine. An unostentatious frog, no poison reds or blues, but with a quiet woodland beauty of its own.

It pulses its throat enigmatically. It must be weighing up its options: to leap or not to leap. The essential frog question.

Such fragile creatures, frogs: the delicate webs between their toes, their liquid eyes, the soft flesh of their undersides, and above all their tender skins...Easy to see how the slightest shift, a fractional drying out of the world, would affect them violently, with such a moist and flinching barrier between their insides and their outsides. The strength in the legs always comes as a surprise.

"Mom says you two used to keep these. As pets."

Surprising, that Alma's told him this. "They're quite good company," she says. "Although they don't keep you warm at night."

It's evening by the time they get home, and Katya's tired and irritable after the long day. Lights are burning upstairs in her house. Toby brings the van to a halt and sits there, eyes flickering to the bedroom window and back.

"So," he says, and does a drum roll on the steering wheel. "Hey, check it out. Derek the man."

There on the opposite side of the road stands the forlorn figure of Derek, today wearing a pink shawl over his head and with his left leg cocooned in a floral scarf. Still clinging on.

"Ahoy, Derek!" cries Toby, pushing open the rusty window.

Derek totters around in a three-sixty, confused. "Ahoy," comes a feeble cry when he spots them. "Got some smokes?"

"Nah, sorry."

"You give him cigarettes?"

Toby shrugs. Over on that side of the road, new brick walls have thrown themselves up overnight. "Holy shit," she says, "It's going up fast, whatever it is."

"Think it's flats," says Toby. "So, anyway, you know that girl?"

"What? What girl?"

"Tasneem. From up the road. You know, the one we met outside."

"The crack chick. What about her."

"Well, actually..." But he doesn't have to continue. His telltale eyes keep creeping up to the lit window. Ah, she thinks. Romeo. Juliet. Christ.

"She's here? Toby, in the house?"

"Well, ja. Just for a few days, though, she's been helping out. With the work and stuff."

"With the *work*?"

"Ja, she's really good. At taking notes, and that. And the money."

"With the money."

"She does accountancy at school. She's great, you'll see, you'll really like her."

"Look, it's been a long day, let's just get inside, shall we? Get this shit out of the van. Actually you can do that by yourself. Put it all in the garage."

"Jeez." Toby stalks off towards the garage door, which he despises even more than she does.

There's a bash on her passenger-side window, and a mangled bird beats the glass with gray feathers.

"Derek," she says wearily. Knocking on her window with one bandage-swathed fist. She cracks the window down two thumbs. "Got nothing today, man."

He steps back but keeps her fixed with a disapproving stare as she gets out of the car and steps around him.

There's a rumor that Derek once had a life, a job as a civil servant. And there's something about him that makes this plausible. Right now, for example, his expression is that of a summons-server for traffic court: unamused, unbending, perhaps a little disappointed in her. Derek's bandages don't cover real wounds, or not physical ones anyway. He always has them on, and they move from limb to limb according to his fancy. But still, swathed as he is, he is an eloquent figure of suffering pride. He's followed her to the gate, is standing too near. He is a tall man, even powerful, when you stop to let yourself consider it.

"Nothing today," she says again, irritated. "I'm sorry." She opens her door and goes in quickly without looking at him again.

It's immediately clear to her that something has happened. Some alien force has passed through the house like a shockwave. There's a freshness. A sense of space and light. As if the walls and ceilings have stepped back from each other a few paces. The sensation is so acute that she stands for a few moments, uncertain, the key still in her hand as if there is another, invisible door that still requires opening.

But she can't investigate the odd sensation just yet because the girl, Tasneem, is in the front room, standing on Katya's couch with her knees braced against its back, one hand splayed on the wall, looking up at the ceiling. She twists around to smile at them. It's a pose that shows off a limber body: white vest creeping up, camo shorts. The backs of her knees are slightly paler than her taut shins, as are the soles of her bare feet. A pair of slip-slops lie on the carpet.

Toby wriggles through, mongoose-like, to insert himself next to her. Both of them stand there smiling at Katya – the girl lightly, Toby with a kind of naked pleading. He so wants her to be kind! Katya can see he's stretched tight: damage might be done by the lightest pinprick.

"This is Tasneem. Tas, Auntie Katya."

The girl bounces down from the couch and sticks out her hand, a grabby strong handshake, and smiles to reveal large porcelain teeth. "Ja, we met. Whoo, you guys smell really bad," she says.

"Mongoose piss," says Toby authoritatively. "It reeks."

The girl points up at the wall above the couch. "See it?"

"See what?" Katya twists to look.

"See? Big one, too."

"What?"

"Crack," say Tasneem and Toby in unison. The girl's bounced up onto the couch again, demonstrating.

And Katya does see. The crack has grown huge. Shit, it's a finger wide, and not quite dark in there: there's a leak of illumination, a slight stain of sunset light spreading from some fissure in the outside wall. Toby steps up onto the couch, puts his ear against the wall to listen, then holds his hands out as if warming them at a ghostly braai.

"Check, there's a breeze," he says.

Katya reaches between the bodies of the two young people. She put out a palm, experimentally – not touching, just holding her hand before the crack. From the guts of the building, a light wind stirs. She pulls away, almost stumbling as she steps backwards off the couch.

"Does that mean it goes right through? All the way? Katya?"

"I don't know. How should I know? Shit." It's chilled her, that breath coming through the crack.

The kids bounce off the couch again, getting in front of her, getting in her way. She pushes past them, walks through into the kitchen. Drops her bag and stands and stares.

It's like a strange dream. It's her house, but changed. A suspicious quantity of light seems to be billowing in through the windows. The blinds are gone, that's it. The panes are clean, clear as water. And the filing cabinet, the old gray steel one that used to hunker just here, at the inconvenient corner of the staircase and the kitchen nook, where she used to bash her thigh on it in passing – it's vanished. The side table, the pine one with the chunk of wood under one leg to stabilize it: also gone. Everything is shining unnaturally. The floors, luxuriating in the air, gleam. It takes her a moment to realize that this is due to the absence of rug. Everything is stripped down, spare, scrubbed. Has she only been away a few days?

"I feel like Rip van Winkle," she says. Blank looks from the kids. "What happened?"

"Looks good, eh?"

"What have you done? Where's...where is the goddamn filing cabinet?"

Why, of all precious things, she should fix on this dour item of office furniture to accuse them with strikes her as farcical even as it comes out of her mouth. She doesn't care. "Toby, the bloody carpets? Where the fuck is everything?"

"We thought you'd like it," says the girl quietly, behind Toby's shoulder. But not without a certain pious tone.

"We did! We thought you would! Come on, Aunt Katya, don't freak out! Don't freak out!" Toby takes her hand, coaxing, consoling, desperately grinning. "Come on, it looks great, doesn't it? We cleaned everything! Check! Check!"

She pulls her hand away. Now he's flipping open kitchen cabinets, flicking on lights, showing her lined up cereal boxes and sorted silverware. Somehow she's close to tears. That poor old filing cabinet, with its constipated paper guts. It's awful old jammed-up sliding drawers, hanging skew. Its patches of black rust.

"Where is it?"

"No, don't worry! We have it, it's in the attic!"

"*Attic*? What attic?"

"Look – look! Let me show you! We haven't thrown anything away, it's just – we did a little feng shui on this place, just while you were gone. We thought it would be a surprise for you."

"What?"

"Feng shui," says Tasneem at his shoulder, holding back a laugh. She darts her eyes at Toby. "Gee, some people pay to get their houses cleaned."

"Is that so?" Katya turns on the girl. "Should I write you a check?"

"Hey!" Toby steps between them. "Jeez!"

A panic is growing in Katya's chest, but at the same time, some distant part of her marvels at the touching spectacle of this kid, this soft-headed youth, stiffening his resolve: she can see him straightening his spine to defend his girl. He makes brave eyes at Katya. She has never seen Toby infatuated before, but of course: he would be one of love's heroes, indomitable.

She's shaking her head. "Fuck."

"Katya ..."

"Fuck it, Tobes! You cleaned the *house*!"

Toby's frantic: he's pointing at something...what? Her notebooks. They've been taken out of the filing cabinet and lined up on a newly cleared shelf. Propped against them as a bookend – and what perverse genius led them to this? – is the picture of Sylvie. Shining behind glass now, in a cheap clip-in frame of red lacquered wood.

She doesn't feel herself grabbing the picture, but it's in her hand and she's hurling it overarm – beautiful! – with a surge of *relief* as the power in her arm translates into the throw and the missile spins out of her grasp. Clean follow-through! She's not aiming at anything, but the frame barely misses Tasneem's head and smashes instead into a clay bowl filled with fruit Katya did not buy, and everything shatters on the bare floor, and there's oranges and apples all over the place. The sound is great, perfect, just the right pitch and reverb to satisfy, and she feels it shuddering through her, and she hears too the voice that comes out of her, a bellow of rage: *"I don't even like fucking fruit!"*

And then the kids are gone, and she looks around in some confusion to find them all the way over on the other side of the house, by the front door, eyes huge, shrinking together and gripping each other's arms like a hapless couple in a horror movie. It's funny: she laughs.

"Okay,' says Toby, his voice a breath. "I think we'll go now." And then he's scrabbling with the locks, and the girl's flashing a look over his shoulder, and then they're out of the house.

She stands there for quite a long time, looking down at her raised hand. There's blood on her knuckle. A single bead of it, perfectly round and red, and she watches as it inches down her finger and then over the back of her hand. There is no pain. She doesn't understand how it could have got there. She can't really remember what's happened, but she feels calm, peaceful almost, like this has all happened a million times before.

She wipes her knuckle, looks again. The blood is not hers.

What?

It must have spattered onto her. From one of the kids. A piece of flying glass, perhaps.

She goes down on her haunches to pick up the broken glass and pottery. She picks up one, two, three pieces, and then she drops them again and lies down in the middle of the mess and she puts her head down on the floorboards and she groans.

"Oh fuck," she says, "Oh fuck, oh fuck, oh fuck." There's a shard digging into her forehead, but she doesn't move. She presses her face into the pain.

The frog is still alive in its tin – that's something, at least. She carries it upstairs, very careful not to trip on the steep climb.

There's a square outline of a trapdoor in the ceiling above the landing. The attic. It has, she dimly knows, always been there. She must've seen it a thousand times, but she can't say that it's ever occurred to her to go up there. But the kids saw the possibilities; saw that the house has other dimensions, that it might expand. That it might be larger than its known volume.

She rinses her hand. She tells herself it's not so bad. A bit of throwing of objects. Some people do it all the time.

But not at Toby.

Her throat clenches in shame. Somehow, hours have passed: it's dark outside. Too late to call Toby now – she'd hate to wake Alma. Too late in every way.

Fortunately, the kids didn't clean out her upstairs cupboards, and she still has the necessary equipment stashed away: an old fish tank, a dish for water. Little trick: how to calm a frog. You flip it on its back and tickle its tummy, and it's putty in your hands. True. She eases it down into the cool dampness of the tank. In a bank bag in a special drawer, a supply of dead flies. She drops half a dozen into the tank. Some frogs are picky, insisting on live running insects only, but this one eyes the flies with interest.

From her bedroom window, she has a melancholy view of the construction site. It looks like World War One down there, with water standing in the trenches. Already, it's hard to remember the shapes of what was there before. On the other side of the park, the residential streets give way to warehouses and workshops, which the trees in the park once concealed. Now, though, the shabby backsides of these buildings are exposed. The sodium streetlights show up flaws in the plaster, ragged rust-holes in the corrugated iron. Decayed, but monumental: living the cold mysterious life of buildings after hours. Buildings that nobody loves or lives in, that were not built for that.

She positions the frog tank carefully next to the bed. Strange what a little company can do, even if it is the humblest of creatures beside you in the night. She remembers that from childhood: falling asleep with a small, doomed pet in a box by her pillow. The darkness tamed, the loneliness held back.

11
ALMA

In the night, the cracks in the walls get worse.

A giant crowbar reaches into her sleep to prise apart the world. So sudden, and so suddenly over, that on waking she's sure the noise was in her dreams: one of those nightmare eruptions that leave one with the sense of a damped explosion, as if the skull were a padded box in which a tiny bomb has been detonated.

She sits up, switches on the bedside light, listens. Nothing. Except that the water in the square tumbler at her bedside is moving, trembling slightly from some aftershock. She watches the nested squares of ripple in the water, their lines of interference. She turns to face the wall, and sees that a new black crack has snaked down behind the bed. A wide one, a proper chasm. It sunders the wall between the two nails that once must have held a previous occupant's pictures, which she's never thought to replace with her own. The tiny fragments of plaster and paint that rim the crack seem to tremble – is it true? – in a breeze as soft and even as a sleeper's breath.

Is that a creaking? A seismic moan? A rolling grunt, rhythmic. Which stops dead; and then, after a moment's silence, she hears quite clearly: "Jesus Christ." A husky voice, dry with infinite irony.

"Toby?"

But the noise is coming through the wall. She bunches the sheets to her chin, sits up and leans over the headboard, pushing her eye to the wall. Looks inside. Dead black in the crack. Is this a load-bearing wall, whatever that is, exactly?

A cough.

Dad?

Her bedroom lies over the garage, and she's always been able to hear the shadow noises of the alleyway through the wall: the rattle of bins, the rubbish men's whistles. But now she can hear new things, in exquisite detail: the rasp of breath, a low mutter.

"Ohhh," moans the male voice. "Oh Christ. Here we go, here we go a-bloody-gain." A world-weary tone, tragically amused.

It's Derek. The voice she knows, but the tone is unfamiliar: where is the wheedler, the beggar of coins and coffee, the collector of toothpicks and paper cups? Who is this other Derek? Her mouth is open against the crack, ready to call his name; but then she closes it again. She's shy.

Another creak and snap from inside the wall. On the other side, someone farts – she hears it distinctly – and someone else moans: a woman's voice, she thinks. Plaster dust floats down on her head from the ceiling, like the most delicate confetti.

Is the whole thing going to come down on top of them? If she steps out of bed, will the building crack open like an egg? Should she go downstairs, crouch under the solid kitchen table? She can't remember what you're supposed to do in an earthquake. Should she call out to Derek's gang, bring them inside? Or would outside be safer? But the sky through the window is glittery and exposed, full of sharp things.

No word comes from the other side of the wall, but after a while she discerns breathing: a clogged, open-mouthed snuffling. At length it modulates into a doggy snore. She puts out her bedside light. The crack in the wall persists, a seam of charcoal a shade paler than the wall. Dawn must be on the way. She lies there, separated from Derek and his companions by only the width and height of a fractured wall. How many are sleeping there? How many breaths? She tries to count the snores. Is her own breathing audible in the night?

It's an old house, solidly built, has stood for nearly a century, despite the shifting foundations. She cannot imagine any real danger, the walls actually falling on top of her. She lies on her back, staring at the ceiling. Now she's seeing the walls hinging open smoothly, like a Tiffany egg or the housing of a giant telescope, leaving her high and dry beneath the stars. Like those pictures of houses after airstrikes or earthquakes, beds suspended, undisturbed, with walls and ceilings gone. Her bed tips lightly this way and that, a boat rocked on a midnight sea. And in the corner, in accompaniment to her dreams, there starts up a rhythmic belling. Her little frog, singing out in the dark, a long way from its marshy home.

In the morning, Katya comes downstairs and sweeps the floor and puts away the bruised fruit, and looks around at what Toby and Tasneem have achieved. She sees what has always been concealed under the grime and clutter, surfaces she's never actually touched before. Someone has arranged fronds of fern in a glass bottle on the kitchen counter, as well as clear glass jars of foodstuffs: rice, some kind of yellowish flour, nuts. It looks good.

She can't find anything: objects have been packed away and organized by some alien intelligence, Tasneem's no doubt, according to unfamiliar schemes and categories. She sees the scissors hanging by a new piece of string from the side of the cupboard. Fridge magnets lined up in a row. Old newspapers folded up and slotted under the sink. It all makes perfect sense.

Clearly, someone has barked a command to clean up and shape up, and every small object in the house has shaken off the dust and hopped to obey: the magazines lined up in a crisp-edged pile, the wine glasses standing to attention. Tasneem! So young, and already a powerful drill-sergeant of the material world.

It's strangely exhilarating, being in this transformed space; but Katya doesn't really know who this house belongs to now. Like she's housesitting for a different version of herself, from some other universe.

Breakfast, that's what's needed.

The cereal bowls she eventually locates stacked in the bottom drawer of the dresser, but she can't see the spoons. At last she locates filter paper, coffee, milk and the rest. She starts the day with a huge mug of really strong coffee, thank you very much, and contemplates how much of the slightly heightened strangeness of her last few days might be attributable to a lack of caffeine.

When she finishes eating, she finds herself washing the cup and bowl and putting them back where she found them. She shifts the skew chairs so they stand straight at the table. She takes her bag, some clothes, the frog in a box. Locking the house behind her, it is as if she's leaving a hotel room, some place she might never see again.

It's a measure of their relationship that the route does not come automatically to her: she doesn't often go to her sister's home in Claremont. The houses in Alma's road are modern, single-story with generous front and back gardens, all beautifully maintained. There is not one shameful façade in the row. Alma's is particularly trim, the wall newly painted.

It seems strange, sometimes, that a child as generally slapdash as Toby could have emerged from this orderly nursery. She knows this troubles Alma too. Alma keeps an eye on their slippery lineage as expressed in her son: always remarking on the shape of an ear, a hand, trying to trace the bits and pieces of Dad, of Katya, of Mom that may have slithered into the mix. She has never revealed who Toby's father was – part, Katya thinks, of her desire to quarantine Toby, to keep parts of him for herself alone. Her new babies, the twins she's had with her plump husband Kevin, have broad, vividly colored faces and chestnut hair and, like Toby, look nothing like Grubbses.

It's quite hard to get into Alma's house, and not because of broken garage doors. The barriers here are rather more deliberate: high wall, electric fence, no bell: it's been removed so that beggars don't disturb the family. She rattles her keys against the security gate. No result. "Alma!" She hooks her fingers over the top of the wall and hauls herself up, toes scrabbling at the joints between the Vibracrete panels.

"I'm here," Alma says, rising suddenly, garden trowel in hand. Their faces are a foot apart. "That wall's just been painted, you know. You're scuffing it."

"Well then let me in, why don't you?"

But Alma makes her climb. Childish, on both their accounts. She holds her hand up, as if to help Katya, but doesn't touch her as she scrambles over the wall. It's high, but Katya's strong in her upper body. She jumps down and her feet land in dug-up flowerbed soil.

It's always like this, her and Alma. Both of them, alert to a battle undeclared. Alma lowers her weapon and digs it into the soil.

Behind her, the garden lies defeated. Every plant knows its place. It is not so much a growing garden as a mosaic: a pattern of concrete inlaid with panels of lawn, outlined with narrow borders of small-petaled, undemonstrative flowers where required. Alma is very proud of it, but Katya has never seen such a collection of dispirited, beaten-down plants. And lawn, lawn, lawn: not big and ostentatious like the Brands', but squared off into diamonds and parallelograms. At the center of four converging paths, there's a concrete birdbath. It's so clean, there isn't even any algae on its sides, and certainly no birds.

It's been a while since Katya's been here. With sidelong glances, she inspects her sister: Alma dislikes being looked at, and always knows when someone's doing it.

Still so thin. Katya's not a large person but her sister always makes her feel puffy, inflated, pressing at her clothes. Alma's wearing white, all white, and her pale hair is plaited neatly down her back.

Who gardens in white? Katya recognizes it, though, as a uniform of a kind.

"You've come to apologize," Alma says.

Katya looks away. "Is he here?"

"He was very upset yesterday." Alma quirks an eyebrow in the direction of the half-open front door. "They're through in the back."

Katya follows her sister's neat rear into the house and down the passageway. Somehow, Alma managed to find a house as symmetrical as herself. A long corridor into the back, doors to left and right. At the end is a kitchen set at right angles, with the back door centrally placed between two big windows.

Everything gleams. The window glass is perfectly clean, the shades pulled down exactly one-fifth of the way over the glass. Outside, more lawn, and another Vibracrete wall, its rectangular slats as regular as the empty cells of a spreadsheet.

"Hi, Annabel," Katya says to the nanny, who is doing the washing up.

"Hello my darling," she smiles. Annabel is a woman about her own age. Katya's not often in this house, but when she is she always chats to Annabel. They smirk at each other about Alma's little ways, behind her back of course. Sometimes Katya fantasizes about stealing her from Alma and setting her up as her secretary, but the sad truth is that she could not afford to pay the woman as much as she's getting right now for changing diapers.

It's dim in the kitchen, but the world outside the kitchen window is aflame with frank and innocent light. There they are, her nephews and niece: Toby sitting on the grass with his legs in a sandbox and the twins playing around his feet. A sandbox! Katya can't remember the last time she saw one of those; it seems strangely outdated, like camper vans and Porta-Pools. She remembers one from her distant past, in a nursery school somewhere. Nobody played in it because it had dog turds in it. But there are no dogs or cats to spoil the silky consistency of this sand.

"You upset him," says Alma again. She talks very freely in front of Annabel, as if the woman is not really there.

"He upset me."

"Oh for god's sake, Katya. The kids did what they thought was a nice thing for you. Toby's fixed three million things in your house and you've never complained. But now he tidies up for you and you, you *freak out*." Alma folds her arms across her narrow chest. "And don't raise your eyebrows at me like that."

"Let's not fight, Alma. I can't stand fighting with you and Toby, all at the same time. And I did actually come here to apologize, by the way."

"That'd be a first. How about apologizing to him for everything else, while you're at it? All this work you make him do –"

"Hey, you're the one sending him round all the time."

"Not that work. *Your* work. He's covered in bites! My god!" Her dry voice cracks, is for a moment a girl's voice, high, almost singing with distress. "And I think about Mom ..."

"Alma."

"This life. It did her in."

Katya's heart lurches into the cold pause that follows. She repeats, miserably, "Alma."

"No, no...I'm not getting upset, I won't get upset. No." She breathes, a deliberate in and out, and when she speaks again her voice is colorless. "Do this for me, Katya. Look at your hands."

Despite herself, she looks down. Her hands are nicked and scuffed. Scabbed and bitten.

"That's what you've given yourself with this life. Think about that."

And she knows what Alma means. They're Dad's hands that she's looking at. And she is silenced: it is another unanswerable thing.

"Let's go out," Alma says. "They've made salad."

Katya dawdles a second in the back doorway, watching the twins play. They're lavishly provisioned with educational toys, and the sandbox is filled with plastic earthmovers and trucks in red, yellow and blue. The toddlers are mashing them eagerly into the ground, but the sand is not ideal for excavation: try though they might, the diggers make no impression. The dry sand keeps running back and filling in the pits, covering the plastic vehicles and the plump hands holding them. There must be all sorts of things lost in that sandbox, lost forever. Katya wonders how deep it goes. Toby's bare feet are completely buried in it, up to the ankles. Every now and then he reaches out a long arm and hooks back an errant crawler. Tasneem drifts behind the group, holding a glass bowl in her hands.

Alma scoops up the girl twin and cradles her. Katya cannot help but be filled with pride and admiration for her sister, despite everything. She is so neat. So clean, so precise. Her clear features, her tightly bound hair, her symmetry. Is this illusion? Are some people's features genuinely more balanced than others? But there is no other way to describe it: Alma is notably bilaterally symmetrical, like a pale but exquisitely patterned moth.

Which is curious, of course, because she is not. Symmetrical, that is.

Her sister always wears the same kind of clothes. It's one of the things they have in common: they don't wear dresses much. Alma doesn't like them because they often lack pockets, and she wants to be able to hide her hand. There are many people, casual acquaintances or even friends, who do not know this thing about Alma: the two fingers on her right hand that are bent into a claw. She broke them badly, a long time ago, and the bones never set right. She waited too long before seeing a doctor. Or perhaps she never did see one – Katya's never heard the whole story. It is a testament to Alma's grace and self-control that she's able to conceal her injury so well. You might know her for years and never see it. She used to be right-handed, but now she holds her pens in the left.

Katya looks at Alma walking through her garden, child on hip, and she sees her sister's subtle loss of balance: invisible, surely, to anyone but her.

It's sunny out there. Alma's not one for the inconvenience of shade trees, shedding leaves and pushing up the lawn. Katya sighs and steps down onto the grass. They all turn and look at her: Alma, Toby, the dark-haired twins and Tasneem. Kevin's not here – he's often away on business – but that hardly seems to matter; Alma and her offspring are a family, complete in themselves. Able to absorb Tasneem, it appears, but not quite Katya.

"Hello, all," she says.

Toby flaps the boy toddler's arm back and forth in a wave.

"You look smart today," says Tasneem, annoyingly. Katya's wearing nothing special: new black jeans, a fitted shirt. Perhaps the girl thinks she's made a special effort.

"Sorry about yesterday," Toby says at once. "The house, and that."

"Ja, well." She gives the twin a skew smile. "Anyway. Maybe you could tell me where you put the goddamn corkscrew."

"Third drawer under the sink," says Tasneem, although her eyes are appraising: Is Auntie Katya panicked about her corkscrew? Does she drink too much?

In turn, Katya watches the teenagers, covertly examining their exposed skin. Alma was exaggerating, of course, about Toby being bitten all over. He's porcelain and sea glass. How on earth did the Grubbs's dingy genes recombine to create such a specimen? Both Toby and Tasneem seem unscathed, in fact. Fresh out of the box.

But then Toby turns his head and Katya sees a small cut on his cheek, a thin stroke of red just below the eye. She can feel her own cheeks and the back of her neck go cold at the sight.

She waits until only Toby's eyes are on her, then touches her face with a fingertip. He shrugs and makes a face.

Apologies. Katya is not, she's been told, very good at them.

At least the blood was not Tasneem's. Some comfort in that, a drop of sick relief. At least it's all in the family.

They've set up a trestle table. With knives and forks and napkins. Katya allows herself to be led, like an invalid, to her seat, and for the first few minutes there is a careful silence.

Salad! What bizarre children are these? They eat the salad, what's more, with great seriousness, concentration and invention. Toby lays out bowls of greens and chopped reds and pureed yellows, and proceeds to construct elaborately layered lettuce parcels. Tasneem punctures the skin of a tomato with her fine incisors. Toby's jaw grows huge when he chews, and his Adam's apple bounces as each masticated bundle goes down.

They have both recovered their perfect good humor. Perhaps an aunt's fury, like a messy house, is easily defeated with youth and resilience. Katya meets Tasneem's eyes across the table, and they conduct a rapid, wordless truce, sealed with a blink on Katya's part; on Tasneem's, a dab of the lips with a paper towel.

Katya can put all this greenery into her system but she will never be made of the same flesh as these pure children. They would never have touched that bully beef – food of the underworld. Perhaps, having eaten it, she now must return again and again to Nineveh.

The noise of their eating, full of snaps, rasps and crunches, adds an air of briskness to proceedings. It would become intolerable if they had to share very many more meals like this, but for now, she's just grateful for the lack of conversation.

All the kids look like pretty insects to her: busy little garden helpers, mandibles moving. Toby is lean and long, with those giant eyes and triangular chin, mantis-like. He even has his hands held up and clasped, unconsciously praying for something. Why has she never seen it before? The twins: tight grubs. Tasneem is beetle-like, glossy, busy.

Compared to them, she feels too soft to be an insect herself, too indolent. A moth at best, quietly molting moth-matter in the corner. She dips her proboscis humbly into the salad dressing. All yesterday's anger has dissipated. It's their age, she thinks. The invincible age. How can she deny them anything?

Tasneem, fuelled, is now putting the plates and cutlery through new maneuvers: double-quick, they're stacked and ferried through to Annabel in the kitchen. The table stands at ease, awaiting further orders.

Now Toby has an infant on each knee, and Alma is hovering behind him, and it's like a diagram of reproduction. Katya's in awe: all this new flesh that has emerged from her sister's body!

She's feeling prickly, out of place again. Frogs in her pocket. She has not yet told Alma about her meeting with Dad, and now she doesn't think she will. The risk of another argument is too great. Katya idly picks up a toy from the grass at her feet. It's a plastic frog – you pull a string out of its wide, smiling mouth, and as it swallows back the cord, a tinny song plays. She holds it up with a smile.

Alma returns the smile, but her eyes are severe: she will not acknowledge this, not now. "It's from Kevin's brother," she says. "Cute hey?"

The frog tugs Katya's finger, trapped in the pull-ring, back against its plastic mouth. It's slightly painful. She removes her finger with a sigh. This is all very wholesome, but it's enough. She thinks of Mr. Brand, his venal weight, his gold signet ring, his fine substantial handshake. The others barely look up from their play when she pushes herself away from the table.

"Love you and leave you," she says. "Business calls."

Tasneem smiles and Toby waves, and the twins wave too. But Alma rolls her eyes, and Katya knows why that is: it's their father's voice that Alma hears when Katya speaks like that.

12
SACRIFICE

The lawns of Constantia seem bland and sterile after the less showy, more intricate pleasures of the wetlands. All is orderly, apparently clipped into obedience – but a pest relocation expert can always tell where the pockets of anarchy lie in a landscape. There, for example: those hadeda birds; they shouldn't be here at all. Big raucous loafers with their pterodactyl beaks and their rackety cries. They're immigrants here, newcomers from the north, shouldering aside the guinea-fowl. She feels a certain admiration for these shifty troublemakers. As pests go, they would be worthy opponents.

At the Brand's house, she parks next to the rock garden, shoulders her bag and walks up the lawn. The place seems vast and quiet without a party going on. Blue water laps in the bean-shaped swimming pool. Silvertrees whisper sidelong to each other, flat hands turning to disguise the sound.

The caterpillar tree is looking healthy, if still a little shaken by its recent experiences. A few new leaves are already budding. Out of habit, she pokes around in the flowerbed, looking for ant lions, stick insects, chameleons.

Something zings through the air overhead. Katya ducks, then looks around. Beyond the flowerbed is another, broad plateau of lawn, and placed upon it in the distance is a familiar figure swinging a golf club. How pleasant to spend your days in games and entertainments! Distance reduces Mr. Brand's impressive bulk and he looks merely stocky.

The arc of the ball is beautiful, though, and draws the eye – until one of the hadedas sculls across the sky beyond, mocking the golf ball's dumb trajectory. The man pauses his game to lean on his club, eyes following the bird. The hadeda gives one derisive haw and flaps into a treetop. Katya steps out from behind the flowerbed.

A large stretch of lawn can be a stage, exposing and framing a body placed upon it. Moving across it now, she is acutely aware of the shape she makes, bright green on pale green, notebook clutched to her chest. Walking on grass is silent, though, and it takes a moment – in which she might change her mind, turn, run away – for him to see her coming. He does not exactly react, just pivots on his golf club to face her more directly. He is too distant for her to see his expression.

As she gets nearer, he looms taller, growing more solid with every step she takes. Now she can see he is looking at her with a tightly closed mouth. It might not be a smile.

"Mr. Brand," she says, with a cheerful-worker grin.

"Grubbs," he says. "Grubbs Junior." But like Zintle, he's lost some élan.

"You wanted to see me? You asked me to come."

This is a fuck-up already, she can feel it. He seems tired today, annoyed. Just look what he's wearing: a saggy blue tracksuit. Clearly he's forgotten about their appointment And just look at her: clutching a frog, grinning like an idiot, buttoned up in poison green and burdened with a number of complicated motivations. Not a beguiling package.

What they need here is whisky.

"Marvellous," he says. "Come inside, let's have a drink. My wife's gone out."

Indoors, sniffing the bar no doubt, Mr. Brand recovers some of his earlier vim. The house is cool, capacious, high ceilinged, smelling of wood-polish and lavender. There's a lounge with glass patio doors looking out over the lawns and the pool.

As a child, the orderliness of other people's houses mystified and slightly frightened Katya. It's only now that she can look at a place like this, the high shine on it, and recognize the labor of a battalion of servants constantly refreshing and protecting these immaculate surfaces. A never-ending task: even as she watches, a thin film is forming over things, over the glass coffee table, the dried flower arrangement, over the figure of Mr. Brand himself.

He clatters around in a corner bar and brings two tumblers of neat whisky over to a glass coffee table. There's a couch on one side and two easy chairs on the other. Katya hesitates, takes the couch. She sees him pause and make some quick calculation of his own, then choose the other end of the sofa. The cushion sinks with his bulk, and she feels tipped irresistibly towards him.

"So," she begins. "Something to show you."

She brings it out with a faintly theatrical flourish. For its appearance today, she has transferred the frog out of the tin can and into the smarter wooden cigar box. She positions it front and center on the coffee table.

"In the box?" He takes a small pair of reading glasses out of his pocket and slips them on. They make him look both elderly and shrewd, and the balance of the meeting tips back to business. He is, she realizes, waiting for his employee to open the container: he does not expect to do anything for himself, here.

She takes her time, laying out her notebook on the table, smoothing flat the pages. He'll find her squiggles incomprehensible, but at least they are evidence of some sort of diligence. A bit of ink, spilled by her on his account. In her bag she also has a typed report, which says very little.

She is giving herself a bit of time to think. Because there are several factors here for her to weigh up, certain things to reveal and certain things to conceal. She must remember what she is here to achieve.

"You'll be pleased to know," she begins, "that I've found something very interesting on the grounds of Nineveh. I've obtained a sample." She snaps open the box like a jeweler flashing a ring for a hesitant groom.

She tips the frog out onto his coffee table. Touches it with the tip of her pencil. She's feeling at one with the creature now, like they're in synch, a carnival double act. As if she need only call out a sum, two plus two, for the frog to tap out the answer with one webbed foot.

Mr. Brand looks coldly at the frog, who lets out a surprisingly raucous croak. It is the first time today the creature has broken its silence.

"It's a frog," says Mr. Brand.

"Well, yes."

"A frog. One frog. You bring me one frog. This is what I'm paying you for."

"No, well. This is obviously not your infestation problem, as such. That will take more time. I understand the insects surface after rain." She blunders on: "But this is something special we have here." She herds the frog onto her palm with the shaft of the pencil. Strokes it soothingly with the point.

She looks up and Mr. Brand is staring at her. His head is cocked to one side, his fingers tracing the rim of the glass. "You Grubbses and your frogs," he says with an indulgent air. "Frogs! Your dad tried that one on me, too, you know. Tried to sell me a bucket of them. Why the hell should I care about a frog?"

Already she can feel things slipping from her control. She takes a breath and launches her pitch: "Because it's a complication."

He grunts. "Grubbs, what's your point?"

"My point being that this is a most unusual environment that you have here. With all the endangered animals."

"Endangered animals? What, rhinos?" He laughs aggressively, thrusting out his chin.

"Well, like this one. *Heliophryne roseii.*" She moves her hand towards Mr. Brand to illustrate her point. The frog is cool, still and strangely heavy in her palm. "The Table Mountain ghost frog. Enormously rare. Critically endangered. Only found in a few streams on Table Mountain. And, as it happens, on your property."

He holds his grin, waiting for the kicker.

She gives him an apologetic smile. "The thing is, I'm legally bound...I have to report it to the Parks Board. It may affect things. Delay things."

"Jesus fucking Christ. I've already built a river through the property! For the goddamn frogs! What more do they want?"

"The thing is, you might need someone on the property to deal with this situation. On a more permanent basis. Maintenance staff, as it were."

"Being yourself."

"Being myself. I could stay on in the caretaker's unit. I think you'll find my rates are reasonable."

"How long?"

"Ongoing."

He gives an indignant snort.

She presses her advantage: "Because, you see, you could bring your tenants in right away. If someone was on-site, controlling the situation. Monitoring the complex ecosystem."

He stares at her, and for the first time she feels he's seeing her properly, sizing her up. Something changes, tightens, in the air between them. "You're, not by any chance, trying to pull a fast one here, Grubbs Junior?"

"Not at all, sir."

After a long moment, he breaks the stare and throws back his head in one of those big-dog laughs, slapping his thighs. He looks so easy, so delighted with them both, that she wants to lean over and give that meaty leg a good slap of her own.

He must feel where her eyes are, because now, without preamble or awkwardness, while she's still wondering if they've done a deal, he leans forward on the couch and slides his hand in between the buttons of her uniform. His hand is so big it pops a button; she can feel his grasp taking in the whole side of her ribcage.

"Come off it, Grubbs," he says. "You didn't come all this way to talk to me about a frog."

One part of her is so surprised that she's caught with her hands in the air, pencil in one and frog in the other, a cartoon of astonishment. Frozen, while she decides what she feels about this.

Another part of her, of course, is not surprised at all. The part, say, that decided not to wear underwear with her overalls today.

And maybe it's because of the young lovers she's left at Alma's, or her cracking-up house or the pain of the mongoose bite, but suddenly this is exactly what she needs. She pushes back into his grip, his strong cigarette-advert shake. It is all comfortable and unhurried, as if this is something they had discussed previously, perhaps under the vine in the alcove on the day they met, and she feels at ease to toss the pencil aside and pull his hand out by the hairy wrist and take a moment to lean over and lay the VIP back in the box and then unbutton the other buttons too and take his hand and push it back again. She kisses him; his mouth is broad and hot, much wider than hers, and tastes of whisky. He presses her down on the couch, a gratifyingly full-bodied clinch, and at some point in the ensuing fumble and grope he rolls on top of her and his elbow catches the edge of the table and tips the box off. The catches are loose, the frog springs free. A vaulting leap, straight at Mr. Brand's face.

She supposes it's a natural impulse for a golfer, to swing at something at times of tension. Mr. Brand, who's pulled his arm up in pain, does not hesitate. Reversing the motion, he back-hands the frog in flight. Katya shouts and rolls out from under him, landing on her knees on the carpet.

Her VIP. Splayed on its back, pale belly agonizingly exposed. A leg twitches. Jaunty no longer. She cups her hand over the body and keeps it there, a beat, two beats. With her other hand she holds closed her greens.

Mr. Brand sits back on the couch and takes a measured sip from his whisky glass. "I'll be damned," he says.

She picks up the corpse and puts it carefully back in its box. "Thing is," she says, "it's endangered. As we discussed."

"God, sorry." He's laughing into his whisky now.

Her face remains stony.

"Shit," he says. "Endangered, you say."

"Yes."

"Well, not on my property, it isn't, apparently. Plenty more where that came from, right?"

"Perhaps." she flicks shut the useless catches, one and then two. The moment is slippery with possibility; it could go in any direction now. "So. Should I speak to Zintle then? About a contract. For the maintenance work we talked about."

But he's squinting out of the window. "Oh, sure," he says vaguely, swirling his drink. "Certainly. Have a word with her. She handles that side of things."

She gives it couple of beats. "And what should I do now?"

"What?"

"Should I go back to Nineveh? Do I carry on?"

He seems bored now: the game has grown tiresome. He cracks the whisky glass down on the table. "Well you haven't finished the job yet, have you? One fucking frog."

Katya leaves her meaningless report on the coffee table and sees herself out. So much for that, she thinks.

But then again, maybe she got what she was hoping for after all.

On her way out, she stops the car in the driveway to replace the lost button with a safety pin. As she's sitting there, Mrs. Brand drives up in a Mercedes. Big car, silky engine. The driveway is narrow: Katya watches the gap between the cars close. The Mercedes slows to a crawl and stops. "Shit," whispers Katya. Does the woman really want to chat? If they both opened their car windows, Mrs. Brand would surely feel the heat off her cheeks, smell the musky waft from under her rigged-together overalls.

Mrs. Brand looks at her suspiciously. She's the shrewd one, of course. Katya remembers her commanding presence from the bottom of the garden, the strength in her pure blue eyes.

Mrs. Brand nods, that's all. And then drives on to the house.

"Poes," says Toby when she picks him up. He seems close to tears. "Bastard."

"Yup. And I carried her all that way, so careful." Somehow, in death, the frog has become female to Katya, too. "Come on, stop messing with it."

She's behind the wheel, and Toby is sitting with the box on his lap. She's thinking, poor Toby. This humane stuff, it's a joke really, it will never fly. It's not what people want. Eradication is the future. And this poor boy, he's just not cut out for it.

Katya watches Toby hold the frog tragically on his palm – that long palm, so unlike a Grubbs's – and she wants to take the little splayed corpse away from him, clean his fingers and fold them up.

"Come on, throw it out," she says now to Toby. "Seriously. It's not really endangered – it's just a regular swamp frog. There's lots more where that one came from."

He gives her shocked eyes. Poor child. He is too young to understand. The compromises that must be made.

"Close your mouth," she says.

The sky up ahead is streaked with delicate clouds, high and white, like the veins in the marble of the countertops of Nineveh. Weather's changing.

When she gets out of the van at the gates of Nineveh, she notices the power and intensity of the frogsong. They're going mad out there with massed amphibian jubilation. It's irresistible: Katya's mood lifts, despite the subdued atmosphere in the van. She feels half-frog, half-girl, lapping at the moisture in the air, so dense and rich. Her frog skin is wet and alive. She bounds over to the giant gates on frog legs, clutches the bars with frog fingers, throat pulsing with excitement. Home!

Pascal's putting the leash on the big dog. Soldier seems jumpy, shivering his hide and lifting his paws like he doesn't like the feel of the earth. Pascal pulls shut the door of the guardhouse and slings a faded backpack over his shoulder. He seems less confident without his dark glasses, his small eyes touchingly exposed. He looks distinctly like someone about to duck out of a situation.

"Where are you going? What's up?"

Pascal wrinkles his long nose. "Rain's coming. Look, just look at him."

Soldier is indeed behaving very oddly. The dog is jerking his muzzle to and fro, sniffing the soil and then throwing his head up, ripping at his chain. She can't see any sign of creepy-crawlies, though.

"When are you coming back?"

"Afterwards." He pauses, gives her a measuring look. "You will be okay here?"

"Oh, sure, sure. Except. Well, what happens, if you go?" she says. "What about security?"

He taps the walkie-talkie on his shoulder. "Same story. Press the red button, I will hear."

"But will you come?"

"Someone will come. And I am not far away." He raises his chin in the direction of the shack settlement, and for the first time she realizes that's probably where he lives.

He opens the gates a crack, and slips through sideways. Soldier has to wriggle to squeeze through the gap. Pascal hesitates. "You sure? Maybe you don't want to wait. They are not nice, these things."

She is tempted for a moment. Nineveh will feel naked without a guard at the gates, particularly without the unflappable Pascal. But she resists. "It's okay. Thanks, but this is what I'm here for, after all."

He shakes his head. "Just push this closed when you are finished, yes?"

He leaves the big gold padlock hanging by one arm. Then man and dog start out down the avenue, which has grown somber in the changed weather. The fronds of the palms have lost their glints and hang heavy on their stems like the plumage of great, sodden birds. Soldier pulls ahead, clearly glad to be free of the place. They don't look back. Pins of rain start to prick her skin.

Toby helps carry all the collection boxes and supplies over the wooden bridge and up to Unit Two. Then he extends a pale hand through the driver's side window, and she waves to him as he cranks the van around and heads off into the rainy evening, bearing the body of the unfortunate frog. Katya has a moment of unease when she snaps the padlock shut – but surely Pascal means what he says, that he'll come if there's trouble? And better locked in than out, right?

She gets back inside just as the rain starts for real, and carries her bags through into the kitchen. She feels tense, excited; skin tingling from the damp. She kicks off her shoes and wanders from room to room, looking out from each window. No circling bicycle, no lonely watchman's fire.

Outside, the voices of the frogs build and build, until the rain builds in turn and drowns them out. The rain is what they've been waiting for, what they're been reeling in with their song. They'll be laying eggs soon.

Perhaps that's what it was all about, that strange scene with Mr. Brand. Frog mating season! Laughing still, she falls flat on her back on her bed. She takes the safety pin off her overalls and slides her hand in. She holds her palm experimentally over her ribcage, over her breasts. Her hands are much smaller and cooler than his were. Impossible to recreate that heavy touch. Impossible to recreate any of it: now that she's away from him, the whole incident seems unreal. She cannot imagine, in sober recollection, how it came to be that their two unlikely bodies collided in that way.

A problem, in her erotic life. An inability to imagine these encounters, before or after each event. Her adventures have always been this way: easy to fall into, rather surprising as they happen and somewhat ridiculous immediately afterwards. Her partners are unpredictable, and she never really sees them coming. Or going, as they do.

Her first boyfriend was when she was seventeen. That didn't last long. She was still with her father then, working as his assistant. The boy was a student. She wanted to stay with him, curl up in the grimy hollow in his foam mattress on the floor of his commune and never leave. They fought about it, Dad and her. Len wanted to move on; there was some job he'd heard about in Pietermaritzburg, something a friend of a friend had told him about.

At the height of the argument, she hit her father in the face. It surprised her, mid-swing, how much she wanted to. He hit her back, and broke her nose. That night she bled all over her boyfriend's pillow.

It was the first time the violence between Katya and Len seemed cruel and deliberate, rather than some kind of deranged collateral damage. It felt right. This was the proper way, the only sufficiently emphatic way, to go about splitting with her father. And it had worked for Alma, after all.

Alma's definitive moment of violence happened when she was seventeen, too. Len had moved them temporarily into a rented flat, all three of them together in a room. The girls were getting too big, though: too old for this life, but also too large, and growing daily. There was less and less space between them all. Soon they'd be rubbing up against each other like the branches of a cramped tree, chafing shiny patches on each other's bark. There were more and more fights between Alma and Dad, with Alma retreating ever deeper into the silence that enraged Len the most.

On that day, Katya was sitting on the windowsill, knees up, a book raised between her and the squalls of Grubbs family life, and so she didn't see the start of it. Perhaps it was Alma who hit first, lashing out at last. Whatever she did, Len was faster. By the time Katya looked up, he had Alma's fingers gripped in his hand, bending them back so far you could hear the snapping.

Alma didn't cry, or even cry out. She went very pale and sat down quickly in a chair, her hand held up in front of her. It still looked a lot like her hand, but wrong, skewed. All of them were quiet, and all of them knew: at last, after all the bashing and battering, something had been broken – on purpose, and for good.

Katya doesn't remember Alma's leaving, or if she said goodbye. She does remember sitting with her father in that rented room, that same day or one soon after, Len on the bed fiddling with a butterfly net. Katya was on the windowsill, feet up, noticing how much bigger the room was now that Alma was gone. Len put the net over his head, pulling a face to make her laugh. She looked at all the new space between her and her dad. And she was gripped by a fear, like a child's dread of the darkness under the bed, of stepping down alone onto that expanse of drab carpet.

Years later, bleeding in her boyfriend's bed, Katya felt like she'd finally made that journey across the carpet and out of the room. But after she'd spent a week with the student, his housemates told him she had to go. She was too strange, too rough, too young, and she smelt bad. She remembers stepping out into the white sunlight outside the house, with a small rucksack and nowhere to go, stripped of every connection to every human thing. Her face was still sore and bruised. She never really did fit in with that university crowd, anyway.

She retreated to Aunt Laura's couch in Pinelands. It was at this time that Katya reacquainted herself with Alma, who turned out to be living in Mowbray, not too far away. Katya visited her a few times in her tiny, impeccable bachelor flat – evidently, too tiny and impeccable to accommodate Katya – and held the new baby on her lap. Alma, only twenty then, seemed both exhausted and triumphant, like a soldier returned from a tough campaign. She was further away than ever, standing on the other side of some wide desert of experience, and too tired to call to Katya over the distance. Alma never spoke about Toby's genesis. Katya never spoke about her broken nose, which she'd briefly hoped might be some new bond between them. In lieu of chat, they handed the baby between them.

Toby had not yet gained the robust wriggliness of his toddler years, and Katya was afraid that she might snap an arm or a neck in some gesture of untrained affection. So she sat completely still, the baby growing heavy on her legs, until the sense of paralysis and claustrophobia almost overwhelmed her. Alma, watching with eyes red from sleeplessness, always seemed to wait until just this moment to retrieve the child – deftly, even with her crooked fingers – and let Katya go.

After a few weeks, Katya's residence at Laura's became intolerable to them both. And so – it still shames her to remember this – Katya found out where her father was, and she went back.

Her hands fall still; her chest moves up and down softly. Outside, the wind is folding up the rain into fluted columns. She thinks of her neighbors, not too far away, in their small shacks with the rain hammering on tin roofs. And what about Derek and his companions? She wonders what they'll do in the rain, now that they only have the alley for shelter.

She pictures Derek getting wet, his saturated bandages growing heavier, pulling him to the ground and plastering him there like soggy toilet paper. When she gets home, she'll give Derek some cash, or an old jersey or two. Promise.

One thing she can say about herself: she has never been ungrateful for a roof, never taken it for granted. Roof, bed, floor, walls. It still seems incredible to her that she has them all, all at the same time; that she has got this much right.

The solitude feels precious to her. She is the only person left here, in Nineveh, and the thought fills her with precarious peace. She swung it, didn't she? She thinks she swung it. Zintle will draw up the contract: that's what he said. She can stay.

She remembers the dead frog falling to the ground. A little sacrifice. Small price, she tells herself, for a measure of sovereignty. It's been a long walk from there to here: from the pavement outside the god-awful student digs to a place where she can touch the walls and floors with almost frictionless pleasure, as she does here in Nineveh.

She feels cautiously free, a tool that has escaped its users. She is a trowel tossed in the air, gleaming for a moment with reflected light, uncertain where to fall. Certainly, she no longer feels Mr. Brand's heavy hand upon her: he might be her employer, but he's not her master.

But there's something nagging at her. Some part of it that doesn't feel real, or certain. Perhaps because she knows that tools are not made to be free. By definition, they are used.

And she has a feeling that she knows what's coming next.

She waits.

It doesn't take long.

Rats-in-a-rattrap, squashed-flat!

The knock comes loud and clear, resonating through Unit Two and waking her from a doze. She's on her feet at once.

Could it be Toby? Come back to drop something off, some item she forgot in the van. But the gate is locked, and she knows it's not him.

Everything is very dark. She feels her way through the flat to the front door. She's getting to be quite good at this; she hardly needs her eyes. Through the peephole, she can see that the motion detector has triggered the light, but it only backlights a hunched shape. Not Toby. Toby's silhouette is tall and slim: when he comes to her front door at home, he wavers in the pebble glass like a piece of seaweed teased by the current. Too short to be Pascal, too burly for Reuben. No, this silhouette is something else. The shadow figure raises a fist and hammers the door.

She knows that if she stands very still in the unlit hallway, she will not be heard or seen. She barely breathes. The visitor is undeterred. He presses his face close to the peephole, blacking it out. Then he withdraws. He slaps the door, swears, and seems to move away.

Katya waits, paralyzed, hands clasped in front of her, completely still until the motion detector has once more relaxed its vigilance and switched off the light outside.

But she knows he'll be back. She will not have to wait for long. She cannot sleep now.

An hour later, again:

Rats-in-a-rattrap, squashed-flat.

And this time she opens the door.

13

RATS IN A RATTRAP

"About bloody time, I'm fucking freezing out here."

He comes in busily, pushing her aside, bringing the breath of the swamp. It's too dark to make out his face, but there's no need for that. He seems hump-backed: some kind of bag on his shoulder. She closes the door slowly behind her.

"Hello Dad," she says. "Thought it might be you."

"Hello my girl," he says. "This storm's a bastard, eh?" He moves, with surprising speed and accuracy, down the dark passage to the bedroom. She hears the bed creaking, as if under a great weight. Her dad always commanded more gravitational force than his actual mass would suggest. She follows him wordlessly. He's sitting on the edge of her bed, back bent and hands between his knees: a dark shape against the white of the duvet. In the dim light from the window she can see his forehead shining with rain.

"Dad. What are you doing here?" And how did you get in, she wonders.

"I'm fucked, my girl," he says, and his voice sounds frail, older. "We'll talk tomorrow, eh? I need some shut-eye."

"Okay," she says. "Tomorrow."

He gets the bed. She takes the couch in the lounge. It's not uncomfortable. She doesn't sleep, though. She doesn't take her clothes off. Although they're in different rooms, all night she senses him:

he sleeps deeply and loudly, rasping, farting, moaning in dreams. She smells him. Outside the rain comes down.

Oh, but she'd forgotten how he was in the mornings.

She wakes to find him putting on a show for her, striding barefoot up and down the lounge carpet like he's on a catwalk. Lips pursed in a soundless whistle. Any minute now he's going to turn up the volume.

Of course he knows she's awake and watching. He's put on the overalls – her overalls – and is twitching and adjusting them as he prances, shrugging them back into their original shape. His ankles show, and he bends – neat bend, neat body, he always had a trim physique – and rolls down the legs to match his slightly greater height. Wiggles his shoulders around, flexes and releases his pectorals: the fabric that strains over her breasts falls loose on him. He rolls down the cuffs over his bony wrists. He tugs at the collar, smoothes the lapels.

Still half asleep, she sees herself: aged, desexed, capering. It's an old, familiar mirror and a cruel one. Dad.

Len lifts his feet one by one and cracks the joints, curling his hairy toes. Gunshot knuckle cracks, his old morning chorus. "Fits like a glove." He grabs her ankles through the blanket. "Get up, you lazy Katyapillar! Cup of tea for your old dad? Come on, stick on some clothes. You're not decent!"

Her throat is swollen. A frog without a croak.

When he wants to, Len can be still as stone. She's seen him creep up soundlessly behind a rabid bat-eared fox, and watched him wait unblinking for a wasp to remove itself from his eyelid. Right now, though, he's the noisiest man alive. Karrump, karrump, stomping through into the kitchen, bashing things around in the fridge.

She is sinking, heavy as stone. She lies there considering. The sense she had earlier, of being a tool free in flight, of falling through air and light: it is gone. What she feels is that she has been tossed from one iron grip to another; one man has thrown her and another has caught her. A sure grasp. A familiar one. And she feels what a tool feels. She feels gravity. She feel inevitability. Because that is what a tool is: something designed to the purpose of the workman, to extend the workman's hand. To receive the dirt from the palm of the holder. To be dug into the ground.

She is a child, a five-year-old. She is tiny, and she is heavy enough to drop right through these floorboards and into the mud.

"Get out here!" he yells from the kitchen. "Haven't you missed me?"

Even in his chipper, sarcastic voice she hears her own. She sleepwalks through to join him. In the kitchen, he's switched all the lights on and he's sitting on the stool as if they're back in a bar, his legs bent jauntily, the green jumpsuit straining against his knees. He looks at her with bright eyes. Same glass green as Toby's – funny, how she never saw that before. And despite herself, she has to laugh (always): he's got out the bully beef and he's digging in. With relish. It's not lost on her: this is the prey she was luring, with her silly cubes of meat. She might as well have put tobacco out, or left whisky. He's drinking the red Sparletta too. As she watches, he drains a bottle. "Lovely," he gasps, pulling his mouth away with a plop. "Aren't you going to make your old man some tea?"

"No teabags. Anyway, I see you've helped yourself. How long have you been up?"

"Oh, hours. Early bird gets the worm, eh?" He nods at the paling window. The rain's still coming down, if less heavily. "Now's the time to get working."

"It's my job, Dad," she says. "Mine." Her voice is a bit too loud, and she's leaning forward, hands clenched on the edge of the table. That's better: she's waking up. Ready to fight – eager for it, even. A long time since she's felt this.

He snorts in mild amusement and lunges forward, dabbing at her left shoulder. What he brings away is something gaudy, greenish-blue, clinging to the backs of his fingers. He holds it up close to her face. It's her friend from the vlei, the funky, iridescent beetle with the jointed feelers.

He lets it run over his clenched knuckles, then cups his fist loosely around it. It crawls out under his thumb. "Little cutie," he says. "*Promeces palustris.* Looks harmless, doesn't it?"

That's the gogga?

"Hey ..."

He holds it in his fist again, covers it with his other hand and shakes it like dice in a cup.

"Give that back."

"What? Oh, you want it? Okay." He leans forward and, with a click of his fingers, lets the beetle loose behind her ear. Reverse conjuring.

"Fuck it, Dad." She fishes it, wriggling, out of her collar. He chuckles. She slams the window open and shakes the beetle off her hand into the air, too annoyed to even look at it.

"Whoops, lost one there!"

"Christ. Dad ..."

But he's off again, pacing through the house, combatively clicking his knuckles. That sound, the syncopation of her childhood.

She follows him helplessly through the rooms.

"Good thing you pitched up, Katyapillar. I was starting to lose my grip here, I'll tell you that. My place is not so bad in the summer, but when it's wet! And these bloody guards – bloody Nigerians or whatever – "

"Pascal? He's Congolese. And Reuben's local."

"Whatever. Shit! Try to get them to do anything! And Brand? Total cunt. Never pays anyone. Fuck him."

Len talks and talks and talks. When she was a kid she'd try to keep up: run as fast, talk as loud. Now, though, she's had more experience with temperamental creatures. She must remember to move carefully around him, doing nothing to startle.

"See, I realized that asshole wasn't going to be paying up. But I liked the place, I saw opportunity here. I had my thing going. I had access, coming and going, no problems. But then they took my damn thumbprints off the system. So I had to take the back entrance. The tradesman's entrance, you might say."

She can't stop listening to him, can't stop herself from contracting a dose of his chaotic energy. He's filling the house up with his voice, with his smell. He rolls smoke after smoke, ashing on the carpet. He starts leafing through her notebook, scoffing at this or that. She catches herself laughing, laughter forcing itself out. It's humiliating, like being an overtired child who can't stop the giggles.

She has to slow him down, slow herself down too. Because it's now that the bad stuff happens, now that things wobble a little out of control: the tooth knocked out by a wild swing of a hand, the collarbone snapped. Many times in her childhood, a fit of this high hysterical mood led directly to an emergency-room visit for her or Alma.

"Did you get my little present then? Eh?" He bounces his fist along the tabletop, hop hop, and clicks his tongue. He'd always done spot-on animal impressions.

"Was that you? The frog in the shower?"

"*Strongylopus grayii!* Clicking stream frog, they call it. Nothing special. You always did like those slippery critters. Remember I used to bring them home for you?"

He's got her. Because she does remember; and yes, she did love those frogs.

"So do you want to see it? See where your old dad's been spending his days?" He's eager, like a child. "You want to?"

And actually, she does.

Outside, Nineveh is filling up with watery mud like soup in a bowl. Terrible drainage: that's another thing she could have told Martin Brand for nothing. Her father leads her down the stairs from the terrace to the ground level, and then splashing through the mud around the side. She didn't notice it before, but there's a narrow strip of ground around the back, just wide enough for a person to pass between the building and the perimeter wall.

The units' rear view is blank brick decorated with a tangle of piping, punctured only by two small bathroom windows, one below the other. They pause under the windows. The lower one is just about eye height, but nothing is visible through the textured glass. The rain is soaking them in a way that you're supposed to mind, but which she never has minded, not really. As a child, she spent many hours with her father like this: in mud, in rain, shivering with cold, holding tools for him or keeping a lookout. Now, they stand in the rain as if it isn't really happening.

"Had to find a way around that damn fingerprint contraption," Len explains as he lifts his hands above his head and feels along the window frame. "Beep, beep, those friggin buttons, drove me crazy... " He digs his fingers in under the frame, flexes his wrists and pops the hinged window open.

Something occurs to her. Her own bathroom window, standing ajar, is directly above this one. A drainpipe runs up past both of them. "Dad – don't tell me you climbed up there."

"Unit Two. Bitch to get into. I'm not as young as I once was."

"You're insane!"

"Oh, well, it's not that hard. Gotta be smallish, of course," he says. "I see you've put on a bit, by the way. Just like your mother. Well, give it a go."

He braces his foot on an elbow-joint of pipe and slaps his bony knee. It takes a moment, but then she understands that he wants her to hoist herself up. She hesitates. This is more intimate physical contact than she's had with Len since she was a teenager. But she puts a hand on his shoulder and a foot on his knee and lifts herself up.

It's strange. His body under her hands is so spare. The strength is still there, but his muscles have lost their rubbery resilience; his shoulder feels narrow under her hand and his knee wavers under her weight. Her father is getting old. It is the first time that she's thought of him as anything close to frail. She climbs up his body and grabs onto the window frame.

Relieving them both of the awkward contact, she thrusts upwards and pulls her torso over onto the edge. She peers in at a cool, obscure space. It's clumsy, not the right way of doing it, and she feels like she's going to plunge face-first onto the floor on the other side. But her hands find the toilet cistern, and she somehow worms her way through on her belly and brings her legs after her and unwinds herself in an ungainly manner into the dim bathroom.

Her feet find purchase on a slimy surface. Water soaks into her shoes, enough to cover her toes. It seems that Unit One has been thoroughly flooded. She wades forward a few steps and waits while her dad nips in behind her, still limber.

They're in a gloomy, splashing place. The first thing she notices is the smell. It is not a foul odor, but the smell of living things, their wastes and exudations. Spittle and musk, mold and decay. Intimately linked to the smell is a sense of indefinable disorder. Chaos hangs in the air like a shout. It is like some wild animal has been kept locked up here. Stronger than anywhere else within the walls of Nineveh, she can feel here in this dank apartment the presence of the beasts.

The light clarifies. The bathroom is identical to the one upstairs, but stripped of all its fittings. A grid of grouting on the walls shows where tiles used to be. Katya makes her way through into the passage, hand trailing on one damp wall. The carpet is gone. The floorboards feel spongy, and her steps are completely silent.

The dimensions are familiar: the floor plan is the same as Unit Two's. But it is transformed. What she sees is a strange duplicate of Unit Two, one existing in some degraded alternative world. Or that same shiny apartment in twenty years, fifty – a place that has lain in ruin for decades.

There is very little of the original decor left. The doors have been taken off their hinges. The furniture is gone, except for a simple wooden table and two straight-backed chairs in the lounge, like a scene from an interrogation room. The fixtures have been pillaged. In the kitchen, broken pipes and straggling electric wires poke out from the wall where the plug points used to be. The walls themselves are streaked, their lower margins green with mold: a tide-line. There is mud on the floor, silted in thin ribbons and piled in the corners, as if a secret river has whispered through the apartment and then sunk away. In between are patches of lush moss growing across the wooden floor. Katya can even see small mushrooms – each a parasol of tender flesh – running along the skirting board. It is bizarrely beautiful: a meadow, a glen, a dell. An in-between place, where things overlap, where the vlei steps inside and the indoor world escapes into the wild.

Although the furniture has been removed, the apartment is not empty. A millipede propels its miniature standing wave along the wall. A blue dragonfly buzzes past her, wings shivering. Other, shadowy shapes are heaped in the corners: bricks, metal poles leaned up against the walls. Doors and counter tops and sections of wall-to-wall carpet; a big coil of hose; a stack of the spiny grids of burglar bars. Cold taps, hot taps, sections of pipe.

The place is a warehouse, she sees now, containing the stripped-out ornaments and accoutrements of Nineveh. A strange dim auction-house for subterranean beings, or a kind of museum, a catalogue of objects from the daylight world. She remembers now the odd things missing from the luxury flats – the patches of bare floor, the missing towel racks. If she'd explored the rest of Nineveh more carefully, gone into the upper stories of the other buildings, perhaps she would have seen much greater damage.

She goes to the bedroom; she knows the layout blindfolded. There's a sodden sleeping bag on the floor, like a blue sea slug wedged against the wall. A row of empty bottles. An ashtray on the windowsill and a million roll-up butts on the floor. How long has he been down here? Surely it could only be possible in the dry weather.

She's piecing it together. This is the middle world, lying beneath the clean light and sumptuousness of Unit Two. Below this is an even danker world: the crawlspace under the building. Behind the kitchen counter she finds a ragged hole in the floor. The plank that covered the opening is missing now, and the water level is high. The black surface winks at her from only a few feet below the floorboards. The rains must have pushed the water up all over the wetlands. It would be difficult, perhaps impossible, to move under the building now. Even as she watches, a piece of wooden beading goes floating past.

And then a single beetle crawls up through the gap, over the lip of the broken floorboards. *Promeces palustris.* This is their portal.

She is flushed with a kind of admiration for Len's fiefdom: it's import/export. Beetles in, building materials out. It's the kind of breaching of boundaries that someone like Mr. Brand could not be expected to imagine, or anticipate, or guard against.

"You sly old bugger, you," she says.

There's a clanging sound in the bedroom and she goes through to find her father wrestling with an iron bedstead. He's got it half up on its hind legs but then has somehow got stuck, one arm thrust through the springs, so he can't set it down again. He totters. The whole thing looks obscene, like the bedframe is trying to mount him.

"Need a hand there, Dad?"

He wheezes but won't ask for help. She takes pity on him and steps forward, supporting the frame while he disentangles himself.

"What were you trying to do?"

He gives her a swift little look of dislike. "They'll give me some money for it. Not much, but still. But we need to take it out the front way. Can't get it through the floor."

She's reaching for the cold metal without a thought. The willing tool. Any awkwardness between them is erased by a job to be done: they both seize on it gratefully.

Her father used to get her to carry things often, in the old days. He always made her take the front, often the heaviest part, so that she was walking fast, too fast, with him rushing her from behind, the fridge or bookcase chipping painfully at the back of her ankles. Going down stairs was the worst, trying to outrun the weight of the thing. Now, again, she takes the forward edge. They guide the bed down the passageway and into the hallway, pausing only to let her swing open the front door. They move surprisingly well together. Nothing falls on toes or cuts into ankles or gets set down on fingertips.

They're out in the cold blustery air and she leads him along towards the pedestrian gate. He's weaker than he used to be, that's for sure. She walks too fast for him, and he drags on the burden, trying to slow things down. She presses on. She is strong.

When she pulls up short in front of the gate, Len runs into her from behind. His breathing is ragged, but neither one of them is going to mention that. The door opens for her thumb and they maneuver the bedstead outside. He's gone silent now; a little sulky.

"This way," he says, pulling her off to the side. She lets him take the lead. They are light-footed people but their burden makes them heavy; their feet sink deep into the mud.

They come out in a grassy clearing that she hasn't seen before: a clear patch of grass, decorated with cowpats and hoof prints.

"Here," he says. "Down. Put it down, dammit."

They put the bed frame down and she takes a seat on its bare springs. The metal is cold against the backs of her thighs. Her father clasps his hands behind his back and stretches his arms. *Click click* go his joints.

"Pissing down," he notes, but it's really just a drizzle now. "Actually I need a piss."

Katya watches her father dispassionately in the rainy light as he shuffles off towards a bush. He seems tired out, shrunken. He always had a certain style – dapper, one might even call it, despite his filthy clothes; but now they bunch loosely around his shanks. It looks like he's been wearing her uniform for weeks, and worn it in to his body's requirements: his sharp knees and elbows, his odorous groin and armpits, his miserly old-man buttocks and chest. She can't imagine putting it on again after this.

He returns slowly, doing up his fly. The skin of his face is drawn tight, the cheeks threaded with tiny broken veins. Under the greens he wears a string vest, yellowed, antique. Those broken shoes, one flapping open at the toe. The backs of his hands are speckled with age. She sits with her own hands hanging between her knees, watching the rain bead the bed-frame. With the old, one must be patient. Patient, perhaps even kind.

"Got a smoke?" he asks.

"I don't smoke."

He sits next to her at last with a squeak of springs and fumbles a squashed packet from his pocket.

"Dad. What's going on? What are we doing here?"

"This is where they come to do the pick-up. For the scrap."

"Oh." Brilliant, she thinks. Scrap-metal crooks. She watches him pat himself down for a lighter. "So, do you have some kind of arrangement with these people? An appointment? Do they even want this old thing?"

He shrugs. "They don't like the heavy iron so much. More the aluminum. Copper pipe."

"So this is it. This is what you've been up to, all this time – pinching scrap metal?"

He looks at her sourly. "What else am I supposed to do?"

He looks so downcast and damp, sitting hunched over on the raw bedsprings. She glimpses the loneliness of his existence. The clammy months of hiding and waiting. The pathetic exchanges of rusty scrap that must be his only human contact.

"Okay," she says. "Okay. Jesus. You can help me. Help me with the damn job."

If she was expecting gratitude or softness, it does not come. He sniffs loudly and wipes the back of his hand across his damp nose. "Bloody right," he says. "You need the help, I'll tell you that for free. Ten legs!"

"What?"

He flicks her chest, right on the badge. "How many legs that thing got? Can't even tell your insects from your spiders, my girlie. From your mites! You need the help, oh yes."

And with that he abandons the bed, and is marching back along the way they came. His spine is straight, and he seems to have regained his spirits. Every now and then he shakes his head and chuckles to himself. Ten legs!

Just before they come up against the wall again, he stops short, distracted by something in the bushes. Turning, she makes out a movement: it's the tile girl, dressed in tight jeans and a yellow jersey and carrying a Shoprite bag over her head. She comes towards them and smiles, and Katya smiles back. But it's Len the girl's looking at.

He clears his throat. "See you later, eh Katyapillar? I need to have a word."

And then he's bustling off, a smile cracking his face. She watches them from a distance, watches how they stand talking to each other. Len is clearly making an effort. The girl's friendly and relaxed, hands on hips. She pushes Len's shoulder playfully. She is not afraid of him; not at all.

Katya is lanced by a jealousy she has no guard against, and turns away. When she turns back again, they're walking away. The girl ahead, her father tailing behind. He's carrying her Shoprite bag for her.

At the pedestrian gate, she pauses on the threshold, deciding. At length she goes back, finds a piece of broken brick under the boardwalk and props it in the doorway so that her father, when he's finished his business, can join her inside Nineveh.

Inside the flat, she cleans the mud from the floor. She puts out overalls for him, one of the ironed and folded pairs she brought from home. She looks into his pathetic sack of possessions: a razor, a comb, rolling papers, some scuzzy pairs of underpants. They look awfully like the ones she used to have to soak in the bath for him when she was a child – surely not? As she removes each dreary item from the bag, she feels herself loading up with a greater and greater freight of sadness and unwillingness. Each one of his possessions claims some more space here.

He comes back much later. His mood is still high, and he's chatty. Maybe he managed to flog that rusty bed for a few bucks after all.

For supper they eat the pink flesh of the processed meat. She doesn't even consider making him a different meal, one using the food she bought so hopefully for herself. She knows what Len likes. They swig it down with the last of the bright red syrup. She serves these things to him and she serves herself a helping too. She feels it sliding down her throat, staining her insides. Her dad smokes pungent roll-ups, which he's obtained from somewhere. The rain resumes.

"So that's where you've been hanging out then," she says. "Down in Unit One, all this time."

"Ja, it's been a funny old time. That hole in the floor... things got a bit out of hand." His voice is animated again: he's taking some pride in telling her. "It wasn't a bad little operation. Nobody ever came to check what was going on. I even shipped out a couple of those big bloody plaster lions!" He chuckles soundlessly. "Lions! Down the plughole! Got a good price for them off some lady outside the garden center. Four hundred bucks the pair. Cash."

"Clever."

"Well, thank you. I thought so too at first. But now, well, see for yourself: those goggas have got a goddamn freeway. Single-minded fuckers, they are. Won't take no. That and the rain, and the damp coming up, well. That's why I started coming up to Unit Two, you see. Plus the toilet's fucked down there."

"So what were you waiting for? Why didn't you just leave?"

He stubs his cigarette out moodily. "And go where? Home? Where's that? I came to your house, you know. Walked past it a couple of times. I've seen you there."

For some shaming reason, her thoughts turn to Derek: her father might have seen her talking to the old man, denying him, turning away. She looks down at her fingers, which are constructing a Derek-esque artifact out of burnt matches and Rizlas on the table.

Len sniffs. "And your sister wouldn't have me. Oh no."

"Can you blame her?"

"What's that supposed to mean? I never did anything to her."

She's speechless for a moment. "Christ, Dad." She holds her own hand up in front of his face like a piece of evidence. "What about this?"

Len stares at it with a kind of cunning, as if it's a half-wild animal, a spider or a crab perhaps, that needs strategic handling. "Accidents happen," he says at last. "Accidents happen." But he seems to feel that something more is needed. "It was like this," he says. He leans forward and takes Katya's hand. His old skin feels warm against hers, slightly oily. His palm and the pads of his fingers are tough. "It was just like this. It's what you do to control a creature, a wild thing attacking. That's all I meant to do."

And with that he separates out one finger, two – the middle and the ring finger – and gently pushes them back until she can feel the sinews pull. Not painful. He holds her hand in that position, his eyes on hers, willing her to understand. "My hand just slipped, that was all, I was too strong. Do you see?"

What she is thinking is that he has never held her hand before. Skin on skin. It is the gentlest touch he has ever given her, the most earnest communication.

She thinks also: he remembers. He knows precisely. Right hand. Those two fingers. He remembers it as well as Alma does. She pulls her hand from his, feeling the irregularities of his skin against hers, his old knuckles across her palm, like length of knotted rope worn smooth from use.

She makes a fist in her lap and covers it with her other hand.

"And Sylvie?"

Len looks up sharply. She's managed to surprise him. "Sylvie?"

"Sylvie. Mom. What did you do to her?"

He gives a huff, as if someone has shoved him in the chest. It's a laugh, but there's nothing cheery about it. "I did nothing to *her*. I couldn't hurt that woman if I tried. Built like a tank. No darling, in case you didn't realize, she left us. Walked out, back to England, back where she came from, bye-bye and thank you very much. Never saw her again."

He looks her in the eyes. One thing: Len has never lied to her.

"So she didn't have an...accident." When she's finished saying this, a marathon sentence, she has to gasp a breath: she's run out of air.

When he speaks, his voice is almost kind. "No sweetheart. She was often running off, you know. It was nothing new."

Katya sits unmoving, balancing this new piece of information very carefully in her mind, a crystal ball. If she moves, it will roll and shatter and possibly slice her to bits.

"Oh."

"Oh, she says." Len folds his arms and shoves his chair back with a squeal. The mood's changed again: he seems angry, but also energized, determined. "Oh is right. I was the one who looked after you back then, you and Alma. And that, Katyapillar" – he slaps a hand on the tabletop – "is why we stick together now! Right? You with me. We start tomorrow on this job. You deal with the boss, I handle the field operations. We're a team."

She stares at the table.

"Up bright and early, eh? Early bird. What's the matter?"

Katya looks at him and she thinks: This is impossible. This cannot happen.

She thinks: I have lived my life since the age of twenty in an effort to get away from this, from this, from exactly this.

14

ARMED RESPONSE

In the early hours, as if a tap is turned off, the rain desists. Katya wakes. In the brief spell of silence that falls on Nineveh, Len's sleeping grunts and moans cease too. His body has always seemed wired to the natural world like this, sensitive to its shifts.

For a brief interval between natural acts, there is a pause, a hush before the orchestra begins. The conductor raises his baton. The creatures of the night wait for the next movement. When it comes, there is no noise. It is rather a change of state – as if the air is charged differently, or has crystallized. Perhaps it is because the moon comes out from the clouds and she sees shadows, washed clean and sharp by the rain, falling on the carpet. Perhaps it is the sense of attentiveness she feels, inside this room and outside, a million small things listening, purposeful, on the edge of some great metamorphosis. Whatever it is, she feels propelled outside, onto the terrace.

Although it's early – what, four, five? – people are already awake down in the shacks, probably getting ready for long minibus taxi commutes; there are glimmers in doorways, the light of paraffin stoves. The moon is still above the rim of the sea, setting alight the patches of water down in the wetlands. From here she can see that the vlei has grown, the smaller pools linking up to form a twisting lake flowing around black islets of ground. In places, the water seems to lap right up against the outer shacks and infiltrate the muddy alleys between them. It must be hellish when it's cold.

The electricity's acting up again. The cold globes of the lamps flicker and revive. There's a soft, rhythmic *clack, clacking,* like knuckles cracking all over Nineveh. It's the locks on all the doors, snapping on and off, on and off, as the electricity wavers. *Clack, clack.* The lights come on. Off. On again.

The mud is shining; it could be groundwater, raised up by the rains and lit by the moon. There are no big puddles, though, but rather a crosshatching of silver like frost on the ground, blazing in the light under the standing lamps. And it's...*crackling.* Like ice splintering.

She takes the stairs down from the upper terrace, the plaster slippery under her bare feet. Nineveh is breathing, flexing in a complex new rhythm that is alien to her: it is not the rhythm of a heartbeat, it is nothing warm-blooded.

The plank path is cool; damp oozes between her bare toes. The silver moon picks up shards of dull light, like pieces of flint embedded in the mud.

What are those things, catching the light?

They're moving.

Swarming.

Between her and the walls of Nineveh, the mud is alive. It whispers and it clicks. She feels a touch on the top of her bare foot, the tentative brush of a feeler. Things scuttle over her toes. The whole surface is alive with tiny creatures, stirring.

Katya walks out among them. The lamps flicker on, off, on, and stay steady.

She hasn't expected the beauty.

She goes down on her knees, she puts her palms flat on the boards. They run over her knuckles. Their carapaces glitter purple, green and gold. Thousands of them. She examines one on the back of her hand. It waves its jointed feelers wildly in her direction, semaphoring something: insectoid exuberance, the joy of the swarm. Or desperate warning. Or mad lasciviousness. Or something. It unsheathes delicate wings from beneath its hard elytra, but then tumbles off the edge of her hand and into the seething tide of its fellows. Not a flyer, then. This exodus is more a march than a flutter.

She tries to make sense of it. They seem to be swarming in one direction, up from the vlei and towards the gates and the road, and presumably on to the built and unbuilt homes beyond. Blind, seeking.

The beetles smoothly lap her wrists, covering her like iridescent scales. They start to come up under her sleeves. She feels a little sting – just a tweak, an experimental pinch – on her upper arm, and she yelps and jerks to her feet, flapping and smacking. Beetle bodies fall off her with a patter, as more climb aboard her feet and start to work their way up.

Retreat: quickly back up the stairs to the terrace. In the flickering circles of light from the lamps, the ground crawls with the gleaming backs of the insects. Seen from a height, it is like the inching progress of some huge multifaceted organism, feeling its way, finding its passage.

She falters. This job is not for someone with only two arms, two legs.

Her fingertips find plastic; she slaps the light switches but they're all dead. She's reduced to fumbling in the dark, finding the right knobs and ridges to guide her through the flat. She stubs her toe painfully on the edge of a cabinet. Left from the hallway. Touch one doorframe, two. The bedroom.

She stands looking down at the body of her father, barely visible in the dark. He sleeps like she remembers him always sleeping: solid, heedless, deep, on his back with his arms flung up on either side of his head like a child's. She wonders what beds he's inhabited since they last shared a roof.

Quietly, she takes the few things she will need: her boots, her gloves. She carries a few collection boxes out to the terrace, and with one in each hand heads back down into the swarm. The sky is growing paler at the edges.

It's like wading through some dry flowing substance, seedpods or grain. Millions of the things. She starts by lifting the beetles one by one, dropping them into the collection box, but soon she's just dipping the rim of the box into the flow, like scooping water. Quickly the box fills with a dozen, two-dozen wriggling bodies. As soon as they're inside the box they go still, as if listening for danger. Or perhaps they have at last found the place they were seeking. They cling to the floor of the box, to its sides, to the underside of its lid.

Two, three, four boxes she gathers in this way. It's senseless: she'll never stem the tide.

Moonlight shows her the empty guardhouse. The door is unlocked. Inside, the chairs are arranged around the table, ghosts in invisible conference. The wooden walls feel flimsy. She wonders if the hut is actually anchored to the earth in any way, or whether the tide of insects might carry the whole box off on their backs. But it's a safe place, out of the way and close to the exit. The collection boxes with their silent occupants slot in neatly under the table.

A patch of yellow light suddenly illuminates the ground: cast down from a window in Unit Two. Electricity's back, and Len has switched on the bedroom light. She wonders what he's doing in there: smoking cigarettes, gorging himself on lurid meats, pissing in the basin. Then the lights snap off again. Has he gone back to sleep? Maybe, just this once, she's got the jump on Len.

She sits in a chair – Reuben's? Pascal's? Worn to the shape of one of them – rests her boots on a collection box and watches the parade through the child's-play window. Her boot tip strokes the wood of the wall, and comes up against a protrusion. It's the big red alarm button, set low on the wall. It looks like something a bank teller might press, surreptitiously, under the counter with a gun to her head. She removes her foot.

Her ankles prickle. When she runs her fingers over them in the half-dark, she can feel tiny bumps where the beasts have bitten her. Itchy. There are creatures in here with her. Her captured friends, and also a few at liberty. Scouts of the main army. There goes one now, a dark shape shouldering its way across the ceiling.

"Snug," she tells herself. "As a bug in a rug."

Bug in a rug. Not Len's words, not his voice. They are blanket-wrapping words, smelling of talc and lipstick. Words that sit you on a lap and rub your back.

Outside, the world is moving, leaving, driven without pause. A liquid rustle like a river flowing past.

Katya reaches out to touch the cool plastic of the telephone on the desk in front of her.

The rings go on for a long time, but at last Alma answers, blearily.

"Kat. What time is it?"

"Early. Al, I need to ask you something. About Mom."

Silence on the other end: the old Alma freeze-out.

"Dad says she went back to England."

Alma is quiet for a long time. "Well, maybe she did."

"I thought she'd had an accident. You let me think that. From when I was little, you let me think that. I always thought something terrible happened to her."

"It *was* terrible." Alma is abruptly alert. "He was *terrible*. To her. You don't remember."

"But why? What about the hospital? I thought she was *dead*."

Another silence. "I never told you that. She was in a hospital, I think. I think...it was some kind of breakdown. But then after that she did leave. And I ..." And then Alma's combative voice stalls, and horrifyingly, she starts to cry. Suddenly, loudly, heartbrokenly. "I was only six! *Six*. Fuck!"

"Oh, Alma." Katya doesn't know what to say to a crying, swearing Alma. She has no precedent. "Alma. Shhh. Shhh."

After some time, Alma's crying sputters and dries up. Katya can hear her blowing her nose. "I suppose we should have talked about this before. I just ..."

"I know."

"It's hard."

"I know."

"Okay, you can stop with the shhh-ing now. I'm not one of your sick...parrots or something."

Katya waits. "So...do you have any idea where she is now?"

"No. No idea." Alma sighs deeply. "God, it's early."

That tired, familiar voice coming down the lines. Katya hasn't felt quite so close to Alma for years.

"So that's it, then," says Katya.

"Yup."

"So Len is really all we have."

"God, please don't say that."

Katya laughs and they say goodbye. After she's put the phone down, though, those last words sting a bit. Alma has Toby, has a husband and babies. And Katya?

Katya has a beautiful plague, an army of insects.

She slouches down in her seat to watch the beetles' progress through the window. The shushing noise is soothing, almost hypnotic. Slowly, the conversation with Alma fades from her mind and she starts to feel the insistent rhythm of the swarm, its secretive white noise. Like the noise and motion of a waterfall, it is random, but within the chaos it's possible to find eddies and troughs and secret tunes, tunes recalling long-ago lullabies ...

Thwock.

She jerks awake from her trance.

There's something big outside: rhythmic, grunting. Coming closer and then retreating.

It does not sound human. It certainly does not sound humane.

She looks through the fairytale window. The sun has yet to jump the wall of Nineveh, and everything is blue with shadow out there. There's something moving across the mud.

It is her father. He is very visible, dressed as he is in the bright green uniform of Painless Pest Relocations, which seems to fluoresce in the dawn light. In his left hand he's flourishing something black and shining: a trash bag. In his right hand is a long, thin stick. He walks out along the boardwalk, concentrating, looking down. And at first it seems like Len is dancing – stepping left, stepping right, a leap, a kick. The dance starts out slow and deliberate and becomes more and more exuberant. Then she sees: it's a golf club in his hand and he's swinging it, up, down, aiming and lashing out with a *crump, crump*.

She is watching her father in his element, doing what he does best: eradicating.

He makes his way across to the other side of the compound, then turns with the golf club held high. He's having a fine old time, she can see. He has regained his vigor, his maniacal grace. He's heading back this way, high-kicking like a crazy drum majorette. *Smack! Smack!* Escaping from his throat are eager hunting cries, obscene in their urgency. Having fun: he can't hope to kill them all this way. At intervals he pauses to scoop, barehanded, the litter of beetle bodies into his rubbish bag.

He heads straight towards her. Right outside the guardhouse, he strikes a pose, golf club slung over his shoulder like a country-club caricature.

He gives no sign of noticing her. The light is strengthening outside, and it's dim in the guardhouse, and perhaps he truly does not see her through the cloudy window. He holds the golf club up, quivering, looks left, looks right, like he can't decide which way to turn. She's utterly still, and so is he, and she can tell from the way his head is cocked that he's listening intently. Her head is bent the same way. Her father can stay still, but she can stay stiller, still as a lizard under a stone, and it is he who moves first, turning away in impatience.

With his sack over his shoulder and his staff in hand, he looks like some despised and disreputable personage out of folklore: rat-catcher, Pied Piper. A ferret or two up his sleeves. The world is a messy business and he is the man for messy business: he's in there wrestling with it, bloodstained and dripping juices. *Got to get your hands dirty, my girl.*

He turns a thick knot into the neck of the sagging plastic bag and dumps it at his feet, then pulls another from a pocket of the overalls. Her overalls, her black bags. He pauses to wipe his fingers on his trouser leg – a streak of brown matter – and turns and lopes off again towards the far side of the property, disappearing between the two far buildings.

She opens the door and steps outside.

There are many of them spilling out of a slit in the side of her dad's killing bag, which is a hideous thing, the living and the dying crawling heedless over each other in the folds of plastic, the walking wounded picking up the relentless march and continuing across the bodies of their brothers.

She picks up one of the dead beetles.

Perhaps she has never looked so closely at the body of an insect, really looked, examined its joints and facets. She has seen many small deaths in her life, and perhaps there is no great tragedy in the destruction of an insect. Or hundreds of them. But it is still a death, and she mourns the undoing of a creature as finely made, as beautifully wrought as this one. It seems hammered out of some rare metal, chased and molded. Knight at arms, tiny samurai; its suit of armor crushed and pulled apart.

She feels the violence in her body. The careless damage. Repair is not possible, but retribution is easy.

Too easy. It's right there in front of her in the guardhouse, at her feet. Katya swings her boot and kicks the red button.

Perhaps she is expecting something more dramatic: a signal, a siren, a shriek that will instantly bring her father to heel. But if there is such a shriek, it happens on other wavelengths. Possibly it disturbs the fine antennae of the beetles, perhaps it blows through them like wind through a field of grass. But she hears nothing. She waits, the only noise the beating of her own heart. Her father is still out of sight behind the far building, and for a moment it's possible to rewind the action, to imagine the button unpressed.

But only for a few moments. Because after that things start to happen very quickly.

Pascal arrives, this time in a car: a proper quick-response vehicle in white with blue trim and a DayGlo yellow stripe down the side, just like a cop car. He looks remarkably official as he hops out, gun – and god, are those handcuffs? – swinging at his hip. Katya's never seen him move so fast, and she feels a twinge of doubt. The first inkling that perhaps, somehow, a mistake has been made.

He opens the back door of the car and another shape appears, straining and panting. Soldier. She'd forgotten about Soldier. The heavy dog lumbers down onto the mud, like a grumpy politician exiting his chauffeur-driven limo. At once she sees he's uneasy. His small ears flatten against his head. He picks up his paws and swings his muzzle from side to side.

A procession of beetles passes through the gates of Nineveh. The flow parts around the wheels of the parked squad car and continues down the driveway, destination mysterious. Dog and man stare at the ground and shift their feet with expressions of equal disgust. Soldier bristles, and you can almost see the hair standing up on the back of Pascal's neck. A deep and richly vibrating growl starts up in the cavern of Soldier's chest. Pascal leashes him just in time: the dog lurches against his straining arm.

"What is it?" says Pascal irritably, peering through the bars of the gate. "I told you these things would come and bother you."

"No, it's not the beetles ..."

"What then?" But then Pascal stops short and lifts his head, listening.

She doesn't have to say a word. Pascal can hear what she can hear: the *crump, crump* of her father's killing blows, distant now, and above that her father's whistle. His happy working song. She knows the tune: it's the one she heard floating up from the beach when she went walking in the swamp that first day. Pascal fumbles with the padlock and comes through, but it's hard to work with Soldier pulling at him, so he quickly shackles the dog to the gate. It takes a few attempts to get the clip on the bars. It's just a plain dog leash, slightly thicker than normal, but still something one would buy in an ordinary pet shop. Katya would prefer to see a chain, specially designed for this weapons-grade animal.

"He is not happy, this one," Pascal mutters. Soldier gives a high yap like a Pekinese. He's starting to drool. Pascal steps back and regards the animal, hands on hips. "I can't take him in like this," he says. He turns his sour gaze 360 degrees, taking in Katya, the insects and the buildings of Nineveh. It's clear he has no stomach for hunting down a trespasser through those infested byways.

"Did you see where he went?" he asks. She just shrugs.

The dog begins to whimper as Pascal starts to pick his way – almost comically, on the tips of his toes – through the debris of dead and alive beetles that strew the mud. Soldier and Katya watch him all the way until he disappears around the back of one of the buildings.

She takes her seat on the bench at the entrance, tucking her feet up and keeping a wary eye on the dog. Soldier is indeed unhappy. A trained animal is orderly at heart, an enemy of chaos, and Soldier is profoundly disturbed. The smell and the touch of the beetles, clearly, is abhorrent to him. As the minutes tick by, he becomes more and more agitated, biting at his toes, pacing left and right, straining at the lead for labored seconds until he seems about to strangle himself.

Minutes pass. The day turns dry. The road leading out of Nineveh is a tunnel of shadow, although the heads of the palms are lit with glassy sunlight. Clear skies again; the frogs are silent. The march of insects thins. Apart from Soldier's whimpering, it's utterly quiet.

Then Soldier stops dead. Stops his whining. Turns, alert but calm, and stares past her, up the driveway. She turns, too, and sees the big silver car rolling down the aisle of palms. It's amazing: at a distance of a hundred meters or more, Soldier has sensed the approach of a figure of authority, an owner, a boss. It has calmed him; he is ready to be deployed.

She stands up nervously, crosses and uncrosses her arms. Then clasps them behind her back.

The car stops just outside the gate. When Mr. Brand emerges, she feels a deep and unanticipated blush welling up from her collarbones and over her cheeks. But she need not worry: if he recalls their indiscretion over the coffee table only the day before, he shows no sign of it now. He's wearing a three-piece linen suit and has become once again completely impermeable. She cannot imagine slipping one of her grubby fingers in between any of those tautly tailored buttons.

She picks her way over the mud to join him. As before, on the grass at the Brands' house, she has the feeling of moving slowly across a lit stage, in full view. The earth on either side is scattered with iridescent bodies.

He's turning a slow circle, glaring. "What a godawful mess."

"Not exactly like the brochure, is it?"

He looks at her as if trying to recall who she is. But then he claps his hands. "Grubbs," he says. "Right, so what's going on? I understand there's been some kind of break-in?"

She feels relief. This imperious man will dig them out of any mess. She briefs him on the situation.

He barely looks at her as he listens and nods, listens and nods. "Well then," he says. "We'd better sort this bullshit out." Such authority: Soldier is entranced. "Where's my security team?"

She hesitates, then points vaguely towards the buildings. "This person I saw – I don't think he's dangerous, exactly ..."

He grunts at her; not quite an acknowledgement. He goes over to the dog and snaps his fingers at the dog.

"Careful, he's nervous," she warns, but there's no need. Mr. Brand's hand is the one Soldier desires: he licks it, presses the side of his jaw against the wrist. Mr. Brand grabs his ears and twists them like rags. Soldier gives an adoring gurgle. A slap to the ribs puts the dog instantly in war mode: pointing his muzzle left and right, staring fixedly at points on the horizon.

At that instant, Len chooses to swing jauntily around the corner of the far building, sack on back, twirling his golf club and whistling. He stops in his tracks when he sees them.

They stand and look at each other, and to Katya they all seem connected, points on the diagram that the guards have been transcribing in the mud for months with their bicycle wheels. Katya and Mr. Brand and Soldier on one side, and her father, the far, wandering point, distorting the square. It is the kind of arrangement that would disturb a lover of order and symmetry. Like Mr. Brand. Or a dog.

Her father shifts from foot to foot. Katya can see that Soldier has fixed on him, is standing with his legs braced, pointing rigidly in Len's direction.

"Dad," she says, but her voice is too soft, and anyway almost immediately eclipsed by her father's, raised in a yell.

"Brand, you cunt! Where's my money?" He lifts his rusty golf club in the air.

She takes a step forward. "Dad."

Mr. Brand's response is a masterstroke. It is deft, minimal, eloquent. He leans down and unclips the leash around Soldier's neck.

For a moment, nothing moves. Then the big dog gives a grunt and a start, as though the air has been whacked from his lungs by a clap on the back, and he's off, picking up the pace as he submits to the ancestral dream of dogs: the hunt, the kill.

It takes Len a moment, but then he too lurches into action. Running across the mud field, comical as his knees lift and fall in the green overalls, his arms pumping. In the bright sunlight it seems like a game, a man and his dog romping across a playing field. Len turns and lashes out with the golf club, but Soldier leaps into the air, paws tucked up like a show jumper clearing the rail.

A noise comes out of Katya's mouth, some incoherent protest, too weak for a shout; the noise simply escapes from her, leaking out like blood from a cut underwater.

She turns her head away.

There's a terrible shrieking, not an animal sound; like the scream of wood going through a sawmill. It stops short and then there is a patch of silence. When she raises her head to see, at first she doesn't understand the scene.

Her father has vanished. It is Soldier and not Len who is cringing, rubbing his muzzle into the mud as if to cool it after a burn. Mr. Brand gives a snort, perhaps of appreciation. "Bastard! Bastard smacked him on the nose!"

Mr. Brand takes few steps forward and then stops, looking down at his shoes. "Fucking mud," he says. He lights a cigarette and goes to sit heavily in the passenger seat of his car. "Where's my goddamn security?" He starts thumbing something into his cellphone.

Soldier struggles to all fours, shakes his massive head as if to rid himself of a fly, and staggers off around a distant corner.

And Katya follows, slipping through the gap between the big gates once again.

15

MAZE

She is running through the maze of a ruined city. A city emptied out by plague, sheathed in mud, scattered with the small, ruined bodies of its meanest inhabitants. Carapaces crunch under her feet as she runs. She can make out muddy human footprints, overlapped by paw prints in the muck.

The architecture seems to have proliferated since she last came through here, growing corridors and portals. She turns left and right and left again, and sees no dog, no guard, no father.

She finds the rusty golf club on the ground. Further on, there's another black bag, spilling its grisly treasures onto the ground. The mud is wrecked with paw prints and claw tracks. Some of the beetles wriggle weakly on their backs. And here: there is blood on the ground, red mammal blood. Footprints widely spaced – running hard.

In a courtyard, there's an angular figure reclining on the edge of a dry fountain. Pascal, leaning on one elbow, his dark-blue uniform as elegant as ever except for rims of mud on the trouser cuffs. He gives her a laconic salute.

"Where is he? Where's my dad?"

He shrugs, flicks his cigarette into the inch of muddy water that has collected in the bottom of the fountain. "Gone," he says. "Anyway, I'm not going to chase that old man. Have you seen my dog?"

She turns and runs in the other direction. She finds the perimeter wall, puts her fingers to it, runs.

She comes out at the back of her own building, in the narrow alleyway, and she sees it immediately: the bathroom window of Unit One is open. A drip of something dark on the plaster below the frame. A shape hunched on the ground below. A dog, sitting patiently. A dog that has treed its quarry.

In one muscular movement, Soldier twists to his feet and comes at her, growling and stiff-legged. There is nowhere to run so she shrinks to her haunches against the back wall and covers her head with her arms. He comes close, so close she can feel his body heat, feverish with the chase. He smells of wet fur and something else, a bitter canine excitement. Black breath on her cheek. A gleam of light strikes his eyeball from the side. Wetness where the flap of his torn ear meets the skull. He grunts softly as he smells her, his massive body tense and trembling, breathing her in.

A faint whistle: Pascal's call. The dog turns its head in frantic relief, races away, leaving her kneeling in the mud.

She waits. It's silent, just her and the black square of that window. She stands and goes over to it. The stain on the window frame is, in fact, a line of beetles, marching out of the house. A slow leak.

"Dad?"

He must have come at a run and leaped up to catch the sharp edge of the window. Agile old bugger, even when wounded. It's too high for her, and there's nothing to stand on. Finally Katya digs her boot-tip into a narrow gap between drainpipe and wall and hauls herself up and over the frame, dropping down onto the bathroom floor.

As she enters the passage, boots sucking on the wet floor, the air grows dim around her. She enters the kitchen. Greenish, underwater light shifts and flexes, and the air is filled with buzzing. The curtains flutter.

Curtains?

There are no curtains. The windows are masked, not with cloth but with a fabric far finer and more rare: the thousand upon thousand twitching bodies of beetles, jeweled, swarming, flicking their wings, coating the room like crystals of amethyst inside a geode.

They cluster on the floor, the wall, the ceiling. Katya reaches out a hand, setting off a chittering flight. As beetles drop from the windowpanes, the light shifts and redistributes, swirling like cloudy water. She walks through to the bedroom, opening up windows, scattering a chaff of insects.

In the lounge, the air is dark and murmurous.

At the wooden table sits a figure, quite still and upright. There is something wrong with his skin, his hair...A human shape perhaps, but built of insect wings. Beetles crawl across his skin.

She can hear the *drip drip* of water. *Tick tick* of insect locomotion. And something else: a ragged rhythm, like air sucking through a punctured straw. Struggling for breath. She goes to the seated figure, reaches out. The insects flutter off him and for a moment, seeing the wetness beneath, she thinks they are flying away with parts of him, that those lightly grasping feet have somehow plucked from him an outer layer of skin. But her father's face emerges. His eyes are closed. She lays her fingers down gently, gentle as insect feet. The labored breath stutters and resumes. She feels her way in the dim light, careful. Here is the dip below his throat...Her fingertips move across to his shoulder, find a ragged indentation, tender. Something oily and warm.

With a gasp he comes awake, glaring. "Katyapillar," he says. "What the fuck did you do?"

She sits down opposite him in the straight-backed chair. Their image in a hundred thousand compound eyes, watching from the walls.

"Oh shit, Dad, shit, he really got you there." The blood has saturated his left sleeve from shoulder to elbow.

She reaches over the table again. Len flinches away. Fair enough. She does not trust the gentleness of her own touch. Perhaps it would hurt him more than help.

"You need a doctor."

"Ah," he says, rotating the shoulder and flinching. "Dunno. Should be okay. Seen worse, had worse."

For the first time in her life, she wonders: is it her father who plagues her, or is it she who plagues her father? Perhaps all this time she's been the one: the pest, the infestation, the thing he cannot winkle out or shake off or eradicate. The one that keeps on turning up again, spoiling things. And look at this pain she's brought him now.

A loud thump rattles the table and she jerks her chair back, startled. Is the floor giving way? But it's coming from above: footsteps. Someone is moving back and forth upstairs, in Unit Two. It sounds like things are being moved around, thrown down. Someone going through her stuff.

"Fat bastard," says Len. "Listen to him."

Together they listen as the raps and thuds reverberate through the building. Is she this noisy? Has her father been listening to her every thump and grunt, her nighttime monologues coming through the boards?

Katya wonders if Mr. Brand will think to look for them down here. One thing about having a belief in the fixed nature of things, in walls and floors: it gives you a certain disadvantage. Mr. Brand, for all his solid confidence, in fact because of it, cannot look beyond the obvious, cannot see past the evidence of the concrete world. He can't consider that perhaps the walls are false, or that the floorboards might conceal strange depths. Despite his rage, he would not think to punch through a wall: it would not occur to him that walls are breachable. In Mr. Brand's world of certainties, such an in-between place is hardly possible; it barely exists.

The noise pauses and then returns louder, closer: it's down on this level, at the front door. They hear the clack of the lock coming open. They wait in the dark.

Mr. Brand is angry. He bangs the front door as if a culprit might be hiding behind it. He's stomping through the house now, swearing, exclaiming in disgust and horror at each new depredation. "Will you look at the floors! My god! How the hell could this happen!" There is an answering voice, too, a diffident echo to each of his barks of disgust.

She's unimpressed by his rage. In her father's presence she has witnessed far more extreme displays. Len is no respecter of boundaries – not of walls, or persons – and she's seen his fist thrust through many flimsy obstacles. This man now blundering around the house is a lamb in comparison.

Katya and her father meet each other's eyes. His whole arm now glistens red with blood. But nonetheless, he cuts a figure of surprising authority, sitting there straight-backed and serious. She always imagined him a misplaced creature, but in fact he seems quite at home here: a man at his own table, under his own roof. In pain, but in possession. He has a strength she always underestimates.

No wonder, then, that when Mr. Brand does step out into the living room where they sit, followed by Pascal and Soldier, there is a disturbance that goes around the room: a confusion of authority. None of them really knows who the boss is here, who owes what allegiances. Soldier, certainly, is not going to risk a move. He skulks behind Pascal's heels, showing them the whites of his eyes, chastened. Perhaps he's never bitten a person before.

Mr. Brand is gasping in his rage. "You pair of bloody crooks!" he yells. "The two of you! Grubbs!"

As he steps forward, the water-damaged floorboards give way beneath his weight, crumbling like soggy toast, and with the sound of paper tearing he plunges all the way through, up to his waist and then his armpits, and his mouth gaping in indignant shock. Mr. Brand has fallen through a hole in the world.

They all look at him. Katya, Len, Pascal and Soldier. Katya lets out an involuntary cough of laughter. Len, too, gives a snort. Then he turns his attention to the guard.

"Pascal. Howzit."

Pascal's scanning the room, eyes shifting from person to person, assessing the situation, making decisions of his own. He raises an acknowledging eyebrow at Katya, but his gaze settles on Len. He nods, and Katya sees at once – of course! – that between them lies a history, an understanding. Perhaps a business arrangement.

"Old man. You need a doctor," says Pascal.

"Could be, could be," says Len. He pushes back his chair and stands, unsteady. His leg, too, is slashed and soaked in blood. Katya puts out a hand to him but he ignores it, clutching the back of the chair as he straightens. "Eina," he whispers.

"You too, yes?" says Pascal to Katya.

She hesitates. Behind her, Mr. Brand, up to his armpits, moans in pain and fright.

Pascal looks coldly at his boss. Then he whistles for Soldier, nods briskly at them all and leaves the room.

"Give me a hand with him, Dad? He's stuck."

But Len's already following Pascal, limping after the dog.

"Dad!"

In the doorway, Len turns. "Not coming with us then, Katyapillar?"

He gives a little smile and half a wave, a sketch of a salute with a bleeding arm. And then her father is gone.

The silence leaves her feeling calmer. What she sees before her is a situation she recognizes. A situation for which she is trained. It is a problem of too many categories of things colliding, of things in wrong places. It requires some sorting, some relocation. Humane, inhumane, whatever.

She goes on her knees next to the hole. He's wedged in pretty tight, but between his body and the broken wood she catches a dark glint of water. There's a brown stain starting to creep up the fabric of his linen suit, and up through the white shirt beneath it. His face is flushed and slick with sweat. His chest must be uncomfortably compressed. She wonders about splinters.

"Are you okay?"

He swallows, opens his mouth to breathe. "Help me here." His voice is constricted.

"Wait." She takes an arm and tries to lever him up, but it's useless even to try. It is as if Mr. Brand is made of some denser material than flesh; he's much too weighty for the flimsy foundations of Nineveh. Certainly he is denser than Katya, and she is powerless to stop his decline. The more they struggle, the deeper he sinks.

"Are you standing?" she says. "Are you standing on solid ground?" He must be, surely; the foundations were not that deep to begin with. But her question introduces a new shade of horror into his expression. As if the world has that second given way completely beneath his feet; as if he's just understood that the void over which he hangs, the muddy vault, is bottomless.

"Mr. Brand," she says, in the slow, firm voice that she uses to calm a frightened creature. "Can you pull yourself out?"

No. No, he cannot.

There's the sound of a car starting up. Pascal and Len, leaving the sinking ship. And then comes the gush of the rain beginning again, and with it a lapping, sucking sound, as if a tide in the mud is tugging the heavy man down into the foundations. His eyes are clear and wide with fear, and he puts out his hands to her, but even before she grips them – slippery, their texture like cold plastic – they both know it's hopeless. He's wedged in, the mud is claiming him. She crouches on her haunches, holding his hands, and considers what is to be done.

"Wait here," she says, unnecessarily. "I'll get help, okay? Just hang in there."

He grips her harder, nails digging into her wrists.

"No," he says. "No, no. No."

He goes on in this way for some time, his hands tightening around hers and the mud soaking into his clothes, moving upwards by capillary action. It has quite extraordinary wicking qualities, that quality fabric. The harder his cold hands grip hers, the faster the damp rises. Seized by a dread of that creeping stain, Katya pulls her hands away from his, and he gives a moan that seems grasped right out of his chest.

She wrenches the rotten floorboards away from around him – they break easily – and flings them to one side, until Mr. Brand is standing in a dark pool with the skirts of his jacket floating up around him.

She sits on the floor, out of reach of his panicky clutch, and unlaces her boots. Pulls off her socks, exposing pale feet. Carefully, she lowers herself down beside him. It's a bit of a squeeze, but there's space. The water is numbingly cold. She feels it in her feet first, and then it reaches her knees, her waist, her chest – until she's standing on fairly solid mud.

She's up close to Mr. Brand now, almost embracing him. She can feel his heat coming through the soaked cloth, despite his shivers. It feels like they're really touching each other for the first time: two animal bodies, seeking warmth.

"Come," she says, taking his hand. His stiff fingers twitch in her grasp. "We should go. Head down."

She puts her hand on top of his head and eases him lower; then she too ducks under the level of the floorboards and together they shuffle forward, stooped. She keeps one hand in his and the other on his back.

A submerged lake. Dark at first, and then she makes out a narrow bar of fuzzy light, which must be coming in under the boardwalk. The water is murky and fouled and it's impossible to see anything below its dark surface. It was foolish to come down here barefoot. Under the water her toes touch solid objects, both squishy and sharp, one of which slithers away. Leading Mr. Brand by the hand, she wades forward carefully, with side-sweeping motions of her feet, as if she's dribbling a small ball very slowly along the bottom.

It is a strange journey through a low-ceilinged underworld, oblique light reflecting off the tilting surface of the water. It's hard to know if they're going in the right direction, but the water grows deeper and they're gradually able to stand more upright. Around them a cold soup swirls. Afloat in it are beams of wood and swatches of carpet, and cold slithering things that wrap around their legs. Flotsam and jetsam. The water slops up and down in wavelets but there is plenty of air, a good layer of breathing space. Underfoot, the mud sucks at her soles. She has little sensation in her feet now. If she stops moving for a second, the lower half of her body feels cut away, painlessly dissolved. At times in the dim light she can make out the bodies of beetles, clinging to the underside of the floor above their heads. Crawling ever onwards, into Nineveh.

It takes them a long time to traverse the building. The ground slopes down beneath them until Katya is submerged almost to her chin, and then they pass under the boardwalk and ascend out of the murk until they're standing on muddy ground with a light rain falling around them. Katya feels like she's been holding her breath in the dark for a year.

Strewn all around is a collection of random objects: towel rails and wooden beading and chair legs and sections of melamine countertops, haphazardly washed out onto the mud. And more fundamental objects: bricks, chunks of concrete.

She sees: the place that once seemed so stable is not steady at all. It is rushing, swirling, all its bricks and tiles and phony lions flushing out. Nothing can be contained. And as the substance of Nineveh unravels, the swamp winds it up like yarn into a ball. Knitting new patterns, weaving Nineveh into the shacks and the city beyond.

Distracted, she lets go of Mr. Brand's hand.

The girl from the side of the road is sitting under a tree in the rain, with a clear plastic bag arranged over her head and a pile of things on the ground in front of her. Shiny objects: pieces of pipe, bolts and washers. She's busy with a rag, cleaning a bathroom tap. Startled, she looks up and stops her polishing. She twists the rag in her hands and waits.

"Hold on," Katya says to Mr. Brand, and walks over, stiff-legged in her muddy greens.

The girl takes the time to tuck the piece of metal into a Shoprite bag. "Where is the old man?" she says.

"He's not here. What's your deal with him, anyway?"

She shrugs. "Usually he brings me things from inside, and I pay him. With food, sometimes. Cigarettes." She holds up the weighted bag. "Do you want this back now?"

"No, no it's okay. Take it all, take what you can. The old man isn't coming any more. And this," – she gestures at the hole in the wall – "is going to be shut up. So take what you want."

The girl nods and stands, twisting the plastic bag. Her see-through shroud is beaded with moisture. She smiles unexpectedly, and is flushed with prettiness. "I'm going home," she says. "You should go inside too. When the rain stops, oh!" And she widens her eyes and flutters her fingers in a familiar gesture, and shudders. "These goggas come again! It's terrible!" And with a laugh, she's off again into the veils of rain, her feet, Katya notices, sensibly encased in blue rubber gumboots like the ones they wear in a slaughterhouse. Katya's own feet are almost the same color.

She looks around for Mr. Brand and spots him walking fast into the bush. She meant to bring him back in through the pedestrian gate, but he seems to be heading out on his own compass bearing, away from Nineveh. She trots to catch up.

He strides forward through the flood waters like an automaton. His suit is dark with muck. His face is pale in the rain, jaw clenched, eyes wide, hair plastered to his scalp. Just as the floorboards of Nineveh proved too flimsy for Mr. Brand, so too the faerie geography of the wetlands cannot hold him. Unhesitating, thrusting forward with great purpose, he finds a straight path through the shifting waters. Katya scuttles after him, overalls dragging, plants whipping her face, following his buttocks – which, molded by the wet cloth of his suit, are magnificently muscular and rounded. Her bare feet are still numb, and although she realizes that they're being pierced and torn, the pain feels distant, theoretical. She sees no birds now. Perhaps they're frightened by the thrashing of Mr. Brand's determined march. In an amazingly short space of time, they're on the beach.

It is only when he's walked far out onto the sand that Mr. Brand stops and stands, glaring out at the sea, fists balled at his sides.

The beach is beyond Nineveh's witching zone. They have broken through. Katya looks around, and the regular topography reasserts itself: here is Noordhoek beach, and there the familiar hump of the mountain with the houses and the road at its base. They have re-entered normal time and space and gravity, deposited on the shores of an ordinary planet. Like spacemen, they are weak and stunned from their journey.

Even the weather's different here: the sky has cleared. A man comes jogging past, dog at his heels. Two young women, deep in conversation, give them an odd look. With their filthy, torn clothes, it must seem as if they've been blown here on some desperate storm.

Mr. Brand sinks to his knees on the white sand. He seems worn out. He pushes back the sleeve of his suit jacket, holds out one pale but substantial arm and stares at it. At first she thinks he's looking at his watch, but he holds the pose too fixedly.

She sees what it is: a tick, dark brown and the size of a lentil, is crabbing across his forearm. It pauses, sizing up an especially succulent patch of skin.

"Hold still," she says, and puts out a hand to tweeze it off.

"No," he says, pushing her away with his other hand. "Leave it."

And the tiny parasite sinks its mandibles into his flesh.

Strange to be back on a tarred pavement, with taxis speeding past. Katya seems to have lost the knack of moving on tar. The surface is too rigid for her swamp soles. Her soiled uniform dries on her, a mud sheath like a chrysalis. Her fingernails and toenails, she notices, are gray with rinds of mud. At length, she finds herself once again walking across the giant's hopscotch squares of the parking lot outside the mall. The car guards dubiously observe her approach.

Through the glass, she sees the shimmering surfaces of the mall. But her reflection lies across this vision like mud on a polished floor. The image in the cool glass is not one she recognizes. It is a wild thing she's looking at, disgorged from some swampy depth, bedraggled and scratched and smeared. Her uniform is completely saturated with mud, her face pasted with weed-like strands of hair. She can smell herself, too: that ditchwater odor that she first sniffed, days ago, in the pit of the excavation opposite her home. She's transformed, like something that's lain under the earth in larval form through a long damp season, waiting to emerge.

She feels in her pockets, looking for a set of keys, something to clutch for comfort, but she has nothing. No equipment. A couple of coins, that's all she can find. They feel like archaic and not obviously useful artifacts.

She did try to bring Mr. Brand with her. She explained that she was walking down the beach to find telephones, taxis, help. But he hardly seemed to hear. She had no power over him, no more hope of moving him than she would a bull seal or a boulder. So she went alone, glancing back to where he sat gazing out to sea, dirty gray suit against beige sand, growing smaller and smaller.

He'll be okay, she thinks. Men like him don't get lost. In her mind she entrusts him to the joggers, the dog-walkers, the lifesavers, those attendants of the real. Because Katya does need to go home.

She steps forward towards the glass, with no confidence that the sensors on the automatic doors will see her, will let her in.

16
LEAVING NINEVEH

The Constantia house looks much as it did before, if disheveled. The swimming pool has gone a delicate shade of apple green, and the grass has grown tall enough to cover Katya's feet.

The same tree is afflicted – those insurance caterpillars making a nuisance of themselves, right on schedule – and once again Toby and she do their collection routine. The work goes quickly. This time the crop is meager; one box of caterpillars, merely. Even the beasts seem to realize that the returns from Mr. Brand are diminishing.

The house is on auction, and Katya's employers this time are the estate agents. As far as she can gather, Mr. Brand had to leave the country in a hurry, pursued by bankruptcy and lawsuits. He's quite notorious now. It was in all the papers. Zintle, who now runs her own PR company, emailed her – with conspiratorial glee – a few of the news links. Nobody ever did get paid.

There are no gardeners in sight: the property seems deserted. But as they're heading back down to the van, catch in hand, Katya glances back up the slope of the lawn, and stops at the sight of a distinctive figure against the sky: sturdy, and dressed in buttercup yellow. Mrs. Brand is standing facing away from them. Perhaps she's come to fetch some last possessions, or dig up loot buried in a corner of the garden. She seems to be studying the grass at her feet. Is she contemplating her past mistakes, her future hopes? Or caught in the moment, wondering what's going on under that green surface? Easy to think of a lawn as sterile and controlled; but the pest relocation expert knows there is a world beneath. To the smallest creatures, Katya imagines, Mrs. Brand is but a shadow in their skies, as vast and inconsequential as a cloud passing.

On the way out, Katya doesn't bother to toss any insurance into the bush. She can't imagine that she'll want to come back here. As Katya and Toby and the caterpillars head on out onto the highway, she has the feeling that all of them have pulled off a great escape.

"Where shall we take them, then?" he asks. "Back to the forest? That didn't work so well before."

"No. I know a better place."

They walk in from the beach side. It's a bright day; winter with its storms has passed, and it looks like it's shaping up to be a hot Cape summer, after all. The beach is full of people, swimming and sunbathing and walking their dogs.

Toby's taken his shirt off, revealing a few more hairs on his still unmuscled chest, and is running up and down to the surf, looping back all sand-crumbed and eager. Katya carries the small catch-box and keeps her eyes on the dunes, trying to spot some landmark. They've been walking for a good half-hour and she's starting to wonder if they've overshot. The sand is monotonous; it's hard to tell where anything is. Hard to imagine the shacks, or the acres of housing estates, just over the rise. The recession has not been good to anyone, and a lot of the luxury estates are failing, lying half-empty, waiting for people to start buying again. She imagines everything gone: Nineveh erased. She'd rather find a hole in the ground than a waste of empty buildings with not enough life or history in them even for ghosts. Then she sees the black hump of the shipwreck, half-submerged in the high tide, and orients herself. And there – a gap in the bushes, a rudimentary path, and a flash of white. A piece of Nineveh. One step back, one step forward and you'd miss it, but just here she can see the topmost corner of its battlements.

"Tobes," she calls. "In here. Put your clothes on, these bushes will murder you."

The wetlands are different now. The water has sunk back, leaving slick mud in places, and there's new growth over the fire-cleared ground. A forest of blue gum saplings are shooting up. Soon this whole area will be shoulder-high in alien vegetation, ready for the flames again.

"See any likely trees?"

Toby answers with a cry. His bare foot has found something sharp. "Is it old?" he asks, handing her a delicate handle attached to a curved section of china.

The broken cup might be from any time at all, from any moment in the last three hundred years, passed from hand to hand, brought here by land or by sea. She drops it back into the mud.

Nineveh's prow lifts above the bush. The shacks are out of sight, although she can smell wood smoke. As they come closer, she sees that things have changed here. For one thing, the wall is not all ice white any more. It's smudged black and brown, as if by fire. The plaster has cracked in places, showing sections of brick. And she'd been wrong about the hole in the foundations getting fixed. The whole boardwalk has collapsed and someone's shoved coils of razor wire into the gap under the building.

The back gate is still locked, though. She presses her thumb to the pad, but the door refuses to click. Maybe it's Katya who's changed. Through the wall she can hear new sounds: a child's shout, a car engine revving and failing, revving and failing.

They walk along the wall to where the driveway heads off at an angle towards the road. Toby follows her silently. There's a hole knocked in the bricks here, giving access to the main entrance. Katya hands the collection box to Toby and ducks through.

Half the gate is gone, perhaps taken for scrap metal, and the remaining half is hanging off its hinges. Inside, someone seems to have inhabited the guardhouse: there's colored cloth up in the windows. Outside Unit One, a group of young men bend over the engine of an old Chevrolet, tormenting it. Some children are playing soccer in the central space, where grass grows patchily. The apartments are also clearly lived in. People lean through the windows, and a line of washing has been suspended between two of the buildings. The place is not as muddy now: here and there, people have sunk half-bricks and pieces of wood into the muck, to step on. And is that a cow?

Katya smiles. There she'd been imagining the apartments standing empty, pining for human attention. How swiftly places change, with just a little pressure of water, time and human need.

Over on the other side of the courtyard, a woman sees her and raises a hand. When she comes over, Katya recognizes the girl from the side of the road, in a denim skirt and scarlet blouse. Some invisible line of adolescence has been crossed, it seems, since they first met. The girl has become more rounded and confident, and has the look of a young woman and not a child.

"Got any tiles?" Katya asks.

The girl smiles back openly – no anxious glances over her shoulder now. "We do car parts now. Do you need?"

"No, but I'll keep that in mind."

"You want a dog? We've got a dog here." She looks around vaguely.

Behind Katya, Toby is scouting down the avenue. "What? Oh, no thanks. We better go, anyway."

"How's the old man?"

"He's the same," Katya says. "The same."

"He talks too much, that one," the girl laughs. "Tell him, he must come visit us. Tell him Nosisi says hello."

Katya smiles. Now the girl has a name. "Why, are those goggas giving you problems again?"

She shakes her head. "No, no, we haven't seen them at all. It's much better now. I think they have gone forever."

Katya wants to say that nothing is certain. Although that is maybe not true for Nosisi: she seems to stand squarely on this ground, sure of her footing.

"Do you remember Pascal?" Katya asks. "Is he living here?"

Nosisi shakes her head, her face unreadable. "No, I don't know him."

And Katya wonders how welcome he was here, the man from the DRC.

Toby calls: "Look!" Behind her, he's peering up into the crown of a living palm. Katya glances back, but the girl is already turning away, forgetting them.

"They like it," says Toby as she approaches. The caterpillars are marching straight up the trunk.

They watch it together for a while, this tiny triumphal procession, unnoticed by the world. Then she touches his shoulder. "Come on, Toby, let's go home."

"Okay. Is that thing coming with us?"

"What thing?"

The force hitting the backs of her thighs knocks her to the ground. She struggles to her haunches, enveloped in a fug of doggy breath. The creature's licking her face, butting at her groin, burying his muzzle in her belly. His claws rake her arms.

"Soldier?"

He's half the weight he was, all ribs, and there's a frayed length of rope around his neck. In his eyes is the desperate gleam of dog pushed past the limit of endurance.

"Wow," says Toby cautiously, stepping back. "That dog stinks."

Soldier rolls over on his stomach and shows them his rude and tender nether side.

She parks across the road from her old house and watches as Toby feeds Soldier in the back of the van: two extra-large cans of Husky and several liters of water, served in old ice cream containers. She's going to have to find a place to wash the animal, too.

"You sure you don't want a lift home?" she asks.

Toby shrugs. "It's cool. Hey, what's this duvet thing doing in here?"

"What? It's not a duvet."

But it is, inarguably. Cream in color, covered in tiny elephants, rumpled and showing unmistakable signs of having been slept in. But Katya doesn't want to discuss that.

"Oh. Well, it's getting mud on it." He runs his nails down Soldier's knobby spine. The dog wheezes and arches, ecstatically kneading the duvet. "Coming in?"

"No."

"He wants you to come in for a cup of tea. He always says."

"God, please."

Across the road, the terrace of old houses still stands, slumped and disreputable. Next to the van looms a new, shiny four-story apartment block, featuring overpriced studio and one-bedroom flats. It fills in the old park plot all the way to the pavement. The road feels shadowy and overhung with buildings, and still lopsided. They need to balance it out, somehow: bulldoze the other side of the road, too, and build something to match. Already there is a developer's billboard up outside the old house.

Turns out that Katya's landlord, a big letting agency, also handles the new building. When it became clear that structural damage had made the old houses unlivable, the tenants were offered smaller but flashier apartments over the road. So all the residents – Tasneem's family, the retired couple from the end – were scooped out of their shells and poured into new accommodations across the way.

Katya doesn't know exactly where they all stay, though. She looks up at the square windows with their identical silver trim and railings, and has no idea which belongs to Tasneem, to the old couple – or even to herself. She's never been inside.

That's because she's not living there. Len is. No doubt stinking the place out with his smokes, his dirty pyjamas and the scattered crumbs from his sour meals. Canny old bird, shrewdest beast. He never was going to be eradicated that easily. But relocation, it turns out, he was amenable to. They all decided it was for the best: "I don't want him dying on the pavement outside my front door, after all," said Alma. Toby goes round to see him, brings him his teabags and cigarettes.

Len got to keep the greens too, there was no getting them off him. He wears them often now, washes them seldom. One sleeve was shredded by Soldier, but Len solved that one by simply ripping the arms of the overalls away at the seams, so his stringy biceps are exposed at all times. He also tore off the breast-pocket badge. "Bloody stupid," were his words. "And it's not to scale."

Now she frowns at Toby. "You're not letting that old man push you around, are you?"

Toby just laughs. "Granddad and me, we're good."

"Ja, well, you just watch out." She tries to soften her tone. "And how about Tasneem? How's things?"

He shrugs. "Ah, we're not going out any more. She was a bit – dunno, strung up? You know?" He glances at her confidentially.

"Stuck up? Highly strung? Anyway, your mother liked her."

"Yup."

"Well, I'm sorry."

"Nah, it's good. We're good." He stretches his long arms, fingers interlaced, and cracks his knuckles. "I'm good," he says, and beams her a smile of radiant self-delight.

Really, there is no way, no way at all, to discomfit this child.

As he waves goodbye, Katya turns the van around and comes back down the street, slowing to eyeball the garage door. She regards it with grim respect: her old, unbowed enemy. If the whole neighborhood collapsed into dust around it, that garage door would still be standing.

As if her mind commands it, the door starts to shiver and buckle, and then pops open a few feet at the bottom. There's a long silence; nothing else gives way. A ragged gray figure ducks out under the lip. Derek: wearing a familiar coat of oily gray tweed that she could swear once belonged to her dad. A strip of fabric wrapped around his right arm. Poison green.

"Ahoy Derek!" Toby calls from across the road, and Derek acknowledges him with a shaky hand.

Katya rolls down her window. "Derek. What are you doing in there?"

He squints at her as though she's a million miles way, pondering whether she's worth the effort of crossing the pavement. Then he saunters over. Tilts his head. "Speak up, girlie."

"You know that building's dangerous – it's going to come down. And doesn't that door drive you crazy, anyway? It doesn't even have a handle."

He smirks in a superior manner. "Drop of oil, that's all it needed. Drop of oil. It's not a bad door. Got a cigarette?"

"Don't smoke."

"Cash? I'll be needing six rand thirty-five."

Six rand thirty-five, huh. She wonders what that buys: a very small coffee at McDonalds? She fetches out a ten-rand note. She's aware of the momentousness of the occasion. This is, she believes, the first time she's ever given Derek any money.

He examines the note, passes it back to her through the window. "Six rand thirty-five."

She can't think of a reason not to do what he says. She fishes around in the ashtray on the dashboard and comes up with the exact amount, largely in small brown coins. He counts it scrupulously.

"Can I have a receipt?"

"Eh?"

"Never mind."

The door swings up gently behind Derek – not sticking at all – and in the gloom of the garage she makes out a figure. Sitting on a plastic crate, smoking a roll-up, dressed in green. Len touches the thumb of his smoking hand to his forehead in a salute.

Katya nods back. She hasn't spoken to her father for weeks. A spiteful demon tells her to show him Soldier, who is now snoozing on her duvet in the back, but she doesn't know which of them would get the bigger fright.

Her dad is not quite what he was. He really does look like someone who's been through a battle. Soldier managed to do damage to the left shoulder and upper arm, and take a chunk of tissue from the calf. So Len's got a limp, too, as well as handsome scars running down both his bare old arms: puff adder one side, dog the other. Extravagant stigmata he's only too happy to show to strangers: "Had to beat the bugger off!" What with Derek's bandaged limbs, the two of them look more than ever like veterans of some particularly grueling war.

But Len is no longer fierce. This last battle has exhausted him, it seems, and when Katya looks at him she see an old man, far more wounded than she will ever be. Scars form a kind of barrier between them now: out in the open, on the skin, clear for anyone to see.

Now Len cranes his head towards her. "What you up to, my girl?"

"Just dropping Tobes off. He's come to see you."

"Good boy. Been working?"

"Yup. A swarm. *Pachypasa capensis*, actually."

"Huh. Well." He flicks ash dismissively. "They're easy. But what I'd actually like to know..." He peeks at Derek, starting to grin.

"What, Dad?"

"What I'd really like to know is," – big gap-toothed smile now – "Was it *painless*?"

The two old men crack up. Katya rolls her eyes over the cackles. Len seems to find her hilarious these days. Could be worse. She shakes her head at them and drives on.

Before she turns the corner, she gives the old soldiers a little serenade on her car horn:

Rats-in-a-rattrap. Squashed flat!

The further she drives, the better she feels. She likes to put distance between herself and her father. It's necessary, she thinks, for both of them. She is like a ball of string unraveling, always connected, but lighter the further she goes. She turns left and right down familiar streets; up over the Main Road, past the hospital and onto the highway. She drives, she drives. There is no rush now, no particular place to go. No permanent address.

Katya's sleeping in the van these days. Nights are warm. This might seem dangerous in a place like Cape Town, but actually it's surprisingly easy. In the back of the van, nobody can see her; she parks in quiet suburban side streets. The van has bars, after all, and can be locked from the inside. And who's going to hijack a van with cockroaches painted on it? Especially now, she thinks, with Soldier on board. It's all she really needs. She doesn't need to fill up more space than this. She cleans herself in shopping-center bathrooms. It isn't the easiest way to live, but it's also not impossible. At least she doesn't have to deal with the sodding garage door.

Sleeping in the van is really not too much of an adjustment. A car smells like home to Katya, like nighttime; those smells of car leather and petrol must have entered the folds of her child's brain long ago, sleeping in her dad's bakkie. A lullaby of sorts. The van fits her perfectly now; the hollow in the seat is the shape of her body, nobody else's. She's pushed the seat forward, she's swiveled the rear-view mirror to exactly the right position. She doesn't even let Toby drive these days: it's too disruptive.

What she's realized is that people like them – like her and Len – they're not homey. They don't have homes, they don't really fit in them. That whole idea she had of Nineveh, of living behind walls that would never crumble, safe within the armed guard's circling lights: a dream, as grandiose and doomed as Mr. Brand's visions.

The suburbs are safer, but sometimes she takes a chance and parks further out, where waking up is more of an adventure. Somewhere near the sea, or with trees. Now she drives up onto Tafelberg Road and stops at one of the viewpoints. It's lonely here at night, and a little eerie – what with the memory of those unfortunate goldfish, and the rock face looming at her back, lit dead silver by the floodlights like a mountain on the moon. But it's a beautiful view, the city spreading down to the harbor, cradled in the arm of Signal Hill. All softening in the evening light, pricked with street lamps, stained further out with puffs of sodium pallor. Directly below the road, she's sometimes seen a group of Rastas, washing their clothes in the stream above the fancy houses. Further out, she can make out the Castle and the bare patch that used to be District Six. Far to the right, the suburbs begin, and beyond that the railway yards and warehouses.

At this height, no people are visible. Except for the constant shuttling of cars along the threads of roads, it might be a city emptied of humans. But she knows they're there. She wonders where Pascal's ended up, patrolling what perimeter; and with no dog at his heel. She has a new habit of examining the faces of tall car guards and night watchmen, as she once looked for her dad in the derelict figures of street people. And Reuben, he must be out there too. She guesses he lives in a suburb she barely knows, far from the center. She sees them all, tucked into pockets of the city. Mrs. Brand and Nosisi and Len and Zintle, and Katya herself, and all the rest. Each one of them in a subtly different Cape Town, waving to each other, meeting occasionally in the places where such cities overlap. Zones where the world is taking form; where things get mixed up and wander from their positions. Ninevehs.

Out there, Katya sees many such places: domains of uncertain ownership. Unfinished boulevards, the smoky glitter of settlements still to be named, the nebulae of black between the lights. Everything's in motion, changed and changing. There is no way to keep the shape of things. One house falls, another rises. Throw a worn brick away and someone downstream will pick it up and lay it next to others in a new course in a new wall – which sooner or later will fall into ruin, giving the spiders a place to anchor their own silken architecture. Even human skin, Katya has read, is porous and infested, every second letting microscopic creatures in and out. Our own bodies are menageries. Short of total sterility, there is no controlling it.

What conceit, to think that she could capture any of this with her bags and nets and boxes. Painless Pest Relocations survives, but she's lost her faith in this job. This fruitless work of trying to keep things in their proper places.

She climbs into the back of the van, makes sure it's locked up tight, and tucks the duvet around herself. Soldier seems to fill a good two-thirds of the space, and she feels the dog's comforting pressure against her side. He gives a long, wheezing sigh. Katya closes her eyes, and waits for the tides of the city to drift her away.

ACKNOWLEDGMENTS

Thank you to Olivia Taylor Smith, Chris Heiser and the great team at Unnamed Press, and to Jaya Nicely for the brilliant cover art. Thanks as ever to my agent Isobel Dixon, and to Jared Shurin for helping to bring *Nineveh* to publication in the US. I'm very grateful to everyone at Umuzi who worked on the original South African edition, and to all the kind friends who read the manuscript.

Various organizations generously provided time, space and funding to work on *Nineveh*: Akademie Schloss Solitude; the Caine Prize; the Lannan Center for Poetics and Social Practice, Georgetown University; the Karoo Boeke Trust, Hantam (Calvinia Boekehuis); the Caldera Arts Center, Oregon; and the University of Cape Town.

On the epigraph page, the verses from Zephaniah are from the Authorised King James Bible. I have omitted the last line of verse 15. Ningal's words are adapted from "The lament for Urim" (Ur), lines 275–291. Black, JA, Cunningham, G, Ebeling, J, Flückiger-Hawker, E, Robson, E, Taylor, J, and Zólyomi, G, *The Electronic Text Corpus of Sumerian Literature* (http://etcsl.orinst.ox.ac.uk/), Oxford 1998–2006. Darwin's words are from a letter to John Lubbock, September 1854. *Darwin Correspondence Project Database*, www.darwinproject.ac.uk/entry-1585 (letter no. 1585).

PHOTO BY MARTIN FIGURA

ABOUT THE AUTHOR

Henrietta Rose-Innes is a South African writer based in Cape Town and currently based in Norwich, UK. *Nineveh* was shortlisted for the M-Net Literary Award and *The Sunday Times* Fiction Prize, and in 2015 (in French translation, *Ninive*) it won the François Sommer Literary Prize. She's previously published a collection of short stories, *Homing,* and the novels *Green Lion, Shark's Egg* and *The Rock Alphabet*. In 2012 her story "Sanctuary" came second in the BBC International Short Story Prize. In 2008 she won the Caine Prize for African Writing, for which she was shortlisted in 2007. Also in 2007, she was awarded the 2007 South African PEN award for her short story, "Poison".

BY THE SAME AUTHOR:

Shark's Egg, 2000
Rock Alphabet, 2004
Homing, 2010
Green Lion, 2015 (US 2017)

CPSIA information can be obtained
at www.ICGtesting.com
Printed in the USA
LVOW12s0526161116
513179LV00003B/3/P